Praise for the Rhona MacLeod series

'Forensic scientist Rhona MacLeod has become one of the most satisfying characters in modern crime fiction – honourable, inquisitive and yet plagued by doubts and, sometimes, fears . . . As ever, the landscape is stunningly evoked and MacLeod's decency and humanity shine through on every page'   *Daily Mail*

'Lin Anderson is one of Scotland's national treasures . . . her writing is unique, bringing warmth and depth to even the seediest parts of Glasgow. Rhona MacLeod is a complex and compelling heroine who just gets better with every outing'   Stuart MacBride

'Vivid and atmospheric . . . enthralling'   *Guardian*

'The bleak landscape is beautifully described, giving this popular series a new lease of life'   *Sunday Times*

'Greenock-born Anderson's work is sharper than a pathologist's scalpel. One of the best Scottish crime series since Rebus'   *Daily Record*

'Inventive, compelling, genuinely scary and beautifully written, as always'   Denzil Meyrick

'Hugel   thology)
Jame

Dark Flight

Lin Anderson is a Scottish author and screenwriter known for her bestselling crime series featuring forensic scientist Dr Rhona MacLeod. Four of her novels have been longlisted for the Scottish Crime Book of the Year, with *Follow the Dead* being a 2018 finalist. Her short film *River Child* won a student BAFTA for Best Fiction and the Celtic Film Festival's Best Drama award and has garnered more than one and a half million views on YouTube. Lin is also the co-founder of the international crime-writing festival Bloody Scotland, which takes place annually in Stirling.

By Lin Anderson

Driftnet
Torch
Deadly Code
Dark Flight
Easy Kill
Final Cut
The Reborn
Picture Her Dead
Paths of the Dead
The Special Dead
None but the Dead
Follow the Dead
Sins of the Dead
Time for the Dead

NOVELLA
Blood Red Roses

Dark Flight

LIN ANDERSON

PAN BOOKS

First published in Great Britain 2007 by Hodder & Stoughton
An Hachette Livre UK company

First published in paperback 2008

This paperback edition published 2020 by Pan Books
an imprint of Pan Macmillan
The Smithson, 6 Briset Street, London EC1M 5NR
Associated companies throughout the world
www.panmacmillan.com

ISBN 978-1-5290-2479-1

3 5 7 9 8 6 4 2

A CIP catalogue record for this book is available from the British Library.

Printed and bound by CPI Group (UK) Ltd, Croydon, CR0 4YY

Visit **www.panmacmillan.com** to read more about all our books
and to buy them. You will also find features, author interviews and
news of any author events, and you can sign up for e-newsletters
so that you're always first to hear about our new releases.

ACKNOWLEDGEMENTS

Thanks to Ted Coventry for his Nigerian input, and to Dr Jennifer Miller of GUARD for her help with bones and botanics.

To Detective Inspector Bill Mitchell.

SANNI DIVED LEFT into thick undergrowth. The big four-by-four vehicle made a 180-degree turn, splattering red mud in a semicircle, and followed. Thorns tore at Sanni's face and chest. He tasted blood. If he could only make the river. The rainy season had swollen it and the fast-moving water would carry him away from his pursuers. He smelt burning diesel as the vehicle stalled, its wheels churning the soggy clay. Sanni broke through the bushes that lined the river bank. *Rua.* Water. *Rua, da godiya.* Thank God. His small slight body stood, indecisive, on the high bank, as big black river ants ran up his thin legs, biting him savagely. Sensing someone behind, he sprang forward. But it was too late. His arm was gripped in a fist of steel. Sanni screamed, but there was no one to hear.

Day 1

Monday

I

'YOU CAN GO outside, but stay in the garden. Do you hear me, Stephen?' His mum's voice was shrill, like a witch's.

Gran's bedroom smelt of pee. His mum was stripping the bed, while his gran sat in a winged armchair, her hair a fluffy white halo. She winked at Stephen as he left the room. His gran was sick, but she wasn't cross.

The garden was tiny and surrounded by a high hedge. Once, when he came on holiday, he'd helped his granddad cut the hedge, but now it was so tall it blocked the light.

Stephen stood on the closed gate, humming to himself . . . until he saw the bones.

They lay in the shape of a cross, on the pavement just outside the garden. Excitement beat the pulse at his temple. Already his active imagination was writing the bones into a story of pirates and treasure. He looked up and down the empty street. Whoever had dropped them was gone. Probably they would never come back. Conscience assuaged, Stephen dropped to his knees, slipped his small hand through the black bars and stretched his arm as far as he could. He grunted as the metal dug painfully into his armpit, his face squashed sideways to the gate. Out of the corner of his eye he could see his fingers wriggling disappointingly short of the bones.

He withdrew his arm and rubbed it, muttering under his breath in a decisive manner, 'I'll have to go outside. I'll just have to.'

He sneaked a look at the kitchen window. What if his mum was at the sink? His heart leapt. The window was blank. A mix of excitement and fear coursed through his veins and he swallowed hard.

He conjured up an image of his mum's angry face if he disobeyed her and he wiped his mouth anxiously. She would go bananas, raving on at him about not doing what he was told. It was a scary thought.

But if he was quick? He saw himself zip out and in again almost instantaneously like Billy Whizz in the *Beano* comic. The bones were tantalisingly close. And it wasn't really going outside, he told himself firmly. Not if he was *very very* quick.

Stephen slipped through, snatched up the bones and stepped swiftly back inside, pulling the gate quietly shut behind him. He stood stock-still, his heart thudding in his chest. At last he let his breath out in an exaggerated gasp. He had done it!

He smiled down at his prize.

The bones were about the size of his first finger, tied together with red thread. He held the cross to his nose and sniffed. They smelt like the garden when his granddad used to dig up the weeds.

He placed the bones in his left palm and ran his

finger over them, studying the three lines scored at the top of each one, which could be a magic mark.

A muffled voice made him look up guiltily. Had his mum seen him go out of the garden? He whistled through his teeth, and shuffled his feet, waiting for the shout that meant trouble.

But no shout came.

When he felt brave enough to look directly, the face that stared at him through the glass was his mum's, but it didn't look like her. Stephen's mouth dropped open and real fear grabbed his stomach. His mum's face was chalk white, her mouth twisted in pain. Behind her was a dark shadow.

Stephen dropped the bones.

'Mum?' His voice emerged in a whimper.

She opened her mouth as if to scream at him and he waited, rigid with apprehension. Then her face jerked towards the glass, once, twice, three times.

Stephen stood rooted to the spot, watching her neck whip backwards and forwards. Then it was over.

She caught his eye and held it. Her mouth moved in a silent exaggerated word.

RUN.

2

DR RHONA MACLEOD ignored the metallic smell of blood mingled with stale urine, and raised her eyes to the ceiling, where cast-off bloodstains formed an arc.

Short heavy weapons tended to swing slowly and in short arcs. Judging by the spots on the ceiling, the instrument used to kill the old woman was probably long and light.

The body sat in an old-fashioned winged armchair, head slumped forward, fluffy white hair stained dark red. The skull gaped in a line from crown to neck. In the opening, contusions bunched like black grapes.

Larger drops splattered the slippered feet and surrounding beige carpet, their tail direction suggesting the victim was attacked from behind.

Rhona wondered if the woman had even realised her attacker was in the room. She secretly hoped she hadn't. To die such a violent death was terrible. To anticipate it, even worse.

The hands that lay in the lap were small and pearly white, a threading of blue veins running like raised tributaries across the crêpy flesh. A worn gold wedding band hung loose on the fourth finger of the left hand, a delicate gold watch circling the thin wrist.

She wore a pale blue nightgown, a knitted shawl about her shoulders. Had it not been for the blood, it was as if she had fallen asleep in her chair and would waken with a crick in her neck.

The room had a threadbare quality, while retaining an aura of gentility, despite the gory contents. Every surface held an ornament, most of which looked like good china. There were three small, ornately framed paintings on the walls, dark oils of highland scenes.

The chair was placed so the woman could see the small television that sat on a chest nearby. A remote lay on the floor beside her, as though she had dropped it. To the left of the chair, the bed had its headboard against the back wall. The bed was newly made, crisp white sheets spoiled by crimson spray. On a bedside table sat a radio and three pill bottles.

Rhona lifted one with a gloved hand and read the label. Sleeping tablets. The other two might be medication for water retention and circulatory problems, but she would have to check. She bagged the bottles and labelled them.

It looked as though the old woman never left this room. And even here, she hadn't been safe.

Detective Inspector Bill Wilson appeared in the doorway, his expression brightening at the sight of Rhona. 'You got here fast.'

'I was in the car when the call came through.'

Bill assumed an official air. In the midst of carnage it served as a survival mechanism. 'The Procurator's been. Decided he didn't need to look in detail to give us the go-ahead. The duty pathologist pronounced death, via a view from the window. He'll wait until we ship them to the mortuary to take a closer look. McNab was keen to restrict access to the scene in case of contamination. Seems sensible.'

The name startled Rhona. She hadn't realised DS McNab was back in town. 'McNab's the Crime Scene Manager?' She tried to keep her tone light.

Bill gave a cursory nod. It was a name well known to both of them. 'Want to take a look in the kitchen?'

The room gave onto a long narrow hall, which led to a back door. The layout was straightforward. A two room, kitchen and bathroom flat. The front room, normally a sitting room, had become Granny's bedsit. According to the other SOCOs, the smaller bedroom at the back was filled with a three-piece suite circa nineteen fifties.

Aluminium tread plates had been laid throughout so no one would leave their own imprint on the scene. Unfortunately, whoever laid them had a longer stride than Rhona, and she had to jump from plate to plate. In other circumstances she might have laughed, but this blood bath held no place for humour.

A younger woman lay face down on the kitchen floor, her skirt pulled up to her waist. The blood had left her severed carotid artery in a series of spurts that corresponded to the beating of her heart. The arterial gush had hit the kitchen surface near the sink, leaving a large stain, several centimetres in diameter. Secondary splattering peppered the front of the kitchen unit.

Rhona felt her throat tighten. Even after all this time, she had to remember to immerse herself in procedure.

Only that saved her, and the other members of the team, from losing their minds, or their emotional well-being, in the face of such violent death.

The woman's sweater had been pushed up. Between the shoulder blades, her attacker had carved a diagonal cross. Her legs and arms had been spread in a mirror image of the same shape.

'Who is she?' Rhona asked.

'Not sure yet. The old woman had a pension book. Enid Cavanagh, seventy-eight years old.'

'Are they related?'

'We think they might be mother and daughter.'

Rhona crouched and shone a torch between the spread-eagled thighs. A smeared mix of blood and what looked like semen had dried in strips down the pale mottled skin of the legs. She peered more closely, directing the torch on the bloodied vaginal area. The clitoris and adjacent labia had been cleanly removed. The extent of the mutilation made her gasp.

'What?'

'She's been circumcised.'

Bill swore under his breath.

He hated all deaths on his patch, but sexual mutilation suggested a sadist. And any study of the psychology of murder identified sadists as good planners, with a degree of intelligence that kept them one step ahead of the law.

Rhona indicated the contact stain of a long blade on the woman's discarded underwear.

'Looks like he wiped the weapon clean on those and took it with him.'

She glanced around the room, trying to get her bearings from the blood spatters and position of the corpse. 'If he attacked her from behind, he could have avoided the main gush of blood. Which means he could be virtually blood free.'

Rhona shone a light obliquely down either side of the body, looking for foot or knee prints. The beam picked out a partial imprint in the V-shape between the victim's left arm and leg. 'Take a look at this.'

Bill stepped across the treads and joined her.

The print was smudged, but distinguishable.

'This looks like a child's footprint.'

The colour drained from Bill's face. He had two kids of his own, teenagers now, but always kids in his eyes. Margaret, his wife of over thirty years, was always giving him a hard time about letting them grow up, especially his daughter, Lisa. Every time Bill was called to a female murder victim, he imagined Lisa in her place.

'Did she have a child?'

Bill stood up. 'We'd better find out, and fast.'

Left to her own devices, Rhona began the slow laborious job of evidence collection. She concentrated on the kitchen. Her assistant, Chrissy McInsh, would finish working the bedroom. Two other scene of crime officers were dealing with the remainder of the small flat.

She swabbed the woman's mouth. Dr Sissons would deal with vaginal and rectum swabs in the mortuary. The tongue was swollen and bloody; her teeth had bitten into it in fright. If the woman had screamed and there was a child nearby, it might have heard and come running in.

Rhona glanced out of the window. What little light existed was masked by a tall hedge. In the middle of the hedge, a metal gate squeaked back and forth, as crime scene personnel moved in and out.

She had a sudden image of herself as a little girl, swinging on their gate, her mother shouting at her to get off, in case she broke the hinges. Had a child been in the garden?

Once she'd finished with the body, she tackled the rest of the room. It was small, a kitchenette rather than a kitchen. She suspected it had been cleaned recently. Beneath the scent of death she discerned the faint aroma of disinfectant. In the sink, a dishcloth was soaking in bleach and water. A teapot lay open and ready for boiling water, a fresh teabag damp inside. Two china cups and saucers sat nearby. A washing-machine door was partly open. Inside were sheets smelling of old sweat and dribbled urine. The woman had changed her mother's bed and cleaned the kitchen then set about making a pot of tea. A normal domestic scene one minute, carnage and death the next. Rhona didn't want to imagine the scenario, yet knew she had to. Understanding the choreography of a crime was as important as collecting the forensic samples associated with it.

She imagined herself standing at the window, maybe checking on a child in the garden. Did the woman hear the intruder in her mother's room? Rhona listened to the soft movement of Chrissy next door. Only a narrow hall divided kitchen from front room. Bill had said the television was on when they arrived. Loud enough for the old woman to hear. Maybe the sound had masked her death?

There had been nothing beneath the younger victim's nails. No skin or hair or blood. When she bagged the hands she could smell bleach from them. It didn't look as if she'd fought her attacker. Why not?

A knife at her neck, perhaps . . . or to protect her child?

Rhona enhanced the child's part-print impression with a protein dye and was satisfied she had enough to distinguish pattern, size and wear. A careful examination of the remaining linoleum revealed a poor partial adult print near the door. Maybe Chrissy would have more luck with the beige carpet.

She stepped her way through the hall. Chrissy had finished photographing the bloodstains and was taping the carpet, looking for fibres or residue. A fringe of bright auburn hair was visible beneath the hood of her white suit.

'How's it going in here?'

Chrissy glanced up. Without the usual make-up, the face looked five years younger. 'Fine. Where are you going?'

'I want to take a look outside.'

Chrissy turned back to the task in hand. Rhona didn't have to ask her to check for footprints. It was a routine part of the job. Chrissy might have a sharp tongue and a somewhat cynical view of the world, but she was a stickler for protocol.

There was a forlorn air to the small garden, as though it had once been loved. The remains of spring daffodils poked out from beneath the too-thick hedge, their heads shrivelled and browning.

A circular bed of spindly roses, badly in need of pruning, suddenly reminded Rhona of her father's garden on the Isle of Skye. She'd felt ashamed of the neglect when she went back after his death. Somehow, seeing the abandoned garden brought home the reality of his passing. Until then she'd imagined she only had to lift the receiver and dial his number and he would be there to answer it.

The gate was black metal but hadn't been painted in a while. Flakes of rust crumbled on touch and sprinkled the concrete path with orange-red dust. She swung the gate shut and crouched on one of the aluminium treads on the short path. The gate was divided in two. The top half consisted of two semicircular bars enclosed within a square. The bottom half was made up of vertical bars, wide enough apart for a small foot.

Between bars three and four, and five and six, were the imprints she sought. She took a series of photos before she attempted retrieval. The imprints were partial of the weighted soles of shoes pressed between the bars. Crouched on the path, she figured she would be just below the height of a child swinging on the gate. She could hear movement from indoors and spotted the top of Chrissy's head in the bedroom.

The kitchen window was left of the path. Assuming the woman had been assaulted at the sink, a child swinging on the gate would have had a clear view of her face when her attacker struck.

Rhona imagined a scream and turned abruptly, as a child would have done . . . and caught sight of the bones.

They were lying half hidden among the shrivelled daffodil leaves. She reached out and picked them up, her heart beating with the excited curiosity of a scientist.

Lying in the palm of her gloved hand, they were immediately recognisable as human half-finger bones, tied tightly together with red thread in the shape of a diagonal cross. The length from the proximal to the distal joint was shorter than her own, suggesting an adult with small hands, or a child. Just below each knuckle, there were three striations cut cross-wise.

She put the bones in a sample bag, then examined the short path to the front door. The perpetrator could have entered the house this way or used the back alley, which involved climbing a wall. According to Bill there were no signs of a forced entry. So he had a key, or both doors were unlocked. There was no back garden, just a shared area of grass with a wooden bench. If the child or assailant ran out of the front door, then there could be blood on this path somewhere.

But the path proved to be clear. Her only reward for a careful search was a wad of chewing gum just outside the gate.

Chrissy appeared at the front door, pulled down her mask, and inhaled deeply. 'The old woman was incontinent. The carpet's reeking.'

'Anything else?'

'Someone pissed on the body.'

'You're sure?'

'I'm sure.'

'Her attacker?'

'Who else would piss on an old woman?'

Drugs and their metabolities were often detectable in urine for longer periods than in the blood. If the attacker was high on something, they would find evidence of it in his urine.

'McNab wants a word.'

'Right.' Rhona tried to keep her face expressionless. The attempt wasn't lost on Chrissy. Not many people knew that piece of Rhona's history and she wanted it kept that way.

'He's in the hut.' Chrissy indicated the mobile crime scene office set up across the road.

'Okay. I'm finished in the kitchen anyway.'

'Ten minutes, then we go for a drink?' Chrissy suggested.

Rhona stripped off the suit, boots and gloves, composing herself as she did so. DS Michael McNab. A moment of madness a couple of years back that had lasted three months. Her dad had died and she'd felt like a boat without a rudder. Sleeping with McNab had made her temporarily forget the emptiness. When she broke it off, he was the one all at sea. He got angry. Tried everything to get back into her life. Rhona still felt bad that she had encouraged him to think there was more to them than sex.

She pulled on her jacket. The spring sunshine had gone and she shivered in the cold April air.

When she pushed open the door of the hut, she was relieved to see McNab wasn't alone. Bill Wilson was there, in his hand a mug of coffee with skin on its surface, just the way he liked it.

McNab had done a good job as Crime Scene Manager. Rhona congratulated him.

Seated at a computer, he accepted the compliment in silence, an inscrutable look on his face. '*We* always did make a good team.'

She ignored any hidden message in the reply and asked if there was any word on the child.

'We've established the younger victim as Carole Devlin, the old woman's married daughter,' Bill told her. 'She has a boy of six called Stephen. A neighbour says Carole often came to help her mother. She brought Stephen with her.'

'So where is he now?'

McNab shook his head. 'We don't know.' He pushed a photo in a silver frame across the desk. 'This was on the sideboard.'

A live and animated Carole Devlin sat beside her mother on a settee. Between her knees perched a boy, wearing a blue school sweatshirt. He had the creamy chocolate-brown skin of a mixed-race child. Handsome, with big brown eyes and a cheeky grin.

'Is there a dad?'

'No idea. The school badge belongs to the nearby primary. DC Clark is contacting the headmistress. We have an address from Carole's handbag that could be her own flat. It's in Gibson Street.'

Gibson Street was a stone's throw from Rhona's lab,

about a fifteen-minute walk from the granny's flat in Dowanhill Road.

'We'll know more by the strategy meeting tomorrow,' Bill said

'There's no sign of the boy, apart from the footprint beside the body and two on the gate,' Rhona told him.

Bill said what she'd been thinking. 'If the attacker took him . . .'

Neither of them wanted to say it, but they feared the child might already be dead.

'There's something else.'

She showed them the bagged finger bones.

McNab examined them through the plastic, his face puzzled. 'They look human.'

'They are.'

Bill gave a weary sigh. 'So, we have two dead women, one of them mutilated, and a missing child . . .'

'And a cross made of human bones,' Rhona finished for him.

3

THE CLUB WAS beginning to fill up. The band didn't perform till later. Now the place echoed with shrill voices just released from a day's work.

Chrissy and Rhona made straight for the bar. A stout man with glasses and a petite pretty brunette Rhona recognised from the mortuary, moved along a bit to give them room. It was Sean's night off, or he would have been here already, setting up for the band, his saxophone on its stand in the corner of the stage. Tonight he would be at the flat, cooking a meal. Rhona knew she should have gone straight home, but didn't want to. Better to sit with Chrissy for a while, until the real world seeped back into her system.

One thing about her line of work: telling your partner what you'd seen and done in the previous six hours didn't make for a comfortable evening.

Guilt made her flip open her mobile. The phone rang out four times then switched to answerphone. She left a message about being kept late at work and rang off.

The club was busy with Glasgow University personnel, including staff from the nearby forensic medical sciences department and a couple of forensic anthropologists from GUARD, the University's Archaeological Research Department. This wasn't a police hang-out, so she didn't have to face McNab, although Bill, a keen jazz fan, often came in.

She dismissed thoughts of Michael McNab from her mind. She hadn't told Sean about that liaison. In fact they never discussed previous relationships, although she suspected Sean's list was a lot longer than her own.

Rhona ordered a white wine from Sam the barman. Chrissy screwed up her face at that, and went for a bright pink alcopop, reminding Rhona that alcohol served that way got into the blood faster, which is what she needed tonight.

'So, what did McNab want?' Her forensic assistant was nothing if not direct.

'Strictly business,' Rhona told her.

'While he undressed you with his eyes.'

'Bill was there.'

'I bet that pissed McNab off.'

'He's a good CSM.'

Chrissy shrugged and took a swallow. 'If a little obsessive.'

'It was a long time ago.'

Chrissy made a noise in her throat that sounded like a grunt of disbelief. 'McNab has a damaged ego where you're concerned.'

'I'm history,' Rhona said firmly.

It had been stupid getting involved with someone from work. There were lots of affairs in the police force. Unsocial hours, shift work, escape from the horrors of the job threw people together. Most liaisons screwed up the work and the personal life of those involved. It was the only time Rhona had made that mistake and it still bothered her.

When McNab headed for the Fife Police College, it had seemed a perfect time to end it. Numerous emails and phone calls from him had left her feeling threatened as well as angry. So she'd told Bill in confidence. He must have had a quiet word with McNab because the communication onslaught had suddenly stopped. Now McNab was back in Glasgow and impossible to avoid.

As Chrissy drained her bottle Sam appeared with another. He flashed her a big dazzling-white smile. 'I finish in an hour?'

'I'll be here.'

Rhona waited until he went to serve someone else, then raised an eyebrow at Chrissy.

'What?' Chrissy played the innocent.

'You never said you were seeing Sam.'

'I like to give it longer than three weeks before I spread the word.'

'And?'

Chrissy looked like the cat that got the cream. 'Well, you know that story about black men . . .'

'Stop, Chrissy!'

The one thing you had to remember about Chrissy: she always told it like it was.

Sam had left the wine bottle beside her and Rhona refilled her glass as Chrissy headed for the Ladies. Someone had switched on the overhead television. A news flash showed the photograph of the missing boy with his mother and grandmother. Rhona asked Sam to turn up the sound.

The report was short, with little detail. A six-year-old boy, Stephen Devlin, was missing, after the grim discovery of the murdered bodies of his mother and grandmother in a flat in the west end of the city. Anyone with any information on the boy's whereabouts should contact the police immediately.

Chrissy returned from the toilet and glanced up at the screen. 'No sign of him?'

Rhona shook her head. As long as they hadn't discovered a body, they had to believe the child was alive. Tomorrow, she would study the attacker's print against the one Chrissy found. If he was carrying the boy as he left, the difference in pressure should be detectable.

Sam came back to check on Chrissy. She gave him the thumbs up and he deposited another pink bottle in front of her. His ebony skin and high cheekbones gave him the look of an African god. He had told Rhona his ancestors were Fulani, a wandering tribe who herded their cattle through Northern Nigeria and its neighbouring states. He'd been brought up in the northern city of Kano. As well as working behind the bar he played jazz piano a couple of evenings a week and his work in the club supported his medical course at Glasgow University.

'Why don't you ask Sam about the bones thing?' Chrissy suggested.

'The bones thing?' Sam gave Chrissy a suggestive smile. 'This isn't another one of your anatomy tests?'

Rhona didn't like to imagine what the anatomy tests

consisted of. She pulled a notepad from her bag, drew a representation of the crossed bones and pushed it across the counter.

Sam had a look, his expression changing from humorous to serious. 'Are they human?'

'I think they are. A child or small adult.'

He thought for a moment. 'They were tied like this when you found them?'

'Yes.'

'It looks like a juju *tsafi* to me.'

'*Tsafi*?' Chrissy raised an eyebrow.

'A fetish.' He caught Chrissy's eye. 'We're not necessarily talking sex here.' Sam smiled. 'Although they're often for that.'

'An object believed by primitive people to have some magical power?' Rhona tried.

'Not always primitive,' Sam corrected her. 'Lots of well-educated people in West Africa still believe in witch doctors. Let me show you something.' He extracted a folded piece of paper from his wallet. 'My mother sent me this in case I needed a bit of help from the old country.'

He spread out the paper on the counter. There was a name and address at the top: *Mallam Muhammed Tunni Sokoto, 21 Yoruba Road, Sabon Gari, Kano.*

Beneath was a long list comprising fifty-six ways your witch doctor could help improve your life.

Chrissy ran an eye down the page. 'Medicine for a commanding tongue?' she read out.

'Well, *you* don't need that one,' Rhona told her with conviction.

'Mmmm. Now here's one I like. Medicine for love.'

'How did you think we two got together?' Sam grinned.

Chrissy read on. 'Medicine for a tired penis?' She shook her head. 'Don't need that.'

Rhona joined in the laughter. 'So the bones might be some sort of witch doctor medicine?' she asked Sam.

'Bones are important in juju.'

'There were three deep scores on each bone.'

He looked startled. 'Where did you find them?'

'Outside a house.'

He thought for a moment. 'Beats me. But I don't pay much attention to that sort of stuff. I could email my mother,' he offered. 'She would be the one to ask.'

'What if I send you a digital photo of the bones?'

'Sure.'

He wrote his email address on the back of her drawing.

A nasty thought struck Rhona. 'How do the witch doctors get the human bones to make the fetish?'

'Poor people die all the time in Nigeria. In the cities you find the bodies in the streets. In the UK?' He shrugged his shoulders. 'It would be more difficult.'

'Not to say illegal,' Chrissy said.

'Would someone kill to get bones for juju?' Rhona asked.

Sam looked worried by that. 'Human sacrifice is the darker side of juju. In black juju, the organs and bones of children are highly prized.'

On her way to the underground station, Rhona found herself looking at children, reminding herself she had a child, although Liam was a young man now. Eighteen years of age, older than she was when he was born. When she left the hospital after the birth, her heart and her arms were empty. Edward, her lover at the time, had talked her into adoption. They were too young for a child, they had to finish their degrees before they married and had children. There was plenty of time. And she'd believed him.

Edward did get married, but not to her. Fiona had given him two children. A son, Jonathan, and a daughter, Morag. Rhona, on the other hand, had stayed single and for the most part alone, until Sean Maguire had entered her life.

She often asked herself what she would do if she got pregnant again. Every time the thought crossed her mind she determined that this time the decision would be hers and hers alone. No one would talk her in or out of anything that important again. Not Sean, not anyone.

Moroseness settled on her like a thick dark cloud. Bill Wilson would be at home now, in the bosom of his family. Would he tell Margaret what he had witnessed today or would he do as she did? Place that knowledge inside a compartment of his brain and shut the door on it.

She'd missed the commuter rush and the underground train was half empty. Two young teenage Goths sat opposite, noses, ears, eyebrows and tongues pierced. Satanic symbols hung on chains around their necks. They were laughing together, the sweet reek of cannabis clinging to their clothes.

Beside them a young mother struggled with a toddler, a buggy, and a girl of about six. The woman had a frazzled air as though her edges were unravelling. They got off at the same stop and Rhona offered to help her up the stairs with the buggy. When the girl slipped her hand in Rhona's, the trusting gesture unnerved her.

She was surprised and disappointed when she reached home to find the flat in darkness. She checked her mobile. If Sean had called while she was in the club she might not have heard him, but there were no messages, voice or text.

Rhona stood in the hall, wishing Chance, her cat, were still alive and running to greet her, his big black body trailing between her legs, tripping her up on her way to the kitchen.

Sean had encouraged her to get another cat, as though she were replacing a pair of shoes. But Chance's death was still too raw in her mind.

The kitchen was as she'd left it that morning, with dishes in the sink and the rock-hard remains of some hastily buttered toast. Any hopes of meeting the scent of garlic and herbs, the open bottle of a carefully chosen red wine, were dashed.

She tried to remember if Sean had mentioned something he had to do tonight. But nothing came to mind. They normally had an easy routine on his night off, eating a leisurely meal together, then making love. He would play her his favourite jazz tracks and she would dutifully listen, knowing his efforts would never turn her into a real jazz fan. Yet when he played the saxophone, it almost worked: she was seduced by the haunting sound and image, his closed eyes, fingers caressing the keys with the intensity of a lover.

She admitted to herself that tonight she needed Sean to talk to. She wanted him to enter her troubled body and make her forget today.

She rang out for a pizza, then poured herself a whisky and water and opened up her laptop. If she couldn't dispel work from her mind, then she would have to engage with it.

She went online and typed 'female genital mutilation' in the search engine.

The result confirmed what she already suspected. FGM was more of a cultural than a religious practice, carried out predominantly in sub-Saharan Africa, on pre-pubescent girls, designed to reduce their sexual response.

What she hadn't known was that an estimated fifty per cent of all Nigerian girls had been operated on. Some thirty million women in Sam's country had been mutilated in this way.

Whoever killed Carole performed that ritual on her. Although Stephen's father was likely black, that didn't mean he was African. But most murdered women were killed by their husband or partner. If Carole Devlin's husband was in Scotland, then he had to be a suspect.

Much later she was awakened by Sean's key in the lock. The stumbling sound of his footsteps in the hall, followed by the masked expletive, suggested he was drunk. Rhona lay in the darkness, nonplussed by this, because she had never seen Sean really drunk before.

When he didn't come into the bedroom, curiosity sent her to find him. The sight made her stop silently in her tracks. He was in the spare room, a fiddle in his hand. He'd brought the battered case with him when he moved in. When she asked whether he could play, he'd told her all Irishmen could play the fiddle, if not with their hands, then in their hearts. Yet the case had stood gathering dust in a corner. To her knowledge Sean had never looked at it since, let alone played it.

Something made her melt back into the shadow of the hall, so she could watch Sean, unseen.

He began to play, slowly at first, as though trying to remember, then he relaxed and the music came of its own accord. She didn't recognise the tune, yet felt herself drown in its sadness.

Sean stopped suddenly, mid-phrase, and threw the fiddle back in its case. 'Fucking old bastard!'

Rhona stepped into the light, frightened by his vehemence. 'Sean?'

His eyes tried to focus on her. 'I'm drunk,' he said in a mixture of defiance and apology.

She smiled. 'I can see that.'

He staggered past her into the kitchen.

When she got there, he had already poured himself a whisky. 'Is that wise?'

'Who are you? My fucking mother?'

She recoiled, stung by the viciousness of the attack.

He shook his head, as if he didn't know where the anger had come from, then swallowed the whisky.

Rhona mentally calculated whether his blood alcohol

content was at danger level. Sean wouldn't be the first male in Glasgow to die from too much drink.

Seeing the worried look on her face, he pushed the glass away. 'My father's sick. I have to go home.'

4

BILL'S RELIEF AT being back home was almost over-whelming. The normal sounds as he slipped his key in the lock; the warmth in the hall after the night air between the car and the front door.

But it wasn't the wind that had chilled him to the bone. It was the remembered sight in that room. The mutilated spread-eagled body of the woman. Her elderly mother, her head bowed almost in prayer. What manner of man could have done such a thing? For he had no doubt in his mind that it had been a man. And the child? The face in the photograph smiling and happy. Where was the boy?

He pulled himself together as Lisa came down the stairs.

'At last. We're starving and Mum made us wait until you came home.' She brushed past him, shouting, 'He's here,' on her way to the kitchen.

A door banged upstairs and Robbie's gelled head appeared, the dark locks spiked like a Victorian street urchin's. He nodded at Bill, his earphones in, the tinny sound of a band escaping.

Margaret's back was towards him as Bill entered the kitchen. Thinking about it later, he realised he should have seen the too-high shoulders, the tenseness in the position of her head.

He placed a kiss in the nape of her neck, feeling overwhelmingly tender towards her. She was his friend, his lover and his soulmate. He could only do what he did because of her. The blackest of days would dissolve as they lay curled together in the bed where his two children had been conceived.

She pointed to a dram already poured out for him.

'You're having one?' he'd said in surprise, seeing the second glass.

Margaret, the daughter of a Presbyterian minister, drank rarely, and never mid-week; the drinking habit had not lasted past student days.

She placed the serving dish on the table and sat down. Bill threw back the whisky, not wanting to delay the meal any further.

'I saw it on the news,' Margaret said, to make it easier for him.

'Saw what?' Lisa piped up.

Margaret gave him a look that said: Tell her enough to end the questions.

'A wee boy's missing. We think he ran away when his mother and grandmother were murdered.'

Lisa had the emotional intelligence of her mother and could read situations and people's reactions as clearly as a written page. She gave her dad a look of sympathy and went back to her food.

Robbie's earphones were still in. Bill was about to remonstrate when Margaret silently shook her head.

They ate in relative silence. By now Bill sensed something was wrong, something more than what had happened in his day. A creeping realisation came when Margaret reached for the water jug and he saw her hand tremble. He was shocked beyond comprehension.

Robbie cleared his plate first, muttered an 'excuse me' and was allowed to depart. Lisa hung on a little longer until Margaret reminded her that her favourite soap was about to come on.

She waited until Lisa had shut the door behind her, then pushed her plate away.

'What is it?'

She composed herself. 'I saw the doctor today . . .'

He was about to interrupt, ask her why, but her hand fluttered like a trapped bird asking him to wait and hear her out.

Bill's heart took off, punching his chest so hard it hurt.

'I have a lump in my right breast. The doctor has requested an immediate appointment at the breast clinic.'

The words out, Margaret looked relieved.

Bill moved his chair towards her, but she drew back. 'No! If you put your arms about me now, I won't cope.'

She got up and began clearing the table, taking refuge in the mundane.

Bill sat in silence, as helpless as a child without its mother, his throat full of words he dared not let himself speak. 'You're sure?' It was a stupid question but he had to ask it. He wanted her to say no, she wasn't sure.

He wanted the hands of the clock to tick backwards to the beginning of their meal.

'I wouldn't have told you tonight only . . .' She paused.

She was apologising to him for telling him that she was ill. Apologising because she sensed in him what he had faced that day and knew the demons that would haunt him through the night.

He felt an overwhelming sadness at the stupidity of men and a matching wonder at the emotional strength of women.

He went quickly towards her before she could retreat and wrapped her in his arms. The tightness of his grip took both their breath away.

The tenseness of her limbs flowed into his taut muscles. He felt her body relax and she sighed, resting her face on his shoulder.

He shut his eyes and saw a bright white line stretching into the distance. He found himself praying, absurdly muttering words to a God he didn't know, mixing Margaret with the missing boy as though they were one and the same.

Her tears dampened his shoulder. He thought of other times when she had wept on his shoulder. Some of them happy and some of them sad. He realised with a sudden clarity that his strength came directly from her.

'The missing boy. Did he see the man kill his mother?'

He wanted to tell her no. But he could never lie to her. 'We don't know.'

'But you think the murderer has the child?'

'We hope the boy got away and is hiding somewhere.'

In her mind, the child's ordeal had become greater
than her own. 'Tell me everything.'

He shook his head. 'I can't repeat it.'

She drew back and looked him in the face. 'Tell me,'
she said.

She was asleep. He had watched her close her eyes, had
seen her mouthing words of prayer. Margaret, daughter of a Scottish minister, had married Bill Wilson, a
lapsed Catholic. She, unlike him, had never lost the
core of her faith in a God.

In his own mind he bullied her God, demanding that
he look after someone who had never knowingly
harmed a living soul, who brought joy, humour and
intelligence into a dark world. Then he thought of the
child. Alone and terrified, or already dead.

And he wept silently in the darkness.

Morning brought some semblance of normality. Margaret had always been a fighter. Her mindset had
moved from despair and fear to determination. Whatever she had to do to confront this thing she would do.
The possibility that the lump might be benign was
there, but Margaret had already contemplated the
worst scenario and decided how to deal with it. If
the growth was benign, that was a bonus.

Before she slept she'd given him her instructions.
The children were not to be told until the lump was

examined. If it was benign they need never be told. If it wasn't they would be told the truth.

'They are old enough to deal with it,' was what she'd said.

She would not hear of Bill coming to the hospital with her. 'If you are with me, I'll have to think about you. I'd rather be there on my own. We'll meet up afterwards, away from the house.'

He had taken her instructions without question. She would tell him when the appointment came through. He had other things to think about just now, she'd insisted.

She saw him off at the door. The scent of her skin as she kissed his cheek swamped him. Ever since she told him, he had grown conscious again of everything about her. It was as though he were back thirty years.

'Find the boy' were her last words to him as he got in the car.

Day 2

Tuesday

5

o'clock.
bodies
the partner or a
Bottom, there
Strathman
daughter had
Rhona looked up.
Also Culler thinks
...

BILL GLANCED AROUND the table. Rhona looked bleary-eyed. He suspected she'd had as much sleep as himself, which wasn't much. This strategy meeting was critical in deciding how much they knew and what their next move would be. As well as himself and Rhona, the Crime Scene Manager, McNab, was there. Bill had observed McNab's reaction when Rhona walked in, smart and professional in her navy-blue suit. He had been relieved by McNab's lack of interest, which must mean McNab had returned to the fold minus that particular obsession.

Detective Superintendent Sutherland was there. He would watch the 360-degree live footage of the crime scene while the experts around the table gave him their opinions to date. Dr Sissons, the pathologist, was the last to arrive. As soon as he had taken his seat, Bill began.

'The crime was discovered by chance. A house-bound neighbour, Mrs Cullen, saw the front door lying open and phoned Mrs Cavanagh. Apparently the old lady was bad about leaving her door unlocked. When there was no answer, the neighbour became concerned and called the police station around five o'clock. A patrol car came to check and found the bodies at five-thirty. Mrs Cullen did not see Stephen, his mother or a stranger enter the house. As far as she knows, there is no Mr Devlin. Carole appeared about a month ago. Mrs Cavanagh told her neighbour her daughter had been living abroad.'

Rhona looked up. 'Abroad?'

'Mrs Cullen thinks England's abroad. The child being "dark", as Mrs Cullen put it, she thought Carole had been living in London.'

They watched the footage in silence. The Super tried to remain impassive, but even he paled at the carnage.

Dr Sissons confirmed the mode of death. 'Enid Cavanagh died from a single blow to the back of the head with a long-bladed and extremely sharp knife. The skull was separated into two halves by the force. Subsequent damage to vital brainstem structure resulted in reflex cardiorespiratory arrest and a quick death.

'Carole Devlin had a more protracted end. Lacerations suggest the knife was held to her neck, probably while she was raped. Then the carotid artery was cut, perhaps at the moment of ejaculation. Once on the floor, her clitoris, prepuce and labia were removed, probably with the same knife—'

Bill interrupted. 'There is no question of more than one weapon or assailant?'

'I don't think so. Whoever wielded this weapon was familiar with it and knew exactly what it could do.'

It was Rhona's turn. 'We found footprints for

Carole, her mother, one from a child inside the house and a partial set on the gate. We also have some that might be the intruder's.'

'Fingerprints?'

'We matched Carole's and her mother's to various sets about this house. I found a clear set from a child on the top of the gate. My guess is the murderer wore gloves, which is strange, because he didn't use a condom. We have a semen sample and a lot of blood, none of it, I think, will be his. We believe,' she indicated Dr Sissons's agreement, 'that Carole didn't put up a fight. Her nails were clean and she had had her hands in bleach prior to her death.'

'Maybe she thought that by not fighting she would stay alive?' Bill wondered.

'Or maybe she didn't want her son to hear and come inside,' Rhona suggested. 'Chrissy is working on the trace material from the carpet. Oh, and something else. The attacker urinated on the old woman. If he was high on something when he killed, we should be able to identify it from the urine.'

'So a sexually violent murder, probably by someone who knew the victims,' Bill said, mentally hoping it was a one-off.

'Or,' Rhona offered, 'a ritualistic murder with satanic connections.' Which meant the murderer would more than likely strike again.

She explained the presence of the human-bone fetish near the gate and the possible link with juju.

Bill didn't like the sound of that. The discovery of human bones identified a crime in itself. 'How can we be sure the bones have anything to do with this murder?' he tried. 'They may have been lying in the garden for a while.'

'We can't. However, the bones were dry, although the grass was damp,' Rhona told him. 'I have a meeting with GUARD later today to try to date them and identify the age and gender of the owner.'

Dr Sissons backed Rhona up. 'The practice of clitoridectomy exists in sub-Saharan Africa, an area also known for the practice of juju or voodoo. Dr MacLeod is right to suggest a possible link between the crime and such a culture.'

Rhona said what they were all thinking: 'We must find the boy. He's our key witness . . . if he's still alive.'

Rhona rushed off after the meeting and Bill didn't get a chance to speak to her alone. He wondered if she was avoiding McNab, but had seen no evidence of discomfort between them. More likely she felt the extreme urgency of the investigation. As Chief Forensic on the case, she had a mass of work to get through with her team. He would be better to leave her alone to get on with it. His team had their own work cut out.

In the incident room, the crime scene photos decorated one wall, as a constant stimulant to the thought process, and an ugly reminder of what they were up against.

He had been totally focused in the meeting, but now thoughts of Margaret rushed in to replace work. He tried to push them to one side. The first thing Margaret would ask when he got home tonight was whether he had found the boy. Worrying about her while on duty wouldn't cut ice with his wife.

He headed for his office and sat down in the ancient leather chair that was his thinking post. It squeaked loudly as he turned towards the window. The boy had been missing for around eighteen hours. The best scenario was that he had entered the house after the murderer left and was hiding out alone somewhere. It had stayed relatively mild overnight, so exposure might not be a problem, depending on how Stephen was dressed.

DC Janice Clark came in.

'Well?'

She shook her head. 'We have a constable at Carole Devlin's flat. The boy hasn't turned up there. The photo went out on all channels last night, but no sightings yet.'

'What about nearby security cameras?'

'We're checking those.'

'House-to-house?'

'Progressing, but nothing significant.'

She must have sensed his frustration because she tried for something positive. 'We should have a DNA sample to check against the database soon.'

'Why did he wear gloves and not a condom?' Bill was really asking himself, but Janice answered.

'He's worried we have his fingerprints and not his DNA?'

'Maybe he doesn't like getting his hands dirty?'

'Or the sexual deviance of the attack demanded he spill his sperm.'

Bill tapped the table with a pen. 'Did she have a mobile?'

'There wasn't one in the handbag.'

'She must have had one, if only to keep in touch with her invalid mother. Maybe the kid took it?'

'Or the murderer?'

'Check the mobile phone companies. See if she's registered with any of them. Find out who the old lady's doctor was. They might know something about the family. The Passport Office. Let's find out if Carole Devlin went abroad. And records of births, deaths and marriages. Was Mr Devlin still in the picture? Anything we can get on her, bank statements, credit cards. Did she ever have a joint account? What about friends? Some girlfriend is bound to come looking for her. And the kid's school. Did they ever hear talk of a daddy? Those bits of news kids write in their jotters . . . teachers know a lot more about home life than parents realise.'

Carole Devlin and her son had a life. People knew them. If the killer wasn't a stranger, then maybe they knew him too. Angry, jealous or disturbed men often killed their kids as well as their partners.

6

STEPHEN OPENED HIS eyes to darkness. At first he imagined he was at home in bed and everything else was a nightmare. Then he knew it wasn't. He closed his eyes tightly and the blackness became bright swirling red, like the blood in the kitchen.

He smothered a sob, fearful that he might be heard. Tears escaped from his eyes and slipped down his face. Something terrible had happened to his mum. And his gran. He shivered, his teeth rattling together. Now that his body was awake, pain, fear and hunger swept through it.

When he'd seen his mum's face at the window, he thought she was angry because he had gone outside the gate. He'd expected her to shout at him, but then she had mouthed the instruction to RUN. Stephen stuck his thumb in his mouth, twisting his top in his hand, trying to squeeze comfort from the feel of the cloth. He should have done what she told him. He should have RUN.

When he'd looked at the window again, she wasn't there. At first he'd been relieved, then he heard a funny sound like a groan. That was when he'd thought about his gran. Once before she had fallen in the bathroom and his mum had called for him to get help.

Worry and a desperate need to see his mum had taken him inside, to find the hall strangely still. He'd stopped, unprepared for the feeling that gave him. The door to the bedroom stood open. The smell of pee was stronger, even though his mum had changed the bed. He could see the edge of the white sheet through the open door. He'd glanced inside. His gran was in her chair, head slumped forward.

He'd stood, hesitant, at the door.

'Gran.' His voice was as small as a mouse's squeak.

His gran hadn't looked up. He took one step in, then stopped when he saw the blood. He'd turned and run into the kitchen . . . and saw HIM standing over his mum's body.

Stephen's terrified mind blanked out the picture. A scream rose in his throat, but the sound never emerged to echo around him in the darkness.

7

RHONA STUCK A copy of Stephen's photograph above her desk. It made him seem real and very much alive and that's the way she wanted it.

She had been involved in a number of child abductions and murders in her career. They didn't happen often, thank God, but when they did, they left their mark on everyone involved. Most murders in Glasgow were committed by one villain on another, and they usually involved drugs. Respect for the victim as a person had to be there, although at times it wasn't easy: the murderer and the victim were often interchangeable in their history of violent behaviour. The biggest killer in Glasgow was alcohol abuse. Homicides were at the bottom of the list after suicides, accidents (often drink-related), and drug abuse (at least two a week). Fifty to sixty homicides a year, which meant one a week. This week they had two. She didn't want to think about a possible third.

The disappearance of the child had brought home to her that she hadn't heard from Liam for at least two months. He had promised to keep in touch, but warned her that his voluntary service post as a teacher in a remote Nigerian school didn't allow for regular letters, phone calls or emails. All she'd had since his departure was one text to say he'd arrived safely.

No doubt Mrs Hope, his adopted mother, was in regular contact. Rhona couldn't blame Liam for that. After all she had given up her son when he was days old. The woman who raised him deserved his love and attention, not her.

It was a guilt trip she was used to taking. It didn't help Liam, or herself, and it certainly wouldn't help Stephen.

Under a low-power microscope the thread that tied the bones together was revealed as a generic cotton thread, available over the counter in hundreds of general outlets and haberdasheries. Nothing there to go on, except the likelihood that it was a UK make.

The bones were a different matter. Both bones proved to be forefingers. Neither epiphysis had fused onto the shaft of the bone, which indicated the owner or owners were likely to be younger than thirteen, although girls' bony end plates tended to fuse earlier. To be sure of gender, they would need to perform DNA analysis. GUARD would use radioactive carbon to date the bones, so they would know when the owner had died. The bones would also carry trace indications of the geological region their owner came from. Strontium isotopes remained unchanged in ratio as they passed through the food chain. They were the same in the soil, in the plants that grew in that soil, in the animals that ate those plants and in the humans who ate those animals. The geology of a particular location could be linked to the bone chemistry of a human being. So she would discover where the owner spent their childhood, even if she would never know whose hands the bones had come from.

Such a quantity of information to be gleaned from something so small and fragile. The question was why were the bones in the garden in the first place?

The toxicology report on Carole Devlin had revealed the presence of mefloquine, an anti-malarial taken from one to three weeks before visiting a malarial area and four weeks after coming back. So Carole Devlin had been somewhere recently where malaria was rife. If Carole and her son had been in Africa, did the boy bring the fetish back from there?

Rhona paused for a moment, letting her mind wander from the present to the previous night. So often in her relationship with Sean, she had been the taker and he the giver. She had come home from work needing someone to take away her thoughts of the day. Never in the time she had known Sean had he done the same.

He had refused to come to her bed. 'I stink of drink. It's better if I sleep in here.'

It was as though being angry had drained his blood of alcohol. He'd sobered up quickly, made himself coffee and gone to bed.

At dawn he'd slipped in behind her, his body cool and scented from the shower. He curled his nakedness around hers, flicking her nipples between his thumb and forefinger. There was a speed and desperation about his movements, as though she might stop him.

She thought of Carole Devlin spread-eagled on the floor, the act of love metamorphosed into an act of hate, but the whisper of Sean's voice on her neck had calmed her.

'I love you.'

She was shocked at the words neither of them had spoken before. He hadn't waited for an answer, rocking himself urgently against and with her. She felt his cheek wet on her shoulder and had a sudden rush of tenderness for him. Immediately it was over, he'd risen and begun to pack. Her body was chilled and empty without him.

She sensed his reluctance to discuss the previous night. He was reluctant even to discuss his journey, so she did not question him.

'You can reach me on the mobile,' he'd told her as he called a taxi.

'Are you sure there's a flight?'

'I booked last night before I got drunk.'

And so they'd parted with the awkwardness of a one-night stand.

Even now, thinking back, Rhona could not decide if Sean hated his father, or hated the fact that his father was dying.

8

'HOW DID CAROLE die?'

Bill Wilson regarded the man sitting in front of him. The skin was a deep ebony, polished like teak. The voice was measured and educated with a clipped edge that suggested English public school.

He had turned up at the police office first thing that morning. Shown his passport at the desk and said the dead woman was his wife.

Bill wondered how much information he should give this man who claimed to be Carole Devlin's husband. He could be kind and keep it to a minimum, or describe in detail and watch his reaction. It might be one way of assessing whether or not this man had anything to do with Carole's death.

'Why don't you tell me?'

Mr Devlin absorbed that remark. 'I take it, by your question, that I am a suspect?'

'When did you last see your wife?'

'She left Nigeria a month ago, taking Stephen with her. Her mother was sick and needed her help.'

'You kept in touch?'

'I was offshore. It is difficult to keep in touch.'

'You are an oil man?'

He nodded almost imperceptibly.

'How long have you been married?'

'Five years.'

'Your wife was raped, then killed and mutilated.'

Shock rippled through the ebony features. 'What do you mean, mutilated?'

'The pathologist described it as female genital mutilation.'

'He circumcised Carole?'

'I believe that is a common occurrence in your country?'

'In young girls, unfortunately yes. It is regarded by some as the path to womanhood.'

Bill tried to gauge whether Devlin's show of distaste was real or for his benefit. 'Where were you yesterday?'

'London. I saw the appeal on the news and caught the first flight up this morning.'

Bill accepted this for the moment. The full details of Mr Devlin's movements would become clear in time.

'Would you be willing to identify the body?'

'Of course. What about Stephen?'

Bill had purposefully omitted mention of the missing boy, wondering how long it would take his father to do so. 'We found your son's footprints at the crime scene. We hope he ran away and is hiding.'

It was no more than had been on the news.

'Stephen is not my son. Carole and I married when he was nearly two.'

'Do you know who the father is?'

'We never discussed it.' The tone suggested he wanted to know, but Carole wouldn't tell him.

'To your knowledge, did Carole keep in touch with Stephen's father?'

'According to Carole, Stephen's father never knew he existed. She hated him, I think.'

Mr Devlin was painting Stephen's father as a murder suspect. Bill wondered if he was doing it on purpose.

'Carole and I met in Nigeria. She was working with a British construction company in the north and visited Lagos occasionally. We met at a party. Stephen was a year old by then.'

'You didn't mind that she had a child?'

'Stephen had a nanny. His presence did not affect the time we could spend together.'

It was an odd answer, or Mr Devlin had not understood the question.

'I mean, did you mind that she had a child by another man?'

He looked surprised to be asked. 'It was of no consequence.'

Bill wondered if Stephen was also of no consequence.

Devlin was driving what looked like an airport-hired car, a blue Vauxhall Corsa. He'd agreed to follow Bill to the city mortuary. Bill could have sent a junior officer, but wanted to see Devlin's face when he looked at the body of his wife.

When they got there, Dr Sissons was busy elsewhere. A young mortuary technician called Sandra showed them through. She looked no older than his daughter, Lisa. Filling your day with dead bodies seemed a strange occupation for a young woman. No stranger, he reminded himself, than the job of a policewoman. At least the people you dealt with in here were no danger to your person, provided you wore two pairs of surgical gloves and made sure you did not come into direct contact with infected blood.

Washed, with the effects of the autopsy carefully disguised, Carole Devlin had been given back some dignity. Bill was glad to replace the previous image in the kitchen with this one. In death she looked peaceful, the horror washed away with the blood. The white sheet, tight to her chin, gave the impression of a cold sleep.

Bill watched as John Devlin looked intently at the face. He touched her hair gently, smoothing it back in a gesture similar to Rhona's when she first viewed the body.

'Can I be with her on my own?'

Bill, sensing the emotion beneath the carefully controlled demeanour, agreed. 'I'll be in the waiting room.'

There was a coffee machine that gave you a choice of three different types of coffee. Bill pressed a button at random. The murky brown liquid that emerged was too hot for his liking. He added some water from the water cooler. It tasted foul. He was looking around for somewhere to dispose of liquid and cup when an agitated Sandra appeared at his elbow.

'Detective Inspector Wilson . . .'

'Yes?'

'There's something I think you should see.'

She didn't wait for an answer but quickly led him through to an office that housed a computer system.

On the screen was an image of the mortuary, Devlin standing beside the sheeted body of his wife, head bowed as if in prayer.

'I'd left the camera running by accident,' Sandra explained. 'When you left the mortuary, this is what happened.'

The screen image changed abruptly. The scene was now Devlin making his request and Bill leaving. Immediately the door closed, Devlin looked around, as if to make sure there was no one else in the mortuary, then he pulled back the white sheet and exposed Carole Devlin's naked body. Decency made Bill want to look away, but Sandra gripped his arm.

'Look!'

Devlin was examining the breasts. His hand hovered over a nipple. For a moment, Bill thought he would touch it.

Bill had heard of this before. Bereaved men wanting a last sexual contact with the body they had loved and lost. He was seized with the terrible realisation that if something happened to Margaret he would want the same.

Beside him, Sandra gave a small distressed sound.

Devlin had deserted the breast and was standing at the pelvic region. He reached down and pushed open the legs. Bill's stomach lurched. If this hadn't been a recording, he would have felt compelled to walk in on Devlin, stopping what might happen next.

Devlin was examining his wife's mutilation.

He produced a mobile phone and took three photos in quick succession.

It was over. The sheet was pulled up and Devlin assumed his thoughtful pose.

'Why did he do that?'

'I don't know,' Bill answered truthfully.

Most people wanted to remember their loved ones alive. Photographing a sexually mutilated body seemed abhorrent to Bill. Voyeuristic, even. Or maybe Devlin wanted to see what the murderer had done so he could hate him even more? In the interview, Bill had sensed Devlin was holding something back. Maybe Devlin had an idea who the murderer might be and that idea was linked with the circumcision?

Shock and disbelief at the cruelty of fate often rendered people incapable of standard human reactions. In different cultures, people behaved in different ways. Sometimes with weeping and wailing and beating of breasts. Sometimes with what resembled cold indifference. Occasionally with obsession about every aspect of the death, however horrific.

Bill wondered what cultural background John Devlin came from. From brief research, he'd discovered Nigeria had a number of faiths, including Animism, Christianity and Islam. As well as multiple faiths it had many different tribes, all of whom, it seemed, distrusted and often hated one another. Devlin sounded as though he had been educated in England. How much of Africa still ran in his blood?

When John Devlin emerged, Bill was waiting for

him. Carole's husband had the air of someone who had achieved something positive, however small.

His tone was gracious. 'Thank you for letting me be with her on my own.'

Bill gestured at the machine. 'Do you want some coffee?'

'Thank you again, but no.' He pulled out the mobile. 'I must call my company and explain why I am not in London.'

'Are there any calls between you and your wife on that phone?'

Devlin thought for a moment. 'I talked to Carole briefly after she arrived in the UK.'

'Make your call, then I'd like our technical boys to take a look at your phone, if that's all right?'

Devlin looked perturbed, then nodded. 'Of course, if you think it will help.'

The ring of Bill's own phone broke the moment. It was Janice, her voice trembling with shock.

'They've found the body of a boy.'

Bill turned away from Devlin and kept his voice low. 'Stephen?'

'We don't know, sir. But the boy is black.'

Bill swore under his breath.

'Okay, Janice. Give me directions.' He listened carefully, then hung up, preparing his face and accompanying lie for John Devlin. There was no use telling him about the body until they were sure it was Stephen's.

But when Bill turned, the waiting room was empty. Devlin had disappeared. Bill checked the washroom first then ran outside. The car park was bare apart from his own vehicle and two others, one he recognised as Dr Sissons's. The blue Vauxhall Corsa had gone.

Bill cursed again.

What an idiot. Thirty years in the force and he let Devlin fool him with his posh accent and studied calm. He radioed in and put out a description of Devlin and the car.

The body had been spotted floating at the mouth of the Kelvin. A man had called the Humane Society at their base in Glasgow Green. Their boat, used to picking up suicides and drownings in the Clyde estuary, had radioed the Police Boat, which had provided the high-profile policing on the river since April 2003. Staffed by a sergeant and seven specially trained constables it had plenty of work. The River Clyde was at the heart of 650 square miles of west of Scotland inland waterway.

Bill called Rhona and asked her to meet him there. He suspected, when she picked up, that she had hoped the call would be good news. He was sorry to dash her hopes.

'You think it's Stephen?'

'It's a black kid. That's all Janice could tell me.'

'Does Devlin know?'

Bill related the incident in the mortuary and Devlin's sudden disappearance.

'He was shocked when he learned the truth,' Rhona suggested.

'Or he didn't want me to have his phone.'

'Taking photos of your wife isn't a crime, even if she's dead.'

'It's not just that. There's something weird about Devlin's reaction to all this. Particularly to the kid missing. It was as though he didn't care.'

'Remember, he came to you. Would he have done that if he'd killed his wife?'

Probably not, but then murderers often offered help to get close to the investigation.

The Clydeside Expressway was nose to tail with lunchtime traffic. Distracted by his thoughts, Bill shot past his exit and had to double back. As a result Rhona got there before him.

9

BY THE TIME BY THE TIME Rhona arrived, the body had been dragged ashore. Josh Baird, the man who'd spotted it in the water, had taken it for one of the recently returned seals, with its head missing. He'd been shocked when he learned the truth.

McNab had an incident tent erected as near to the bank of the Kelvin as was sensible, given the tidal nature of the river. The slippery surface squelched under Rhona's feet, the smell a pungent mix of decaying vegetation and river silt. She was grateful for the wellies she always kept in the boot of the car.

This same tributary flowed below her laboratory window. She had stood on many of the numerous bridges that criss-crossed it, weaving a path through the famous Kelvingrove Park. This was the first time she had seen where it eventually ended, swallowed up in its greater cousin, the River Clyde.

An inner and outer cordon had been secured around the incident tent, a constable on the outer cordon logging everyone coming in and out of the crime scene.

Rhona signed in and approached the tent, hoping Bill was already there; but the tent was empty apart from McNab.

When he saw her, his stern expression didn't change, although the way he said her name irritated her. 'Dr MacLeod.'

'Where is it?'

He stood to one side, revealing the object on a metal table. A shock wave ran through Rhona. She had expected horror, but not this.

The small black naked corpse was limbless and headless, just as Josh had suggested. She stepped closer, drawn by disbelief.

The legs had been sawn off at the top of each femur; the arms at the upper humerus. The head had been parted from the body cleanly, perhaps with one stroke. Rhona examined the genital area. The torso was male although the genitalia had also been sliced off.

The final mutilation was a diagonal cross carved in the centre of the small thin chest.

Rhona did a quick mental calculation. The skin had whitened and was heavily puckered. Such a degree of maceration meant the torso could have been in the water between twelve hours and three days. Which meant it could be Stephen.

She let the thought wash over her that all the time they'd hoped, searched and prayed for the little boy, he was already dead and in the water.

The torso showed no sign of hypostasis. No blood had followed the law of gravity and sunk to the blood vessels in the lower part of the body. There were no livid patches so no blood had coagulated. The boy's blood, she realised with horror, had been drained from his body, prior to his immersion in the river.

McNab handed her an evidence bag. Inside was a pair of blue boxer shorts. 'He was wearing these when we pulled him in.'

'That's it?' she asked.

'That's it.'

If the torso turned out not to be Stephen, then a pair of shorts might help them identify the kid, but it was a long shot. And as far as she knew there had been no reports of a missing black boy, apart from Stephen. Scotland didn't have a large black population, but it was easy enough to travel across the border from England.

'You think it's Stephen Devlin?' McNab asked.

'We'll know soon enough.'

One thing she could prove was whether this torso was related to Carole Devlin. Rhona had a gut feeling it was not. Maybe it was just a strong desire for it not to be Stephen. She didn't know. But the feeling was powerful. And if the torso wasn't Stephen, that meant they had a child murder *and* an abduction to deal with.

McNab hovered close by as she took tissue samples. He'd not given her any cause for concern since his return to active duty, but there was something about this pregnant silence that unnerved her. He had always been chatty before. That's what she'd first liked about him. When their relationship had moved into the sexual arena, his attitude remained the same. It had somehow led her to believe he felt the same way about their relationship as she did. When she broke it off, his reaction had thrown her completely. The easy chat had turned vitriolic, full of demands and accusations.

When Bill walked in the atmosphere changed. Rhona was so aware of the change, she thought Bill must sense it as well, but he was too focused on the body.

'Is it Stephen?' he asked.

'I don't know.'

His glance ran the length of the torso, taking in the gaping wounds and the cross cut into the chest. 'The same symbol.'

'Looks like it.'

Rhona explained about the blood letting.

Bill looked haggard, dark shadows circling his eyes.

'Are you okay?'

He didn't seem to hear.

'Bill?'

'What?'

'You look terrible.'

He made a face at McNab. 'Always the kind word from Dr MacLeod, eh?'

The twisted smile was meant to reassure Rhona. It didn't.

He changed the subject. 'So, how soon before we know if it's Stephen?'

'I'll be as quick as I can.'

'In the meantime we keep on looking.'

The school playground was empty. DC Janice Clark glanced at her watch. School was already out. No hum of chat from closed classrooms, no teacher's voice giving instructions.

Schools were peaceful places without kids. The main door was lying open, but reception was manned by a woman in her fifties with a no-nonsense air. 'Can I help you?'

Janice flashed her badge.

The lady took time to study it. No one was going to get past without her okay. 'You're here to see Miss Stuart?'

When Janice nodded, the woman indicated an open visitors' book. 'Please sign in. Your name and the time. You are also expected to sign out.'

Once Janice had signed, she was buzzed through the electronically controlled door. Schools weren't the open places of her day. Since Thomas Hamilton had blazed his way through Dunblane Primary in 1996, killing sixteen children and their teacher, the local authorities were pretty stringent about security. Janice's own memories of doors staying open summer and winter no longer rang true. Then, the kids just thought of getting out of the place at the end of the day. There was no thought of someone wanting to get in.

Miss Stuart's classroom was three along on the ground level. The door was shut and Janice glanced in the small rectangular window to see the teacher sitting at her desk, a pile of jotters beside her. Marking, the bane of most teachers' lives. Janice knew all about it. Her big sister was a teacher. Marking, and stroppy kids. The worst in secondary schools, when the hormones started rioting. As far as Janice knew, the rioting had moved steadily downwards and now took place in many primary classrooms.

She knocked on the door and a clear steady voice called, 'Come in.'

The classroom had been painted bright yellow. One wall held a long mural of an historic battle, 'Bannockburn 1314' blazoned along the top. The combatants were a motley crew. It looked as though the scene had been divided into rectangles and different kids got to draw their own stick-like men. The result was a lot of missing arms and legs, big swords and blood.

Miss Stuart studied Janice's badge of office and pointed to a seat across the desk from her.

'I heard on the news. It's terrible.' Tears sprang to her eyes. She opened a desk drawer and pulled out a paper hanky. Janice gave her time to blow her nose.

'How well do you know Stephen?'

'Not well at all. He only arrived in school a month ago.'

'Does he ever speak of his father?'

'No, but . . .' Miss Stuart rifled through the jotters on her desk. 'This is Stephen's news jotter. The children write a bit each day. He's only six so there's more drawings than words. And he often uses Nigerian words when he isn't sure of the English. I don't know if he spells them correctly.' She looked apologetic, as though teachers were supposed to know everything.

Janice pulled the open jotter towards her and flipped through the pages. Most were headed with the day of the week and a date in big circular letters. There were coloured drawings of the weather, a bus and one of an orange underground train.

'He likes Glasgow underground,' Miss Stuart explained with a smile.

Janice stopped at a picture of a wide muddy-
coloured river, with high banks. *Rua* was written below.

'I think *rua* means water, or river, in Hausa. That's
the language he sometimes uses. There's a drawing of a
man on the next page.'

The figure was tall and stately. Broad but not fat. He
was wearing a suit and a blue tie. There was a thick,
angry pencilled cross drawn through his face.

If this was Stephen's father, he didn't like him very
much.

'May I take this with me?'

'Of course.'

'Where does Stephen sit?'

Miss Stuart pointed to a desk in the second front
row.

'And friends? Who sits beside him? Plays with him?'

'Stephen doesn't have a particular friend. He likes
playing by himself.' She hesitated for a moment.
'Although he does chat to Yana on occasion.'

'Yana?'

'She's black too.' She looked embarrassed to use the
word. 'Her father works at Glasgow University.'

'It might help to speak to Yana.'

Miss Stuart opened her register and wrote an address on a slip of paper. 'I will call Dr Olatunde and tell
him I've given you his contact details, if that's all right?'

'Of course.' Janice nodded her understanding.

'There's one other thing . . .'

'Yes.'

'Stephen is afraid of the dark. Very afraid. Something happened to make him that way.'

'He told you that?'

She shook her head. 'No. His mother did.'

'And she never mentioned a Mr Devlin?'

'No. And I never asked,' she said firmly.

Single parents were apparently a common occurrence for Miss Stuart.

'Did Carole Devlin give the impression she was afraid of something or someone?'

'No. She seemed calm and well organised. If she was fearful it was for her son. She worried whether the other children would be mean to him because of his colour.'

'And are they?'

'Not in my presence,' she retorted angrily.

As Janice left, the teacher went back to her marking. Overtime in teaching wasn't paid for. A bit like CID.

The corridor smelt of disinfectant. Janice breathed it in. For a moment, she was a school kid again and it was just as scary now as it had been then.

10

CAROLE DEVLIN'S FLAT was as neat and tidy as a hotel bedroom and just as impersonal. Bill watched as a team went carefully through her meagre belongings. It looked as though Carole had come here with nothing and had amassed nothing while here. Two suitcases in a hall cupboard. Minimal clothes in the wardrobes and drawers. The kitchen had enough food for a couple of meals. Plenty of cornflakes and milk suggested Stephen was a cereal fan. The flat was a private rent. He'd already spoken to the owner, a Mr Fisher, who lived above. He was elderly, deaf and very pleasant. He didn't like renting to students, he'd told Bill. He could hear their music even when he turned his hearing aid down.

Mrs Devlin and the boy were quiet. She paid two months in advance and had taken the flat for six months initially. She brought him his milk and paper when she went to the shops. In fact she was a perfect tenant. His rheumy eyes betrayed his distress at her demise.

'What about Stephen?' he asked, his voice shaking.

'We're still looking,' Bill told him, trying to sound positive.

They had managed to keep the story of the torso out of the headlines so far. The press was giving them a window to see if the body was Stephen's.

The continuing house-to-house plus the search of the surrounding area had produced nothing. The boy had simply disappeared. If he had managed to get away from his mother's attacker, he had found a good hiding place.

Bill had experience of runaway kids before. A girl of eight had gone missing in the summer of 2004. Molly Reynolds. Her name was written on his soul. Thirty-six hours after she disappeared on her way home from school, he had privately given up hope of finding her alive. Then a night watchman on a building site found her. She'd made a den in a pile of pipes and insisted she wasn't going home until her mother threw out the latest boyfriend, who was sticking his hands down her knickers.

A lost child became a child abuse case. Bill thought about making it a double murder. The stupid mother and her arse of a boyfriend.

'Sir . . .' DC MacLaren handed him a photograph. 'This was in a drawer in the mum's bedroom.'

Carole Devlin stood in a formal pose beside a black man. Both were wearing brightly patterned national dress and smiling broadly. A wedding photograph, perhaps? If it was, the chap beside her wasn't the one who claimed to be her husband and walked out of the mortuary after taking photos of her mutilation.

Bill turned the picture over. A faint stamp read: *Ronald Ugwu, Photographer, Sabon Gari, Kano.*

'Kano?' he muttered to himself.

'Northern Nigeria, sir.'

Bill was impressed.

'My brother-in-law's a civil engineer. Spent some time in Northern Nigeria working on an irrigation project.' MacLaren looked pleased to know something the boss didn't. 'Language is Hausa. Religion, predominantly Islam, with a bit of everything else thrown in, including the witch doctor stuff . . . juju.'

Bill didn't like hearing the juju word again. 'Is your brother-in-law still out there?'

MacLaren shook his head. 'Nigeria turfed out most of the expats. He's in Indonesia now.'

It could have been useful to have someone on hand who knew a bit about the place.

'Find out if there's someone at one of the city universities who's an expert on Nigeria, particularly the practice of juju.'

DC MacLaren appeared delighted to be given a task that didn't involve house-to-house and searching undergrowth.

The autopsy on the torso was scheduled for four o'clock. Bill contemplated a quick call to Margaret, then decided against it. If she thought he was 'on her case' she would give him grief. Better to do what she said and wait for her to tell him any news about an appointment. Anxiety gnawed at his stomach. He didn't like to admit to himself that he might be more worried about his wife than the missing kid. If it was cancer, he was a bystander, dependent on medical people doing their job. And that stuck in his gut.

Margaret was right. He had to concentrate on finding the boy, as long as he wasn't already lying on a slab in the mortuary.

Twice in two days. Bill was beginning to feel as though he lived in the mortuary. Dr Sissons looked up at the clock as Bill entered and gave him a brief welcoming nod. It was protocol for the investigating officer and the Procurator Fiscal to be present at an autopsy. Few Procurator Fiscals came. Too smelly and bloody for them.

Police officers, mortuary assistants and lawyers, in fact anyone who might have to give evidence in a criminal court, were encouraged to take Glasgow University's three-term course in Forensic Medical Science. It prepared you for the worst, covering everything from Forensic Psychiatry to Forensic Anthropology, with Blood Splatter Analysis, Arson and DNA Technology on the way. You needed the knowledge to face the top criminal defence lawyers currently practising in Scotland. Otherwise they would make mincemeat of your evidence.

You also had to have a strong stomach to cope with some of the images they showed on the big screen of the lecture theatre. Wounds from every type of sharp implement Glaswegians could get their hands on. Knives, samurai swords and, in one instance, a whirligig.

One thing the course didn't illustrate was an autopsy.

Sandra, the mortuary technician from earlier with

Lin Anderson

Devlin, was helping. Bill didn't recognise the small slim figure in her overalls until she said a friendly hello.

A second pathologist, Dr Brown, was also present, a requirement of Scottish law. Sissons began his description of what was left of the body, his monotone delivery belying the fact that they were looking at the remains of a child. 'In the water approximately twelve to thirty-six hours, judging by the skin texture.' He recorded the obvious into the microphone: 'Headless, limbless and bloodless. Two incised wounds to the chest, approximately eight centimetres in length, in the shape of a cross.'

He began a meticulous search for other injuries or external signs of disease, then opened up the chest cavity. Bill was familiar with the procedure but the process still horrified him. Once the body lost its shape it ceased to be human and became a carcass in a butcher's shop. But this intricate study of its constituent parts would tell them much about the boy.

'Likely cause of death, decapitation, allowing the blood to be drained out. The removal of arms and legs may have been associated with a ritual or an attempt to make the body unrecognisable. The sexual organs have also been removed. The anus has been swabbed and no evidence of sexual assault found.'

He began the removal of the internal organs.

'If the child has spent time in West Africa, then parasitic invasion is a likely possibility. We should check for schistosomiasis in particular. It's endemic and specific to region, which could be helpful in pinpointing his origins.'

The stomach contents plopped into a basin. What looked like the remains of a gherkin swam in a sea of part-digested meat.

'Looks suspiciously like a McDonald's.'

Sandra took a closer look. 'Judy at GUARD says Burger King crinkle-cut their gherkins. McDonald's don't.'

The juxtaposition of fast-food outlets and ritual murder had a dark kind of irony to it.

'His stomach contents should indicate whether he was in the UK twenty-four hours before his death.'

Finished with the examination, Sissons gave instructions to Sandra to tidy the torso then made for the sink and pulled off his gloves.

The fresh running water sounded good to Bill.

'You were lucky to find him. The next tide could have washed him well downstream.'

The word *lucky* didn't seem to have a place in this room.

Sissons scrubbed his hands thoroughly, then dried them on a paper towel. He turned to face Bill. 'I take it you want to know if this torso is the missing boy?'

'As soon as possible.'

'We can't go on skin tone alone, but judging by the length and breadth, I would estimate this torso to be older than the missing boy. The only way to be sure is for Dr MacLeod to confirm with DNA.'

Bill refused to think of the victim as a torso. He was a boy. And he had decided to call him Abel. The name of Adam's son, killed by his older brother, Cain. The first murder in the Hebrew Bible and the Qur'an.

Bill didn't know whether to be jubilant or distraught at the likelihood that it wasn't Stephen. Odds were, after this amount of time, a missing child, especially one as young as Stephen, was dead. If Abel wasn't Stephen, they had another dead child on their hands.

11

TWO HUNDRED CELLS. The equivalent of holding a pen for thirty seconds. That was all it took to generate a DNA profile.

But samples collected at the crime scene had to be free from contamination. It didn't matter how good the laboratory was, how good the DNA facilities were. If the samples were compromised or of poor quality, the evidence was suspect.

She had used Carole's blood to profile her DNA. For Abel it had to be tissue. If Carole was Abel's mother then her DNA strands would show up in his.

The comparison printout told Rhona what she wanted to see. Abel had genotype 3,2. He had inherited the two-type repeat on his chromosome from his father. His mother had gifted him three repeats in his chromosome pattern. But Carole Devlin didn't have that pattern to give him. The torso they'd pulled from the Kelvin wasn't Carole's son.

She had run the semen-produced DNA profile of the perpetrator through the NDNAD. The murderer wasn't in the national database. She also had a DNA profile for Stephen with the help of some clothes from Carole's flat and a toothbrush. That way she had ruled out the possibility that the man who killed Carole was Stephen's natural father.

So much information and yet still they knew nothing. Two women and a boy dead, another boy missing. The cross on the bodies of Carole and Abel suggested a common attacker, or at least a common theme to the attacks.

Which led to the bones.

Rhona pulled up a photo of the crossed bones onto her computer screen. She had passed the originals found in the garden to Judy Brown, the anthropologist at GUARD. Finding their origins wouldn't be the problem. What they meant, if anything, in the context of the crime might prove more difficult.

She drafted a short email to Sam and attached the photo. Maybe his Nigerian mother could throw some light on their significance.

It was pitch-black outside. Time had rushed by unnoticed in a flurry of forensic activity. Day two of the enquiry at an end and they were nowhere nearer finding Stephen.

When Rhona heard the door open, McNab was the last person she expected to see.

He glanced up at the wall clock. 'Thought you'd still be working.'

He spoke as though he knew her intimately. The idea rattled her. She waited in silence for him to explain why he was here, conscious that her heart had upped its beat.

'I wanted to know if the body was Stephen's.'

'It isn't.'

He gave a relieved shrug, then looked ashamed. 'That just means we have another dead kid.'

Rhona tried to recall what it was about McNab that had made her invite him into her bed. Laughter was one of the reasons. When she was with him she laughed a lot, about work, the politics of the police force, life in general. Sex was hot, long lasting and satisfying. Being with him was like being on holiday, then the holiday ended and she came back to reality.

The silence between them was growing more uneasy with every second. She wanted to break it, but didn't know how. He looked increasingly uncomfortable and she felt bad because of it. That was the trouble with women. They always wanted to make people happy. You can't make an old lover into a friend, particularly if you dumped him.

He noticed the image of the bones on the computer screen and came forward for a better look. To step away would have looked silly. Rhona stayed where she was.

A scent stays in the memory longer than any other sense. It can trigger flashbacks, where visual images would not. Victims of violent crime know that more than anyone. An attacker's scent never goes away. It lies coiled in the subconscious, a snake waiting to strike. A rush of emotions swept through Rhona, sexual attraction followed closely by something resembling fear. For a split second she wondered if this was what abused women felt about the men who both loved and hurt them. Attraction and revulsion inextricably woven together.

'Are you okay?'

By the expression on his face, she had rattled McNab as much as he had her.

'In need of a stiff drink and some food, that's all.'

It was the wrong answer. He would offer to take her for a drink and she would have to refuse. The professional veneer they were operating under would crack and they might have to talk about what was really going on.

'I won't offer to buy you one,' he joked.

He looked sorry and she suddenly realised he was trying to be normal with her. Trying harder than she was.

'There's no law against the CSM buying the Chief Forensic a drink.'

This was how it had to be played. Easy. As though nothing had happened between them, nor ever would.

A weight lifted off his shoulders and he smiled.

'Okay . . . you've persuaded me.'

They walked down University Avenue an arm's length apart. The jazz club didn't serve food, but Rhona chose to go there anyway. Eating with McNab was too friendly. A drink in a busy bar populated by colleagues felt safer.

Sam wasn't behind the bar or at the piano. His replacement answered her enquiry with a knowing look. 'His night off. Meeting his girl.'

Rhona was relieved Chrissy wasn't there making eyes at her over McNab's shoulder, nursing opinions to be served up later, cold and unpalatable. Only

Sandra sat at the bar with her colleague Simon. They were en route to the Western Infirmary lecture theatre for their Tuesday night dose of forensic medicine. They were halfway through the nine-month course. Rhona had given the DNA lecture just after the Christmas break.

'What is it tonight, then?'

'Forensic Odontology,' Sandra told her.

'Paisley, the biting capital of the world.'

'I take it it's the same stories every year?'

'They only repeat the good ones.'

Rhona watched them leave, conscious now that she was alone with McNab. The barman had brought her usual glass of wine and McNab's beer order. The barman's brief enquiry about Sean was difficult to answer. Sean had sent only one text since he left for Dublin, to say he'd arrived safely and would call. Whatever was happening there wasn't something he wanted to talk about and she had been too preoccupied to dwell on it. Sean's family were his own affair. He'd volunteered nothing about them and she hadn't forced the issue.

'He's not sure when he'll be back.' That was truthful enough.

McNab waited for the barman to move away before he said, 'There was a similar case in 2001. A black boy's torso was pulled out of the Thames. D'you remember?'

It had been high profile for a while, making the national newspapers. The investigating team had tracked the child via his bone mineral content to the Yoruba plateau in Nigeria. Despite extensive enquiries there, no mother had come forward to claim she'd lost a child. But there had been a connection to Glasgow. A Nigerian woman had been taken into custody and questioned. Nothing came of it, as far as Rhona knew.

'Could be just a coincidence,' she suggested.

'Or another piece of the same jigsaw.'

They discussed a recent newspaper article that had estimated there were at least three hundred thousand people living illegally in Britain, evading the immigration authorities for years. Many of them had kids now. During the 'Adam' enquiry in London, schools had reported black kids missing from their classrooms. Missing because their families moved on, or missing like Adam and Abel?

'The DI's in touch with the Met,' McNab told her. 'Maybe they can throw some light on our case.'

Rhona's glass was empty. McNab offered her a refill, but she declined. 'I have to get home.'

'Of course.'

She slipped off the stool. 'See you at the meeting tomorrow.'

It was what any colleague would say.

'See you.'

She was conscious of his eyes on her back as she walked to the stairs. Outside she took a deep gulp of Glasgow air. It tasted sweet despite the fumes. The first meeting alone with McNab was over. The next, should it happen, would be easier, the one after easier still. But she wished Sean was at the flat waiting for her. She wanted to drown McNab's scent in Sean's.

★   ★   ★

Rhona called in at the pasta shop and bought fresh pasta and tomato sauce. Mr Margiotta suggested a suitable bottle of red wine to go with it and she acquiesced. Sean was the wine connoisseur. Normally she didn't have to choose.

The meeting with McNab had disturbed her, bringing back uncomfortable memories. He had been one of the reasons she'd avoided forming another relationship.

Sean had changed that. She wasn't sure what love was, yet he had used that word before he left for Dublin. Part of her wished he hadn't said it, knowing they had crossed a line.

Despite the echoing emptiness of the flat, she felt relieved to be there. She locked and bolted the front door in a sudden need for security. In her first few moments in the hall without the soft miaowing of Chance, she made the momentous decision to replace him. She would search out a cat rescue home and find one as soon as possible. A flat without a cat wasn't a home.

She opened the wine to let it breathe and went to shower. The heavy drumming water left her breathless. She bent her head, letting the needles beat her shoulders, easing the tenseness that sent cramps up her neck. Had Sean been there, he would have noticed her raised shoulders and massaged them. His strong thumbs stroking the muscles into relaxation.

From the kitchen window she contemplated the statue of the Virgin Mary in the convent garden behind. Forever serene, bathed in her spotlight.

I am the way, the truth and the light, Jesus said.

Religion wasn't part of her life, but she understood what all detectives knew. A man who could rape and kill had invented an evil narrative for his life where empathy played no part. The more ferocious the assault, the greater the likelihood of a pre-existing relationship between the victim and their attacker. The viciousness of the assault on Carole Devlin suggested she knew her murderer.

The physical evidence didn't lie. That's what she had been taught. But the way the criminal embraced the crime and the way he chose to commit it was also evidence. The murderer had left psychological traces, ambiguous and subtle, but important none the less.

After eating she set up her laptop and located as much information as she could on the Metropolitan Police's investigation into the death of the boy they'd called Adam. What was available online was confined to newspaper reports. Interesting but sketchy. She would have to rely on Bill to give the relevant aspects of the story tomorrow, at the next strategy meeting.

The wine sent her to sleep in front of the gas fire, her dreams haunted by the vision of a child weeping in a dark cold place. The doorbell shattered the nightmare and she sat up startled, unsure where she was and what had woken her. The doorbell rang again, more insistent this time. She stood up stupid with sleep and went to the door.

'Rhona. It's me. Take off the bolt.' Sean's voice was urgent.

He stood with the small holdall beside him, his eyes smudged with fatigue, bristle darkening his chin.

He gave her a relieved half smile. 'Can I come in?'

She stood to one side and let him pass.

'I'm sorry. I should have called, but there hasn't been a minute.'

'Your father . . .' she began.

He pushed the door shut and slid the bolt. The muscles on the back of his neck were bunched as though the action needed great effort. 'Come here.'

He pulled her to him, his mouth fastening on hers, his body crushed against her. He smelt of whisky and sweat.

He groaned and a shudder passed through his body.

She reached down and clasped him, urging him into action.

His movements were swift and frantic as though he were fighting for his life. She met each thrust with her own, exorcising her own inner demons.

Afterwards he mumbled an apology into her hair. 'I was desperate.'

She cradled his head in her hands and touched his lips lightly with her own. 'So was I.'

They looked down at the discarded clothes and laughed.

'Come on.'

He fetched the duvet and they sat cuddled beneath it in front of the fire. His skin glistened in the light. She licked a trickle of sweat that ran down the hollow in his chest.

   * * *

Later, in bed, he talked about his father's death.

'The funeral's on Friday. I have to go back.'

'I'll come with you.'

He looked puzzled as though the thought had never occurred to him. 'I don't know. It would be hard for you. The family . . .'

'Don't know about me?'

'Oh they know about you. It's just they'd have you for breakfast along with the bacon and soda bread.'

'That bad?'

'The Irish are a breed apart,' he said ruefully.

'You don't have to tell me that.'

He acknowledged her attempt at humour.

'Me mam's heartbroken.' He shook his head as if in disbelief.

He had lapsed into colloquial Irish. Rhona liked the sound. It made his voice into a sort of music.

'Da was an ole bastard. A drunk with a silver tongue and a fuck of a temper. Mam tied a string across the stairs once. Hoped he would fall and break his neck. The perfect murder.'

She was shocked. 'You're joking?'

He shook his head. 'I was eight at the time. He was on one of his binges. I saw her do it. But she took it away before he came downstairs.'

'God!'

'God didn't come into it, or else he would have tied the string across the stairs himself and given us all peace.'

It was like a funny story someone would tell in a pub after a few drinks. Only it wasn't really funny.

Rhona examined the deep blue eyes. 'You're not like him.'

'No I'm not. He fathered eight children and I have none.'

There was a note of sadness in his voice. In the midst of pain he always cracked a joke. This time was no different.

'But he and I have the same sex drive.'

Rhona lay close, her arm about him, breathing him in as he dropped into a deep sleep, McNab's scent gone from her memory.

12

THE WATER BEAT his face in steady drips. Stephen opened his mouth and let it dribble over his parched tongue. The oily taste met the back of his throat and he gagged, rolling sideways, coughing and spluttering. Some sick came up and he spat it out.

This is what it's like to be buried alive.

The thought frightened him so much his bladder released and pee ran hot through his shorts and down his leg.

The sharp smell of it made him think of his gran. She didn't cry when she had an accident. He wasn't going to either. He closed his eyes tightly and the tears ran outwards, into his hair. He imagined Gran winking at him and popping a raspberry jelly baby in his mouth. 'Go on, then. Give us a song. That one I like.'

Stephen began in a small piping voice like a bird's.

> *One more step along the world I go,*
> *One more step along the world I go,*
> *From the old things to the new*
> *Keep me travelling along with you . . .*

He faltered at the sound of footsteps in the tunnel. His body began to shake uncontrollably.

Someone was coming.

Day 3

Wednesday

13

SEAN WAS STILL in the deep sleep of the previous night. In the morning light the bruised patches under his eyes were more obvious, as was the smell of whisky. He'd been drinking whisky in an almost continuous flow since he'd left. 'It makes talking easier,' he'd said. 'Everyone talks about a death in Ireland. Too much and too often.'

She made some strong coffee and drank it while she dressed. Day three of the investigation. Stephen had been missing for thirty-six hours. Time was crucial in a missing child case. Twelve hours was the magic number and they were well past that. Yet she carried on believing that he was still alive. Gut feeling or misguided hope? Rhona couldn't tell which.

The lab was empty and silent. Too early even for Chrissy. If she worked quickly there was a chance she would have something on the shorts found on the torso for the strategy meeting at ten o'clock.

The shorts were dark blue with what looked like a foreign label, partially cut off. They had dried in dirty smears from their time in the river and on the muddy bank. She spread them out on the counter. Using a magnifying glass she went over every square centimetre of material, locating stains that proved to be blood, urine, faeces and semen.

She set aside a sample of each of these for testing then looked more closely at the back of the shorts. The material was smudged with ground-in dirt. She removed a small portion of material and examined it under the microscope. The particles looked like a mix of mineral and organic. Unless the mix was unique it would be of little help unless they could match it to similar material on a suspect. And they didn't have a suspect.

Now she carefully turned the pockets inside out and concentrated on the seams. Even submerged in water, something might remain lodged there. Her heart quickened as she distinguished what looked like plant hairs or trichomes. She removed them and slid them under the microscope. There were two types of trichomes, fine and coarse. What plant did they belong to?

'Hey!'

Rhona jumped, startled at Chrissy's sudden appearance.

'You're in early.' Chrissy smothered a yawn.

'The strategy meeting on the torso's at ten o'clock, and I'm due at GUARD again at nine.'

'Have you checked your email yet?'

She had been too busy to think about it.

'Sam sent you something about the bones.'

Chrissy's expression didn't herald good news.

'What is it?'

'You'd better read it for yourself.'

Sam had forwarded his mother's reply.

Rhona skimmed it, then began reading it again with a sense of unease. It was a clear warning that anyone touching the bones was in imminent danger.

Rhona was a scientist through and through, but she knew the power of the spiritual world over those who believed. Sam's mother believed. And she was frightened.

The bleaching light of the meeting room rendered Dr Sissons even more stone-like than usual. McNab threw Rhona a glance as she entered and she acknowledged it. Bill Wilson sat at the head of the table with his usual cup of cold coffee, his mind elsewhere. DC Clark looked nervous, shifting in her seat like a child in a classroom under the watchful eye of a teacher.

If Stephen was dead then it was because the people in this room had not found him in time to prevent it. That was the unspoken thought in everyone's mind, except perhaps Sissons. He was only responsible for telling them how a victim died.

Sissons began his report on the torso. He brought up an image on the big screen, the crossed scars clearly visible. There was an audible intake of breath from DC Clark. She was the only person in the room who hadn't seen the child's torso. Bill threw her a swift look and she shook her head, indicating she was okay.

They were subjected to the story of the decapitation and blood letting, the examination of the stomach contents and internal organs.

'The child died within twelve hours of eating his last meal, which was, I am reliably informed from forensic, a typical Burger King. The boy was also suffering from a parasitic disease known as bilharzia or schistosomiasis. Schistosoma parasites can penetrate the skin of people who wade, swim, bathe, or wash in contaminated water. Within several weeks, worms grow inside the blood vessels of the body and produce eggs. Some of these eggs travel to the bladder or intestines and are passed into the urine or stool. I have sent a specimen to the City Hospital in Edinburgh for confirmation.'

'So the child wasn't brought up here?' Bill asked.

'He could have become infected on a visit.' Dr Sissons motioned to Rhona. 'Dr MacLeod will be able to deduce from his bone mineral content where he was brought up.'

Rhona had spent almost an hour with Judy Brown at GUARD. It had proved an interesting meeting. She told the assembled group what she had found out.

'The crossed bones at the scene of the first murder are male, approximately six to eight years old,' she told them. 'The study of the mineral content suggests an area near Kano in Northern Nigeria. The torso bones are still being analysed. However . . .' and here she pulled out the email she'd received from Sam. She explained Sam's origins and the fact that he'd sent an image of the bones to his mother in Nigeria.

'His mother says,' Rhona read the email out loud: ' "Where did you find these? They are very powerful black magic and should not be touched." '

'Is that all?' Bill broke the disbelieving silence that followed her words.

'No. There's more.' She cleared her throat and read on. ' "The bones choose their next victim." '

'What the hell does that mean?' Bill reached for the email and read out the rest. ' "The bones signify the chosen one. A previous human sacrifice supplies the bones that attract the next sacrifice." '

'Jesus!' McNab muttered beside her.

Sitting next to DC Clark, Rhona felt her flinch and stiffen. When Rhona turned to comfort her, Janice's eyes were wide with fear.

'It is, of course, nonsense,' Sissons's clipped authoritative voice shattered the sense of unease.

'To us it is,' Bill went on grimly. 'But to whoever took Stephen, it is not.'

'There's one bit of good news.' The rest of the team looked at Rhona as though they needed it. 'I examined the shorts taken from Abel. One of the pockets had plant material and soil in it not dislodged by its time in the water. The soil is a type of coal dust.'

They waited while she went on. 'We're still analysing the dust. Mines can have distinctive components in their coal seams. If Abel was kept in or near a coal shaft, we might be able to locate its whereabouts.'

Bill was already going over in his mind how many old mine workings there were in the central belt of Scotland. Dozens in Glasgow alone, most of their locations long forgotten. It was only when housing estates showed signs of subsidence that old mine workings were suspected.

Rhona went steadily on. 'The plant material checks out as two types of trichomes from a plant called

Echium vulgare or viper's bugloss. It's rare and is found on Glasgow bings, the spoil heaps found near former mines. Picking the plant or even brushing against it is painful and causes a rash.'

'Okay. So we think Abel may have been kept near old mine workings.'

'Or in one?' McNab suggested.

'How does that help us find Stephen?' Bill asked.

'I think Stephen was lifted over the wall into the back alley,' Rhona explained. 'The other SOCOs found partial tyre prints. When we lifted these we found coal dust, of a similar make-up, in the tread marks.'

'Eureka!' McNab's exclamation echoed Rhona's own thoughts when she'd found the match.

Bill was thinking out loud. 'If there was a van someone must have seen it. How can you bundle a kid into a van and not be seen?'

'The alleyway has eight-foot walls either side,' Rhona reminded him. 'Only someone in an upper flat would see over the wall.'

'Okay, we go back. We ask again.'

It was Janice's turn to report. She produced the school jotter and flipped it open at the page with the drawing of the man. 'Stephen's teacher insists a father wasn't mentioned either by Carole Devlin or Stephen.'

'Whoever the man in the drawing is, Stephen doesn't like him.' Rhona's use of the present tense brought them all up sharp.

'Stephen had . . . has one friend at school, a little girl called Yana.'

'And?'

'I went round to their house but there was no answer. I've tried twice since. When there was no reply on the number the school gave me, I contacted the university. Dr Olatunde is on leave. He is visiting his family in Nigeria.'

'Did he take his daughter with him?'

'Miss Stuart didn't seem to know he was away. She was going to phone him, tell him I would be in contact about Stephen.'

'And you let her?'

Janice looked confused. 'I thought teachers weren't allowed to give out information on their pupils without—'

Bill cut her off. 'You're a police officer, DC Clark, in case you've forgotten. We don't warn suspects we're coming.'

Janice drew herself up. 'He wasn't a suspect, sir.'

'Everyone's a suspect, detective constable!' Bill snapped.

Rhona shot him a look. His eyes were red rimmed, his skin grey. Bill was a boss who led his troops by example, not by ridiculing their mistakes.

Rhona filled the stunned silence. 'Is there any chance Stephen was taken out of the country?'

McNab shook his head. 'They would need his passport. And he would have to be with a parent or guardian.'

'The guy who professed to be Carole's husband?' Rhona asked.

'No sign of him. But all major UK airports have been given a description,' Janice told her.

If the man who called himself Devlin was using another identity, passport control would be unlikely to spot him.

'The Met are checking up to see if they have anything on our Mr Devlin. The CCTV picture is grainy. The lab's working on it, but without a better image or DNA . . .' said McNab.

'Our contact in the Met is sending up details of their Adam case,' Bill added.

'The forensic reports?' Rhona asked.

'Those too. Okay,' Bill ordered, 'I want a map of all coal mines in and around the Glasgow area as soon as possible. Janice?'

'Yes, sir.'

Rhona stood up. 'I've already contacted the mining museum at the Victoria Colliery in Newtongrange. I'm going down there now.'

'So we need to find a disused mine that matches your coal deposit . . .'

'And has viper's bugloss growing on it.'

14

SAM HARUNA SAT relaxed and easy on the hard chair of the interview room. Bill was more used to seeing him serving behind the bar or playing the piano. They had even talked jazz pianists together. Bill had professed a liking for Bob Alberti and Sam had agreed with him.

'*Everything I Love* CD with Harry Allen on saxophone.'

'Track?' Bill tested him.

'"Drifting".'

Bill liked the young Nigerian. According to Sean, he was a reliable worker. His manner with people suggested he would make a good doctor. Just the sort of immigrant Scotland needed.

He had no reason to ask Sam to come down here, apart from the email. When he'd called the jazz club, Sam had agreed immediately.

'You're not under suspicion of anything,' Bill had assured him.

Sam had sounded relieved. 'That's good.'

Bill had already ordered a trawl for any West Africans living in Glasgow. He wasn't comfortable about it, but it had to be done.

He'd taken Sam into the interview room because

there was nowhere else quiet enough to talk. After the strategy meeting, the station had exploded into action. Bill couldn't help but think that without more to go on, it was mostly displacement activity.

The air in the room smelt of stale cigarette smoke and, faintly, of urine. It wouldn't be unheard of for interviewees to quietly piss themselves while sitting in here. Bill made a mental note to have the cleaners douse the place in bleach again.

'Where did you learn piano?'

'A *Baturi* taught me.'

'*Baturi*?'

Sam smiled. 'The Hausa word for a European. He had a piano in his house in Kano. I had a job as a kid, helping in his garden. I watered the plants first thing in the morning and last thing at night. He loved those plants. He had a big verandah. Blue morning glory and big white scented moonflowers wound all the way up. He paid me in piano lessons.' Sam leaned forward. 'But you didn't ask me here to talk piano or plants.'

'No,' Bill conceded. 'The bones . . .'

'My mother believes those things she said.'

'And you don't?'

Sam thought for a moment. 'Can I ask you a question?'

'Go ahead.'

'Do you pray?'

A week ago Bill would have said no and meant it. But not any more. If the truth were told, he was praying there was a God, praying with all his heart and soul.

Sam was reading his mind. 'Do you believe in God?'

Bill felt uncomfortable. It was a question he'd never been asked, not even by Margaret. He tried to be honest. 'Like most folk I prefer to hedge my bets.'

'I do the same with juju. I could never say I don't believe, just in case . . .'

'Are there many Nigerians in Glasgow?'

'You mean a secret juju society casting spells on the good Scottish people of the city?' Sam grew serious. 'There are a few but I'm not in touch with them. I have become a *Baturi*.'

Bill wondered how true that was.

'But I will say this. The person who made that fetish believes.'

'Believes what?'

'That having sex with a child can cure you of AIDS. That killing a child will make you more powerful. The child's spirit enters you and gives you new life.'

A shiver ran down Bill's back. 'The torso in the Kelvin had the blood drained from it.' He watched Sam's face closely as he spoke. 'What does that mean?'

'Life blood contains the spirit of the child. They will drink it.'

'They cut off his penis and testicles.'

'They will dry them and grind them down for medicine to make men more virile.' Sam covered his eyes. 'I am ashamed to say these things. They are like poison in my mouth.'

Bill pushed the jotter across the table. 'Stephen drew a picture of a man. Can you recognise it?'

Sam's face paled under the ebony skin.

'You know him?'

'It is a child's drawing . . . I couldn't be sure.'

'But it looks like someone?'

Sam was struggling with himself. 'The facial scars . . . three horizontal on each cheek just above the corners of the mouth.'

Bill looked more closely. They had concentrated on the pencilled cross through the head. But Sam was right. Stephen had drawn three scars on each cheek.

'Dr Olatunde has those. They are the markings of his tribe. Oyo, I think. They're very distinctive.'

The same Dr Olatunde whose daughter was Stephen's friend?

'How do you know this man?' Bill asked him.

'He's a teacher in the medical department of Glasgow University.'

On the way to the university, Margaret's text came through on the mobile. Bill immediately drew up on a double yellow line.

Today. 2pm. M.

He leaned back against the headrest, nausea sweeping over him. He never felt sick. Had never experienced that chilly sweat before the rush of bile. Margaret had been sick all the time when she was pregnant with the kids. She used to carry a couple of plain biscuits everywhere with her. Nibbling them when she thought he wasn't looking, to stave off the nausea. Sometimes she would ask him to pull over so she could be discreetly sick in the gutter. The irritation he'd felt then stabbed him now with remorse.

He wound down the window and gulped in fresh air.

A yellow oilskin jumped from a scooter and walked purposefully towards him, notebook in hand. He couldn't have been more than eighteen, his face spotted with adolescent red. 'You can't park there.' There was righteous indignation in his voice.

Bill flashed his ID. 'Get lost or I'll book *you*!'

The red blotches met one another in embarrassment. 'Sorry, officer.'

He retreated to his scooter. Bill felt bad, throwing his weight around. He should save that for the real villains.

'Get a grip,' he muttered to himself. What bloody use was he like this? He texted back: *I'll be waiting*. It took ages stabbing in the letters, his fingers too blunt and sweaty for the keys. He felt like a big helpless child. The experience of feeling sorry for himself was as new to him as the nausea. Both tasted bitter in his mouth.

15

104

THE BIG GASOMETER on the northern side of the M8 no longer wore the Mr Happy sign and the slogan 'Glasgow's Miles Better'. Now 'Glasgow with Style' was a fashion capital, full of chic designer clothes and pavement cafes. But the outer housing schemes had not had the luck of their inner-city neighbours. Glasgow, a working-class city, was divided as never before, with the poor getting poorer and the well-off ever richer.

Rhona tuned into the lunchtime news and listened to Radio Scotland's version of the torso story. There was genuine shock at Stephen's disappearance and the macabre find at the mouth of the Kelvin. Not something for *The Pride of the Clyde* to tell their tourist passengers as they chugged down the river from Broomielaw Quay to the Braehead shopping centre.

Child murder and abduction horrified the public. It was the last and greatest taboo. Even hardened criminals hated men who preyed on children. Everyone had their place on the morality ladder. Child killers didn't even reach the bottom rung.

Rhona turned off the radio when the news ended, giving her the peace to think. She hadn't wanted to lay too much emphasis on the botanical evidence, but it was a breakthrough. Viper's bugloss was rare. Locating the sites where it grew was the best clue they had. Coal deposits were trickier and would depend a lot on what she could find out at Newtongrange.

She had phoned ahead and explained the purpose of her visit. The library was manned by volunteers two days a week, Monday and Thursday. The seriousness of her quest had brought in a volunteer just to see her, despite it being Wednesday.

It took forty-five minutes to reach the Edinburgh ring road. Even Edinburgh's outskirts were tidier than Glasgow's, the ring road enclosing Scotland's capital city like a curved arm. To the right, where the slopes of the Pentlands housed the longest dry-ski run in the UK, flashes of light marked skiers weaving their way down the artificial surface.

She had printed out a route map from the internet before leaving. It seemed pretty straightforward. The first major roundabout after the Lothian Junction. The Victoria Colliery was well posted in brown-and-white tourist signs. Three miles on from the roundabout, she swung right into the Visitor Centre car park.

The library and offices were across the road in what looked like an old primary school or village hall, a big red colliery wheel outside the front door. Mike Davies, volunteer and ex-miner, was waiting for her in the library. A dapper man in a tweed jacket, his fresh-faced complexion belied his years. Behind thick glasses, his eyes were friendly and concerned.

'A bad business,' he muttered when she offered her thanks. 'I'm glad to help.'

He'd already laid out photocopied maps pinpointing former mines in the Glasgow area, and a set of books on the mineral make-up of each.

He left her to it, bringing her a mug of tea and a slice of cake five minutes later. 'We get well looked after here. The cafe in the visitor centre sends over home baking.'

'Just what I need.'

The rich tiffin cake tasted delicious, especially since she had missed lunch somewhere along the way.

Few people realised the previous extent of mining in the Glasgow area. Going back as far as the nineteenth century there were literally hundreds of working mines. By the 1970s there were nearer half a dozen. Each had its specialisation – household coal, splint, Drumgray, Blackband or Virgin.

A walk along the River Kelvin with her father when she was a child had always included the scary story of the young army officer who had tripped and fallen down an abandoned mine shaft in the grounds of a big house, and was stranded there for ten days before being rescued. Children playing in the woods heard him calling, imagined it was a ghost and ran away. By luck or the grace of God, someone out walking their dog found him before he died. Dounane Gardens was built over that eighteenth-century mine. Like hundreds of others it was long forgotten.

Rhona's blood ran cold at the thought of a terrified Stephen, like the young officer, dying alone in the dark.

Or not alone.

The thought focused her on the map. She knew the

make-up of the coal dust and she highlighted any area that came close to her mineral analysis.

There were still too many.

Most species of bugloss preferred sunny, well-drained soils. So not natural citizens of Glasgow. But one did grow here: viper's bugloss or *Echium Vulgare*. Rare but beautiful, a striking blue, it had been identified in four locations. Three on bings at Gateside and Bardykes, to the south of the Clyde, and Kenmuirhill to the north. But the biggest concentration was recorded near Kenmuirhill, on the rubble waste ground at the derelict site of the former Hallside Steelworks. In 1989, it had provided a stunning display in the solidified slag, reminiscent of Tenerife.

All four locations were close to one another, but the Kenmuirhill pit had the closest mineral make-up to their sample.

She called Bill to tell him what she'd found but his mobile was either off or he wasn't answering. So she phoned the incident room and was immediately put through to DC Clark.

'You've found something?'

Rhona rattled off her list of possibilities with Kenmuirhill at the top. 'I'll have to collect soil samples from all the areas for comparison. But I'd recommend a search of any abandoned or derelict buildings around Kenmuir.'

'Right.'

'I can't reach Bill.'

'Neither can I, but I'll speak to DCI Sutherland.'

Mike was hovering at Rhona's side when she came

off the phone. 'Another mug of tea or some proper lunch?'

'Thanks, Mike, but I have to go.'

The old miner was examining her with questioning eyes. She had to give him some reason for hope.

'We have a place to start looking.' That was all she could say.

He appreciated the reason for her reticence. 'If there's anything more I can do, just get in touch.' He swept his arm around the carefully catalogued shelves. 'I'm the search engine around here.'

'Probably quicker than a computer, too.'

'I have six grandchildren, you know.' There was a catch in his throat. 'They're my life.'

Rhona knew what he was trying to say. 'We'll find him,' she assured him. The words *dead or alive* hung in the air, unsaid.

16

THE WOMAN IN the wheelchair resembled an old lady, but when you got up close you realised she wasn't. Her body had simply shrunk inside its skin. Most of her hair had gone, leaving only a wispy brown down. A clear tube descended from her right nostril and disappeared inside her sweater. She sat very still, like a fine piece of china that any slight movement might knock over and shatter.

She sensed Bill's eyes on her and turned. Something resembling a gargoyle smile seized Bill's face.

She acknowledged his attempt with a small smile in return. She was obviously used to his sort of pity.

'Can I help?' A smart middle-aged woman called from the reception desk.

Bill stumbled his way through the words *Breast Clinic*.

'You've come in the wrong way. This is cardiovascular.'

Bill stood stupidly, still in shock at the image in the wheelchair, half listening to the receptionist's instructions.

'Breast Clinic is next entrance along.'

'Thanks.'

Lin Anderson

His legs felt like water. Outside, he leaned against a pillar.

What if Margaret got to look like that woman in the wheelchair? So still and fragile and ill? His body shook with unimaginable horror. He was more afraid than he had ever been in his life before. And had more self-loathing.

This wasn't about him or how he felt. Who the fuck cared if he was afraid? The one who counted here was Margaret. Not the silly bastard she married thirty years ago.

He found himself reaching in his pocket for the cigarettes he'd given up on their marriage day, because Margaret asked him to.

'I don't want to be a tobacco widow,' is what she'd said.

He didn't want her to be either.

And who got the cancer?

Anger flooded his veins. Who got the fucking cancer?

Shut up! He said the words out loud and a woman passing with a kid gave him a dirty look.

He didn't know that yet, he told himself. Except he did. He knew it with the same certainty that he'd known the sex of his kids before they were born. With the same certainty he'd known the moment he met her that Margaret would be the love of his life.

Margaret had cancer. He just didn't know how badly she had it.

He saw her emerge from the neighbouring entrance. She stood and glanced about her, searching for him.

'Margaret!' he shouted. 'I'm here.'

They sat in the car in the car park. She wanted to tell him the facts before they got home. Her hands were clasped in her lap. He knew it was to stop them shaking.

'They've taken a biopsy. They'll contact me as soon as they know.'

Bill realised he was holding his breath and had been since they got in the car. 'How long before we know?'

'A week.' She drew herself up. 'Right. What about the missing boy?'

'Still missing.'

'Alive?' Margaret had been a policeman's wife long enough to know that statistically speaking Stephen was dead as soon as they crossed the twelve-hour threshold in the search for him.

'I hope so.'

'Drop me home,' she told him. 'And get back on the job.'

They drove back in silence. She wouldn't let him come in with her.

'Let me know when you're coming home to eat.' She pecked his cheek and whispered, 'I love you.'

He waited until she was inside and the door shut before he turned on his mobile.

'Wait for back-up before you go on site.'

There was silence at Rhona's end.

'Did you hear me, Rhona?'

'I'm almost there, Bill. I'm only taking soil samples and checking for viper's bugloss.'

'What if he is keeping the kid there? You might alert him.'

She thought about that. 'I'm less likely to alert him than a police unit.'

Which was true. Still, instinct told him that someone who could kill so easily wouldn't like anyone sniffing around. A woman on her own was easy prey.

'DC McNab is on his way. He'll meet you at the end of River Road next to New Carmyle Park. Wait for him there.'

Rhona reluctantly agreed.

The M74 dropped her just north of the train station. Carmyle had retained its village size and character by being confined to a triangle of land flanked by the M74 motorway, the River Clyde and the A763.

Once inside that triangle, city life seemed far away. Even the distant coal bings didn't detract from the neat street of red-brick terraced houses with bright yellow-painted doors. Carmyle Avenue headed downhill towards the Clyde where it became River Road. On one side was typical local authority housing with well-kept gardens and patios with tables. Across the road stretched a wide expanse of cut grass and paths to the river. There were a few mums about, walking kids in prams and chatting to neighbours.

Not the sort of place to house a child abductor and murderer. But it wouldn't be the first neighbourhood in Scotland to wake up and find it had a convicted paedophile living in its midst. And usually after a child had gone missing.

She parked the car and got out for a look. After Carmyle Park, River Road gave onto the former Kenmuir Road. The street sign was rusted and indicated a dead end, its original route to London Road sliced by the M74 extension. On a street lamp was a warning notice that no tipping was allowed. The threat of hefty fines suggested that the local authority was serious, as was the statement that they were monitoring the area with CCTV.

Rhona stepped her way around muddy puddles and walked under a disused railway bridge that began the boundary of no-man's land. Beyond it the road was still visible, but fast disappearing under creeping vegetation, piles of old tyres and rusting household goods. Either the CCTV set-up wasn't working or the council had failed to enforce its threats.

In the distance, low sandstone buildings clustered in a rough circle suggested an abandoned farm, its existence pre-dating the eras of mining and steelworks.

A sudden movement in the surrounding bushes startled Rhona and she jumped aside as a chocolate-coloured whippet shot out and bounded towards the river.

She waited, already conjuring up a story should the dog's owner ask why she was here. He eventually appeared, panting from his exertions in keeping up with the dog. At a guess he was in his sixties. His difficulty in breathing wasn't age, Rhona judged, but advanced lung disease.

He stopped to wheeze for a bit then managed a whistle. The dog reappeared seconds later, ran around him and took off again.

'Wish I had half his energy. Not a bad day for walking the dog.' He glanced at a glowering sky. 'If the rain keeps off.'

He waited for her contribution. If she wasn't walking a dog, why was she here?

Rhona decided to tell a half-lie. 'I'm from Glasgow University botany department. I heard a rare plant is growing on Kenmuirhill.'

He was impressed. 'Aye, it's funny the way poisoned land can produce beauty.' He coughed and wheezed a bit more.

She pulled out a picture of viper's bugloss and showed him. 'This is the one.'

He examined the coloured printout with interest. 'I've seen it. Lovely blue colour, but it stings you if you try to pick it.'

'Can I ask where?'

He pointed beyond the derelict buildings. 'Site of the old colliery. You're too early for the flowers, but I expect you know that already.'

The whippet had returned. It bounded around them both, barking excitedly.

'He doesn't realise I've no breath.' He made his farewells and left, the dog's sharp bark echoing from the archway of the bridge.

Now she knew she was right about the location, Rhona was impatient for a look, but there was still no sign of McNab.

She decided to risk going on her own.

The distant rumble of traffic on the motorway only served to highlight the silent abandonment of the farm ruins. A scattering of discarded syringes and condoms looked recent and the air smelt of burnt rubber and rotting garbage, yet the remains of the old farmhouse retained a stately air in the midst of such modern desolation. Only one full gable end remained of the original stone structure. Halfway up was an arched window, above it a carving, worn smooth by the weather but still distinguishable as a Clydesdale horse.

Rhona began searching the rubble looking for the telltale rosette of leaves. The plant liked to spend its first year close to the ground gathering energy and growing a long black tap root. When summer arrived it would bolt, growing a central header, which became a mass of blue flowers. The rubble housed a sprinkling of weld and wild mignonette but no bugloss.

When she turned the corner of the building, two boys in their teens were sitting against the wall, smoking joints, an empty bottle of strong cider on the ground between them. Both were dressed in white tracksuits, regulation checked caps pulled low. They slowly stood up, feet splayed for balance.

One pointed a tattooed hand at her. 'Who the fuck are you?'

Rhona suspected they were high and drunk, a bad combination, and probably no older than sixteen, despite the feral look. She could either run or stand her ground. Rhona decided on the latter.

'I'm a botanist,' she said, keeping her voice steady. 'I'm looking for rare plants that grow around here.'

They exchanged amused looks. The freckled one emitted a high-pitched giggle.

The tattooed one spoke. 'Rare plants, is it? That's funny. We're here looking for pussy.' He punched his mate's arm. 'Here, pussy, pussy, pussy!' he said in a high miaowing voice.

The freckled one gave a low excited growl. They exchanged looks then walked purposefully towards her.

Rhona turned and ran. With a whoop of delight they followed.

The assault was vicious, intrusive and over in seconds. As they passed her on either side, one shoved his hand between her legs, the other grabbed her breast. Rhona squealed in pain and outrage. Then they were gone, catcalling as they ran up and over the railway bridge to the other side of the river.

Frustration and fury swept through Rhona, intensified by her sense of her own vulnerability. She felt violated and utterly impotent.

She leaned against a low wall and took a series of deep breaths until her heartbeat slowed and her limbs ceased their trembling. Bill was right. She shouldn't have come alone.

Thinking that made her angrier still. This was nothing to do with the case. An assault like this could have happened anywhere, at any time. It could, but it hadn't, until now.

When McNab appeared from the shadow of the

bridge, she was absurdly grateful. She had to stop herself running and embracing him.

There must have been something in her stance or the expression on her face, because he upped his pace as he came towards her.

'You okay?'

'I had a slight run-in with a couple of teenage boys.'

McNab knew her well enough to recognise a lie. He was already pulling out his mobile. 'Description?'

'It doesn't matter.'

'Description,' he insisted.

'White tracksuits, checked caps.' She gave a laugh. 'Which describes half of Glasgow.'

The laugh didn't fool McNab. 'You should have waited for me.'

Rhona didn't want to discuss that. 'Now you're here, can we make a start?' She didn't mean it to come out as irritated as it did.

He snapped the mobile shut. 'A team's on its way. But yes, we can make a start.'

She covered her discomfort by fetching her forensic case from the car. McNab waited for her by the ruins. By the time she returned, she had regained her composure. Seeing McNab as a knight in shining armour had unnerved her. She wanted him at a professional distance, nothing more.

'It's a large area,' he said on her return. 'What are we looking for?'

'I want to locate the plants. For Abel to have traces in his pocket, he must have been pretty close to one.' She showed McNab the printout. 'It won't be in flower yet so just look for low-growing leaves like these. There'll be no plants around it – it doesn't like competition.'

'A bit like myself.'

It was an awkward attempt at a joke, or a harking back to old times. Either way she didn't acknowledge it. Rhona made a show of pulling on a set of latex gloves.

'I'll find the plants and take soil samples. I suggest you check out the buildings.'

He took what amounted to an order with good grace.

She moved in the general direction of the bing. Patches of fresh grass and weeds were clearly visible among the garbage and piles of tyres. If they thought the boy was here, they would have to lift the tyres and go through all the piles of rubbish. It wasn't a nice thought.

The undergrowth became patchy because of poorer soil. This was the bugloss's natural habitat. Ten minutes later she struck lucky, spotting a plot of the telltale leaves near a weird structure like a concrete cylinder with a single door and an inverted cone as its top. It was far enough away from the farm buildings to suggest it played some part in the nearby mine.

The cylinder was part buried in slag at one side, the bugloss scattered over it. She climbed the slag, extracted a plant and a sample of the surrounding soil and bagged them. From her vantage point, the ground near the door looked disturbed by what might be a set of wheels. Glancing back the way she'd come, she could make out a set of parallel lines running from here through the short grass to the tarred track and the railway bridge.

A vehicle had crossed the waste ground to this cylinder and not long ago.

Common sense told her that with all the dumping going on, that wasn't unusual. Instinct told her something else.

She took photos of the tracks from above, then came closer and took some more. Normally she would lift a print immediately, but she desperately wanted to take a look inside the concrete cylinder. If she were careful she could reach the door without disturbing the evidence.

McNab was nowhere in sight, which probably meant he was inside one of the farm buildings.

She listened at the door. The last thing she wanted was to disturb another drink and drugs party, but the only sound was the drip of water.

The handle turned easily enough but the wood was swollen with damp and the door jarred against the bottom half of its frame.

Rhona put her shoulder to it and gave a short sharp shove. The door resisted the first time, but gave on the second try.

A fetid smell rushed out to greet her. Urine, fresh faeces and the stench of decomposition.

17

THE SMELL WAS strong enough to make her gag, but her desperation to see what was in there was greater than her desire to vomit.

Light from the open door was dull and grey, reaching in only a few feet. The rest was thick darkness. She resisted the temptation to rush in. If this was a crime scene it had to be preserved. Whatever was generating the smell had been dead for a while, but that didn't mean there wasn't also something alive in there.

'Stephen?'

The steady plip of water was the only answer to her call. She opened her case and took out a forensic torch. The beam lit up what looked like a small white shoe lying on the concrete floor.

McNab responded immediately to her frantic shout. She watched as he sprang across the waste ground, leaping the piles of rubbish with the ease of a hurdler. He had always been fitter than the rest of the squad, but he must have been in training during his spell at the Police College. He was barely out of breath when he reached her.

His anxious glance moved from her shocked face to the open doorway. 'Is it . . .'

'I can see a child's trainer but it's too dark. I don't want to go in before I put on a suit.'

He peered in, registering the ominous smell. 'I've got crime scene gear in my boot. I'll go and get it.'

'Don't use the track in case of tyre evidence,' she said, as though McNab needed to be told his job.

'You sure you'll be all right here?'

Distress at the possible contents of the building rendered her voice sharp. 'Of course!'

He scanned the waste ground as he left, obviously checking for her earlier assailants. The feeling that he was watching out for her only served to make Rhona feel more vulnerable.

She was pulling on the suit as the threatening sky let go in a sharp burst of rain, plastering her hair to her head and running down her face. Forensically, rain was bad, washing a site clean of evidence. The weather had stayed pretty dry since Stephen's disappearance. That had been their only real luck . . .

Street lights on the distant River Road popped on, bathing it in orange, as McNab's headlights emerged from beneath the railway bridge. The car swerved to avoid a pile of tyres on the remains of the tarred surface then swung left onto the waste ground. If McNab reached her without a puncture he was doing well.

He stayed clear of the rutted track, weaving between clumps of bushes and piles of rubble, the back axle jumping violently up and down, and finally drew in behind the building.

She waited for him to lay metal treads as far as the door. When he was finished she handed him a suit. 'If you're coming in you'd better put this on.' It was her way of saying she didn't want to go in alone.

McNab drew on the suit and pulled up the hood, leaving the mask dangling around his neck.

He produced two high-powered torches, handing Rhona one. It felt heavy and solid. She pressed the switch and a strong beam of light sprang on.

'We should call Bill.'

'I already have,' he told her. 'There's the usual rush-hour traffic on the M8. They'll be here as soon as they can.'

McNab stood back, letting her go first. She ducked under the lintel, hearing him grunt as he ducked and followed her. He directed his beam at the centre of the floor.

The trainer lay on its side, a smear of mud on the white surface.

She swung the beam across the floor, holding her breath.

There was no body.

She heard a muttered 'Thank God' from McNab. Rhona wasn't so relieved.

'Check the walls,' she told him.

Both circles of light danced the back wall together.

'Jesus.' McNab's voice was a hiss. 'What the hell is that?'

The rectangular brick construction was about three foot high and two foot wide. On its surface sat two candles. Between them stood some kind of animal skull, wrapped in barbed wire. There was a red diagonal cross painted on the wall above.

Rhona directed her beam to the left as McNab moved right. There was nothing but concrete wall glistening with water that trickled down in green and slimy trails. Apart from the single shoe and the strange altar, the place was empty.

McNab fetched another couple of treads and laid them in a path to the back wall. He stepped across first then held out his hand. Rhona took it and joined him. They both stared down at the grey bony object on the makeshift altar.

'What kind of animal is it, do you think?' McNab looked to her for guidance.

'I don't know – maybe a sheep or goat.'

Rhona took some camera shots. The flash lit up rusting barbed wire and four six-inch nails that were driven through the bone.

She turned it and took some more shots from a different angle.

'The smell's stronger here,' McNab said. 'Where the hell is it coming from?'

He was right. They had grown gradually used to the scent of decomposition. But it was stronger in the area of the altar. The skull was old and clean, washed almost white and there was nothing on the floor or the walls to explain the smell.

Rhona bagged the skull and the candles, then bent closer to the bricks. 'It's coming from inside the altar.' She placed the bags at her feet and examined the bricks. 'They're not cemented together.'

She pulled at the top front one and it slid forward. She removed it and placed it carefully on the ground.

The smell rushed out at them.

She heard McNab smother a gag.

'Use the mask!'

Officers' vomit was not welcome on a crime scene. The bile was full of DNA.

Above the hastily pulled-up mask, McNab's eyes were watering.

'Maybe you'd better wait outside,' she suggested.

He shook his head.

The space left by the top brick was too small for the torch. McNab held it for her while she removed two more.

This time she could shine her torch inside.

The altar appeared to be built around a hole in the ground filled with stagnant water. A long grey thing floated on its surface.

'What can you see?' he muttered through the mask.

'Dirty water. And something that looks like a stick.'

She caught it with her gloved hand and pulled it towards her.

The resulting sensation was both peculiar and horrific. The surface of the object seemed to part from the whole, stripping down its length like a snake discarding its skin.

She let go and quickly withdrew her hand, realising with sickening certainty what she had grabbed. Disintegrating skin and hair stuck to the pale latex of her glove.

'It's a dead dog,' she told him. 'The stick was its tail.'

★   ★   ★

Lamps had been rigged up inside the concrete structure. It was like illuminating a grave: harsh, unrelenting and without respect.

Chrissy's face was a livid white. In the forensic suit she looked ghost-like, a wraith in a tomb, as she finished sampling the damp walls.

From somewhere in Rhona's memory came the thought that in African culture, buildings were made circular to prevent evil spirits from lurking in the corners. But within this cylinder, evil was in the very air they breathed.

The altar had been dismantled and the dog's body removed. There had been no other body parts in the hole, human or otherwise.

She had collected human faeces, both fresh and old, from the foot of the wall, which also smelt strongly of urine. This place had been a prison, but the lack of blood suggested it had not been a place of torture or death. The red cross on the wall had been made with ordinary household paint.

The shoe could be a match to the ones worn by Stephen. That was all they'd found of the missing boy. Their one stroke of luck: the trainer had a Velcro fastening and everything stuck to Velcro.

'I could do with a drink,' Chrissy exclaimed with gusto. 'A big one.'

'Me too.' Rhona rolled the latex gloves off her hands.

They had gone over the building with a fine-toothed comb. Collected plenty of material, none of it pleasant. And none of it seemed likely to lead them to Stephen.

The light had faded, leaving a faint red glow to wash

the western sky. It had transformed the coal bing into a prehistoric volcano. In the foreground the river shimmered red, like a ribbon of blood. The police divers had managed an hour's search before giving up for lack of light. They would return at dawn tomorrow.

A westerly breeze fluttered the cordon tape. Rhona breathed in its freshness.

A group of teenagers had found their way onto the railway bridge and were peering down on the floodlit scene. Rhona wondered about her attackers. If they used the farm ruins as a meeting place, they could have seen something. She scanned the group, but there were no checked caps or white tracksuits. McNab was approaching them, having had the sense to block their escape across the river with a couple of uniforms.

He waved down at Rhona, gesturing to her to come up.

'Why does he want you?' Chrissy asked, puzzled.

'I saw kids here earlier. He wants me to check if they're among that lot.'

Chrissy gave an exasperated sigh.

'Look, you go on. I'll meet you at the club.'

'I'll be drunk by the time you arrive,' Chrissy threatened, as Rhona walked off.

The final span on this side of the bridge had been demolished, leaving a drop of a metre. McNab was waiting to pull her up.

There were four in the group. Two girls, one blonde, the other a streaked auburn, and two boys, both with blond highlights, all mid teens. Dressed in sports gear, they might have been out for a run, were it not for the intricately gelled hairstyles of the boys and the girls' thick make-up. They appeared defiant and scared at the same time. McNab had that effect on people.

'Recognise any of them?'

Rhona took a good look at the two males. When she said no, there was an audible sigh of relief from the skinnier one.

'Mine were taller. One with freckles, the other had a tattooed hand.'

At her words, the blonde girl tried to exchange a look with the other, who pointedly ignored her.

'You know who we're talking about?' McNab aimed his question at Blondie.

It was the other one that spoke. 'Naw.'

These four needed lessons in body language. What they said and the moves they made when they said it, didn't match. Rhona wasn't the only one who had spotted that.

McNab was moving in for the kill.

'Okay.' His voice had an ominous quality, not lost on any of them. The skinny boy was squirming, his expensive trainers scuffing the stone.

When necessary McNab could lie with ease. 'Since this is a *murder* enquiry, you'll all have to accompany me to the police station.'

'Murder?' Skinny looked aghast at the others. 'Jesus. Malchie's murdered somebody!'

The cooler girl gave him a withering look. 'You stupid bastard.'

'Right, ladies and gentlemen, where does this Malchie live?'

The worried one coughed up the information pretty quickly. McNab told the two uniforms to escort the four home and get their details.

'My dad'll kill me,' Skinny told him.

'Then I'll charge *him* with murder.'

Rhona couldn't disguise a smile as the four left. 'You could have been kinder,' she suggested.

'And not get a name and address for Malchie?'

'This isn't about earlier?'

'Not if you don't want it to be.'

'But if Malchie thinks he might be charged with sexual assault, it might make him talk?'

'Great minds think alike.' McNab gave her the same boyish grin that had attracted her in the first place. 'Malchie and mate like to party in the ruins. Chances are they've seen something and will want to tell us about it.'

Rhona glanced down, searching for DI Wilson among the figures that still criss-crossed the crime scene. 'We should pass the info to Bill.'

'If we don't head there now, someone will get word to Malchie and he'll be gone. If he's there, we'll bring him back with us.'

18

MALCHIE LIVED NEAR the primary school. The only thing growing in the front garden was a pile of rusting metal. The contrast with next door's neat lawn and flower beds must have irked his tidy neighbour every time he looked out of the window.

A woman opened the door to them. She was thin and nervous, her eyes darting from them into the sitting room. Rhona suspected she was about to tell them Malchie wasn't home, when a voice called, 'Who is it, Ma?'

McNab shot Rhona a questioning look.

She nodded. It was Malchie, all right. A coldness crept through her. Facing him might be more difficult than she had imagined.

The woman glanced at McNab's badge then stood aside to let them past. 'My man'll be back soon.' The warning seemed to frighten her more than them.

Malchie jumped up from the settee as McNab stepped into the room.

'You stupid bitch,' he threw at his mother.

The woman shrank back and McNab stepped between them.

'Malcolm Menzies?' McNab flashed his ID.

'What is it to you?' Malchie's expression suggested he wasn't home to visitors, especially the police. That changed when he caught sight of Rhona.

'Is this one of them?' McNab asked Rhona.

If McNab thought Rhona's presence would bother Malchie, he was mistaken. Malchie made a show of licking his lips and slowly looking her up and down, lingering at her breasts and more pointedly at her crotch. Then he squeezed his hands suggestively and gave her a sly smile.

Rhona forced herself to meet Malchie's penetrating gaze, her mouth dry, her skin crawling, blood rushing to her face.

Her voice surprised her by its strength. 'Yes.'

McNab addressed Malchie, his voice as cold as ice. 'You met Dr MacLeod earlier on the waste ground.'

'We . . .' Malchie paused for effect, '*brushed* against one another so to speak.'

'You and another youth assaulted Dr MacLeod.'

Malchie shook his head in amazement. 'No way. We were looking for rare plants. Rare plants grow on those bings, you know.'

McNab was barely controlling his temper. If the mother hadn't been there, Rhona suspected he would have throttled Malchie.

'If Dr MacLeod presses charges . . .'

Malchie liked that idea. 'Two against one. We win.'

'The CCTV footage says otherwise.'

For a moment Malchie was thrown, then he came back, sharp as ever. 'Doesn't work.'

'That's where you're wrong.'

Doubt crossed his face.

'Under-age drinking, smoking dope . . . sexual assault.' McNab gave a disappointed shake of his head. 'And all on camera.'

There was a wee gasp from the mother. 'Malcolm . . .'

'Shut it!' Malchie licked his lips again. His eyes darted from McNab to Rhona and back again. 'What do you want?'

'We want to know who's using the round building on the waste ground.'

For a moment, fear clouded Malchie's weasel eyes. 'I don't know.'

'Think,' said McNab. 'Think very hard.'

'You are the Crime Scene Manager, you are not in charge of the investigation.'

'He was part of the crime scene,' McNab insisted. The stubborn look suggested Bill was being unreasonable.

Malchie stood between two uniforms a few feet away. He was watching the disagreement with relish.

Rhona butted in. 'We were worried someone would warn him before we checked with you.'

If Bill was surprised at her standing up for McNab, he didn't show it.

'Malchie and his mate assaulted Rhona while she was waiting for us.'

'What?' Bill shot Rhona a look.

'We thought we could use that to make him talk . . .' Rhona petered out at Bill's expression.

'And when did you become a detective, Dr MacLeod?'

The question stung her, not because he asked it, but because of the tone of his voice. Bill didn't use sarcasm normally, at least not on his team.

Bill gestured to the two uniforms to bring Malchie over.

He swaggered towards them, the sly look back on his face. 'They threatened me,' he whined. 'Forced me to come down here.'

Bill let him finish, not taking his eyes off Malchie's twisted face. 'Okay, son. Here's the story. I'm detaining you on suspicion of an assault on a forensic scientist working at a scene of crime.'

'Like fuck!'

Bill looked at McNab. 'What age is he?'

'He says fifteen . . .'

'Take him home and pick up a parent,' Bill told McNab. 'I'll see you down at the police station.'

Malchie cursed his way to the police car, the swagger turned to a shuffle.

'I'm sorry,' Rhona said.

Bill's face had collapsed into weariness. 'You'll need to come to the station and make a statement. We can hold him for six hours then we'll have to charge him or let him go.'

'He looked frightened when we mentioned this building.'

Bill glanced around at the dark entrance. 'Who can blame him? It looks like a tomb.'

'But it wasn't,' Rhona reminded him.

★　　★　　★

Chrissy sounded pissed off when Rhona called her. 'How long will you be?'

'I don't know. I have to go to the station and make a statement.'

'I'll see you tomorrow, then?'

'Chrissy – the altar, don't mention it to Sam, will you?'

'As if.'

The altar was significant, but it shouldn't be in the public domain until Bill decided.

19

CHRISSY THREW THE mobile in her bag and picked up the plastic cup, temporarily masquerading as a real glass. She would have preferred a shooter bottle with a straw but Glasgow was contemplating taking its first steps in combating pub assaults with broken glass. A recent report condemning it as the most violent city in Europe demanded some response. Broken bottles were a weapon of choice for many villains, not in here, but in many other bars.

She took a mouthful. Decanting the drink had made it warmer. She would have to start asking for ice.

Sam was on the piano tonight, covering for the absent Sean. Music was one way of trying to forget the minutiae of the day . . . and the smell. 'That Old Black Magic' seemed oddly appropriate in the circumstances.

Sam smiled over at her, sending a pleasant shiver up her spine. If she wanted to go home with him, she would have to last until midnight and she had to be up early. Common sense told her to wait for the weekend, but she felt the need for human company rather than sleep. If Rhona had been here they would have talked it through, laid the day's events to rest, at least for tonight.

Sam threw her a quizzical glance. Did she plan to stay?

Chrissy nodded and ordered another drink.

Rain smattered the pavement with puddles. Sam guided her around them, his arm about her shoulders. She was glad of the dark. That way no one looked at them, or shouted racist comments. Chrissy could give as good as she got, but Sam didn't like her to. He would put his hand on her arm and tell her quietly that it didn't matter. But it mattered to her. She wasn't ashamed of their relationship, she was ashamed of the people of the city she loved, behaving like that.

Tonight there was no anger, just pleasure in walking together through the dark wet streets.

'Does it rain like this in Kano?'

'Much worse. When the rains come, the force of water is strong enough to dig trenches.'

'In tarmac?'

'No, the tarred road becomes a river. But such roads are scarce, especially in the old city. There they are red clay. Concrete in the dry season, mud in the wet.'

'The wet season lasts all year here.'

'You're lucky.'

Chrissy looked up at the rain illuminated in the yellow of the street lamp. 'How can it be lucky to have rain all the time?'

Sam tipped his head back and savoured the drops. 'Because the rain makes things grow. Nothing grows without it.'

Even her vivid imagination could not conjure up a world where rain was welcomed.

'The woman who died . . .' Sam said as they walked on.

'Yes?'

'She was a member of my church.'

Chrissy came to an abrupt halt. 'Your church?' She said the word *church* as though it were poison.

He looked puzzled. 'You are a Catholic.'

'I was indoctrinated as a Catholic.'

'And you no longer believe?'

Chrissy opened her mouth to agree but something stopped her. 'I don't go to church,' was the best she could manage.

'Carole Devlin was a member of the Nigerian Church of God.'

Chrissy gave a silent groan. 'How do you know?'

'Pastor Achebe spoke to me when he saw the photo in the newspaper.'

'Why didn't he call the police?'

Sam looked uncomfortable. 'The church is a place of refuge.'

Chrissy digested that. 'Meaning people go there who are illegal immigrants?'

'Possibly.' Sam was cautious.

'The police need to speak to anyone who knew Carole if we're going to find her killer.'

'I know.'

'What about Stephen?'

'I never saw either of them, but according to the pastor he would come to church with his mother.'

'And the husband?'

Sam shook his head.

'I'll tell DI Wilson tomorrow.'

'Good.' He seemed relieved.

'Where is this church?'

'We meet in a hall on Maryhill Road. I will give you the pastor's mobile number.'

Chrissy tried to control her expression to no avail. So, her latest boyfriend was a member of some sect called the Nigerian Church of God. What would her family priest say about that? The expression 'sleeping with the enemy' immediately sprang to mind.

Sam's face was black porcelain in the wet light. He stood very still, waiting for Chrissy to make an excuse to go home. If she wasn't put off by the colour of his skin, then revealing his religion might have done it.

Chrissy slipped her hand into his and opened her mouth to crack a joke along those lines.

'Don't.' He laid a finger on her lips. 'The pastor teaches us that love is greater than hate. Is that a bad thing?'

The flat smelt of bergamot and cinnamon. Sam had an oil burner lit most of the time. Chrissy had assumed it reminded him of Africa, but now she pondered its religious significance.

He was meticulous in his tidiness. Everything clean, the bed carefully made. Her own flat looked like a tip in comparison. Ever since she'd left home, she'd culti-vated the 'lived-in' look, in contrast to her mother's constant, obsessive housework. It was as though tidying the house gave her mum control over at least part of her life. The monotonous regularity of Chrissy's dad's drunken rages and her brothers' moral messes could never rock the 'cleanliness is next to godliness' ship her mum sailed as captain.

They undressed and lay between the clean white sheets, still scented from washing. The sound of jazz piano on the stereo was their accompaniment, its roving nuances like Sam's black hand across her ivory skin.

His long pianist fingers were both gentle and firm, playing notes on her body that made her cry out with pleasure. Afterwards they lay, not speaking, her head in the crook of his arm. Chrissy didn't want to break the silence nor leave him, but she still stood up and began to dress.

'Don't leave,' Sam pleaded.

'It's better if I go home.'

He swung his legs out of bed.

'No,' she protested. 'I'll call a taxi. You don't have to get up.'

He pulled on his trousers. 'If we stand outside, one will pass soon.'

They waited at the kerb. The sexual intimacy was gone, but there was still an invisible bond between them. He hailed a cab on its way back to the city centre and opened the door for her. She caught a glimpse of the driver's expression and tried to read it, with no success.

'Where to?'

She gave him the address and settled back, fastening

her seat belt. All the church members would have to be interviewed, including Sam. What if he'd never met Carole or Stephen? Chrissy tried to recall his denial. Was he telling the truth?

She watched the rain trickling down the window pane, feeling increasingly uneasy with the decision she had to make. Maybe it would be better not to see Sam until the investigation was complete. The realisation left a hole in her stomach. It would be difficult to explain. Sam would take it as rejection.

Chrissy wondered if her decision was purely professional or whether Sam's religious leanings had tipped the balance. She had fought so hard to break free of the church, and love was, as she knew from bitter experience, its strongest method of persuasion.

20

THE GUESTS AT the Malmaison Hotel experienced chic and comfortable rooms with a choice of CDs for the high quality stereo. The entrance to this former Greek Orthodox church was classical, suffused with that inimitable Glasgow style.

Despite this, the outlook from some side bedrooms left a lot to be desired. A bird's-eye view of Pitt Street Police Station. Pitt Street was renowned for many things, but not a classical entrance or stylish decor.

At the desk, a patient sergeant was attempting to take down details from an elderly man who wanted an ASBO put on his neighbour's budgies. Despite turning off his hearing aid, his flat still sounded like an aviary.

Rhona followed Bill to an interview room, passing Malchie and mother on the way. They were already in Room 1. Malchie had drawn his chair as far from his mother as possible in the cramped space. Rhona wondered if 'her man' had returned, as promised. The woman glanced out as Rhona passed. The sudden intimacy of the look suggested she and Rhona had something in common. Both had suffered abuse at her son's hands.

If she pressed charges on Malchie, what would that

mean for this woman? Who in that house would pay the price?

It made Rhona think of Chrissy, staying too long at home, protecting her mother from her father's drunken rages, spending an inordinate amount of time and her earnings righting her brothers' misdemeanours. Only Patrick, the eldest, had been a real man to both women, and he was gay. Chrissy had kept that secret from her macho father and younger brothers, and particularly from her mother, for whom Catholicism was much more than a prop in a difficult life.

Bill ushered her into Room 3 and shut the door. 'Okay – so what's this all about?'

He listened patiently while she described the assault. It sounded insignificant. Unworthy of the attention it was getting. Yet Rhona could not shake off the feeling of violation that retelling the tale gave her.

She waited for Bill's comment.

'I suggest you make a formal statement. It will, of course, be difficult to make it stick.'

'Two against one; they win.'

Bill looked sympathetic. 'Janice is checking with the council. If they have footage . . .'

'Chances are it won't be pointing my way. Look, Bill, the only reason I'm here is in the hope you can get him to talk about that building.'

'Okay, let's see what he has to say.'

Bill left her with paper and pen. She wrote a brief résumé of events and signed it. The door to Room 1 was firmly closed when she passed. She handed her statement to the desk sergeant and he gave her a file in return.

'Compliments of the Met. DI Wilson said you'd understand.'

When she reached the car, she checked her mobile. There was a voice message from Sean.

'Rhona, it's Wednesday 5 p.m. I'm on my way back to Dublin. The funeral is on Friday morning. The wake will last days but I plan to escape Saturday. See you then.'

She contemplated going to the jazz club. Chances were Chrissy would still be there. She rejected the idea in favour of food and a read of the Met's forensic notes.

Rhona switched on all the lights, walking from room to room in the flat, illuminating the darkness. The silence remained thick and unwelcoming.

She stuck a ready meal in the microwave, trying to ignore the label and its list of chemical additives, including too much sugar and salt. Sean was the cook and he wasn't here. She discovered the remains of a bottle of Sancerre in the fridge and poured herself a glass while waiting for the timer to ping.

Settled on the couch in front of the fire, she ate and read at the same time.

In September 2001, the headless, limbless and bloodless torso of a five-year-old black boy was found floating in the Thames near Tower Bridge. The DI in charge named him Adam. The investigation followed 'the beat in the heart of darkness', or so the newspapers had said.

Rhona leafed through the photos of the exhibits collected on raids on nine houses the following July.

Exhibits that suggested, according to a well-known academic and expert in African culture, the practice of voodoo, juju or black magic.

The first photograph was of an animal skull pierced by a large staple and wound thickly in heavy black cotton. This was followed by photos of evidence bags containing dung, clay and soil samples, and medicine bottles containing wooden crucifixes floating in an oily liquid.

But it was the forensic report that interested her most. When the investigation team contacted the FBI's powerful forensic muscle with what they had, they'd been told to give up. The case was unsolvable.

The London team didn't take the FBI's advice.

Pollen content in Adam's stomach confirmed the presence of particles common to European plant life. From that they established Adam had been in the UK up to seventy-two hours prior to his death. A study of his bones narrowed his isotope signature to three different areas covering five different countries in Africa where Adam might have been brought up. A team from the Met had taken a forensic safari to West Africa to collect soil and animal bones, fresh meat from market stalls and even a sample from a post-mortem examination. When these were compared in the laboratory with Adam's strontium signature they pinpointed Adam's origins to a wedge of land, 100 miles by 50 miles, in south-west Nigeria. At its centre was Benin City, a place renowned for human trafficking.

It was a remarkable investigation, which did not as yet have a conclusion. The question was whether the

Met's Adam had any connection with Abel. Adam's ritualistic death was similar to Abel's. Tests on the samples taken from the cylindrical building could confirm Abel's presence there, although the lack of blood suggested that wasn't where he died. The shoe they recovered might turn out to be one worn by Stephen. She would test that tomorrow. If it was, then Abel's death and Stephen's disappearance had to be linked.

The over-seasoned ready meal tasted bitter in her mouth. She set it aside and took a mouthful of wine. The investigation seemed to be turning just as sour. Bill's difficult manner was more than just desperation to find the missing boy.

Rhona wondered if he was ill and hiding it from them. Or if there was trouble from his superiors. A missing child put enormous pressure on the investigation team, in this case worsened by the double murder of his mother and grandmother. It was enough to make anyone irritable and depressed, even Bill Wilson.

The phone rang in the hall and she went to answer it. At eleven o'clock it was more than likely Sean calling from the bosom of his family.

The voice was Irish, but it was a woman. The tone was soft, almost apologetic. 'Is that Rhona MacLeod?'

'Yes, it is.'

'I'm calling from Dublin.'

Rhona felt instantly unnerved. 'Did Sean arrive okay?'

'He's with his mother.'

This was followed by silence. It was as though the caller wanted Rhona to speak first.

'Are you one of Sean's sisters?' How many did Sean say he had? She knew none of their names.

'No.'

Silence fell again.

'I'm sorry, but can I ask who you are?'

'I'm Kitty Maguire. Sean's wife.'

Rhona felt a surge of something – panic? – and acid rose in her throat. She gripped the receiver more tightly.

'Sean's wife?' she repeated slowly. She knew a reaction was called for, but had no idea what it might be.

'Yes.'

'But I don't understand.'

'Sean didn't mention me, then?'

'I think there must be some mistake.'

'There's no mistake.'

The phone went down with a clatter. Rhona did a swift 1471 but the caller had withheld the number.

Rhona replaced the receiver, not knowing whether to be angry or irritated.

What on earth was the woman talking about? Sean didn't have a wife. Sean wasn't married.

But why would a woman phone and tell her she was Sean's wife if she wasn't? And how did the woman get this number? She didn't give out her home number to just anyone. It was ex-directory. Only Sean and close friends and colleagues knew it. Including McNab.

Rhona dismissed that thought almost immediately.

Even if McNab remembered her number, why would he have anything to do with some mad woman who called from Dublin to say she was Sean's wife?

Rhona realised with an abrupt certainty that she knew next to nothing of Sean's life before they met. He could have been married half a dozen times and she would have no idea. It had taken her long enough to confess to him that she had given up her child for adoption. She only told Sean because of the murdered teenager she'd thought might be the son she hadn't seen for seventeen years.

Rhona sank onto a chair. Were she and Sean nothing but strangers having sex with each other? No, it was much more than that. Why else would she feel so hurt, so betrayed?

Why had she let it get to this stage? If McNab had told her he was married, she wouldn't have cared. McNab's commitment elsewhere would have confirmed theirs as the sort of relationship she preferred. Transient.

The soft Irish voice of the phone call began to assume a face. Probably dark-haired, she sounded younger than Sean. She spoke his name with familiarity.

Sean played gigs all over the place. Had he played Dublin recently? How many times had he visited Dublin since they got together?

Rhona recalled their conversation about the funeral, when she'd suggested going with him. Sean had made light of the idea. His family would have her for breakfast along with the bacon and soda bread, he'd said, making her laugh.

Why did he not want her there?

The wine was finished. Rhona fetched a bottle of Islay Malt from the drinks cabinet and poured a shot.

A mix of wine, whisky and apprehension swam through her veins. What if she didn't mention this to Sean when he called? What if she simply turned up in Dublin on Friday?

Even as she toyed with the idea, Rhona knew she had already made up her mind.

21

MALCOLM MENZIES SAT slumped in the chair, fingers drumming the table.

The desk sergeant had delivered Rhona's statement. It sat on the table in front of Bill. Next door was Malchie's partner in crime. A skinny freckled youth of the same age who went by the name of Danny Fergus. He'd apparently spent most of his time since being lifted shitting himself in the Gents. His father had accompanied him to the police station. To Daniel Fergus Senior, Pitt Street was a second home. He'd been lifted on a regular basis since he was his son's age. History was fast repeating itself.

Malchie's mother looked up gratefully as a PC entered with a mug of tea. Her demeanour reminded Bill of the woman in the wheelchair at the hospital. Withered and weary of life and its painful knocks.

'The tattoo . . .' Bill began.

'What about it?' A flicker of fear shone in the youth's eyes, but he kept on drumming.

'You have to be eighteen for a tattoo parlour to work on you.'

'I did it myself.'

Bill caught Malchie's hand, silencing it.

He tried to pull away, then let the hand go limp.

Bill had a closer look at the diagonal cross between his thumb and forefinger. It was roughly done, more like a scar than a tattoo. 'What does it mean?'

'Nothing. It means nothing.'

'This shape was painted on the inside wall of that building.'

'So?'

Bill suspected that Malchie had spent his entire life talking like this. A mixture of belligerence and defiance. Malchie fought because he knew no other way to live. Everyone was out to get him, and he was out to get them back.

His mother sipped at her mug of tea, taking pleasure at not being the one on the receiving end for a change.

Bill took a moment to glance over Rhona's statement. Malchie went back to his drumming. Bill could have cheerfully chopped off his hand had a machete been available.

He stood up. Malchie regarded him with empty eyes.

'Your mate's here.'

The look clouded with concern.

'Let's hear what *he* has to say.'

'Nothing!' Malchie shouted at Bill's back. 'Fuck nothing!'

Danny was out of the toilet, but looked like it might not be for long. His face was pasty under the freckles, his hand cradling his stomach, his breathing laboured.

The room was airless and smoke-filled. Danny

Senior was drawing on a cigarette as though it was his last, sucking every last drop of nicotine and associated carcinogens with it.

Bill threw open the window and a Baltic breeze swept in.

'Hey. That's fucking freezing!'

Bill gave the fag a pointed look.

Big Danny took a last draw and stubbed it out as though the ashtray were Bill's face.

The blast of fresh air brought some colour to young Danny's cheeks and he was breathing easier. He moved his stomach hand to his pocket and sat up in the chair, throwing swift questioning glances at his father.

These two had had no chance of a private confab between home and the police station. And they hadn't been left alone since they got here. Bill had made sure of that.

'So what do you know about the round building on the waste ground, Danny?'

It wasn't what the youth expected to hear.

He paled, then went red.

He shot his father a quick look.

'Nothing,' he managed.

'The CCTV caught you drinking and smoking nearby and . . .' he gestured to Rhona's statement, 'assaulting a female scene of crime officer.'

Young Danny rushed in. 'She said she was looking for plants . . .' then tailed off, his stupidity reflected in the threatening look doled out by his father.

'Stupid wee git.' Big Danny shook his head in disbelief. 'Takes after his mother.'

'Danny, listen very carefully. There is a small boy missing. His mother and grandmother were murdered. We think he might have been taken to that building, so it's very important you try to remember anyone you've seen hanging round there.'

Even Big Danny drew himself up at the word *murder*.

'You don't think he had anything to do with—'

Bill interrupted his worried words. 'Well, Danny?'

The youth opened his mouth and shut it again, like a dying fish.

Bill raised his voice. 'Well, Danny?'

'I seen a white van, that's all.' Then it came pouring out like verbal diarrhoea. 'I said to Malchie, maybe there was stolen stuff we could get, sell for drink. We waited until the van went away and then we tried to get in, but it was locked. There was this smell, this fucking awful smell.'

'And?'

'And nothing. We couldn't get in.'

'When did you see the van?'

'Friday afternoon.'

'Did you see it after that?'

'Naw.'

'Do you remember the number plate?'

'I didn't give a fuck about the number plate.' Danny had grown braver with his confession, but not for long.

'Right.' Bill made a big show of looking at Rhona's statement again. 'Now let's talk about this sexual assault charge.'

Day 4

Thursday

22

THE FRONT DOOR of 10 River Road was opened by a young woman in her teens, with very straight long blonde hair. She wore jeans with slits across the thighs and a cut-off top that exposed a diamond belly-button stud. A child of about three peeked out between her legs. He had a Postman Pat van in his hand.

Janice gave him a smile and he looked up quizzically at his mum.

Janice showed her ID. 'Detective Constable Janice Clark. We're looking for a missing boy.' She offered the photo of Stephen and the woman examined it with interest. 'We believe he has been in this area. Have you seen him?'

She looked sorry to have to say no. 'There's no coloured kids around here except for the Sikh family, and they've got two little girls.'

'What about a white van hanging around the waste ground?'

She gave a snort of laughter and smiled cynically. Her teeth were pearly white, as though she had had them painted.

'The council put up that sign about fines. Fat lot of good that did. The vans are queuing up here at weekends. If the council have got CCTV footage, they're doing nothing with it.'

Janice thanked her and left. As the door closed there was a wail of anguish from the child and some soothing words of comfort from the mother.

The next three residents of River Road said much the same. No one had seen Stephen or any black kid. They moaned about the dumping, were angry that nothing was being done about it.

'No niggers here!' one large tattooed man told her in no uncertain terms, like an echo of the Reverend Ian Paisley shouting, 'No surrender'. Janice didn't know whether to laugh or cry when he shut the door in her face.

The last house on River Road sported a smart patio table and chairs and pots of multicoloured primroses. When she rang the bell, a dog gave a high-pitched bark. She could see its thin dark body behind the glass.

She checked the name on the door as someone came wheezing through the hall. Janice waited for Mr Martin to get his breath back before she posed her question and showed him the photo.

'Never seen the lad and I walk the waste ground a lot with Chippie here.'

'Have you seen anything suspicious in the area, apart from the dumping?' She didn't want to go into all that again.

He gave her a sharp look. 'Kids hang about the old farm, drinking and smoking dope. There's nothing here for them any more. No jobs now the steelworks and mines are gone.'

Janice brought up the subject of the white van and he thought for a moment.

'There was a van near the concrete building with the funny roof. I thought it was odd. They usually dump on the old Kenmuir Road or at the farm. Is the van something to do with the missing kid?'

'Could be. When did you see it?'

'Monday. Aye, it was definitely Monday. I didn't feel like going out, my chest was that bad. But Chippie here kept on at me.' He looked fondly down at the whippet sitting at his feet.

'What time was that?'

'Teatime. Five o'clock.'

'You don't remember the registration number, do you?' It was a forlorn hope.

'As a matter of fact I do. I thought I'd report it to the council. I tried, but I kept getting that press button one for this, two for that. I got confused and gave up.'

Janice couldn't believe her luck. Who said house-to-house took up too much time and produced nothing?

'S 064 OXO. I remembered it because I'm sixty-four and I like a cube of Oxo in my mince.'

Janice could have kissed him. 'Thanks, Mr Martin.'

'Nae problem, hen.'

Janice called in the registration number to the police station, for it to be traced. She had messed up with Dr Olatunde; this might improve her standing with the boss. She had two streets left to cover. By the time she'd done them, there might be some news, a name and address back for the owner of the van. That might bring a smile, however grim, to DI Wilson's face.

She had made mistakes before. They all had. But the DI had never stripped her down like that, made her feel and look stupid. Anger was something he kept for the criminals. She didn't like what was happening to him. She didn't like the change in their relationship. It made her feel inadequate and not up to the job.

After giving her report she asked to be put through to the DI. He listened to her news, then without altering the tone of his voice told her to meet him right away at the Nigerian Church of God on Maryhill Road.

If she'd expected congratulations she was let down. It was the DI's way to encourage his team whenever possible. Turning up a number plate on a suspect vehicle in a murder hunt was just such an occasion, she'd thought.

Janice bit back her disappointment. Half the reason she enjoyed the job was because of her superior officer. Something was very wrong with DI Wilson and she would never be able to ask what it was. She said her goodbyes to the rest of the door-to-door team and headed for the car.

Through the railway bridge she could see the distant incident tent. The bridge had been sealed off so no one could look down on the scene of crime officers methodically searching the waste ground.

Mr Martin had taken to the river bank with his whippet. He was tossing a stick and waiting for

Chippie to bring it back. A young mother with an empty pushchair followed a wobbly toddler across the grass. On one side of the bridge, normal life ticked on; on the other side, life was anything but normal.

23

CASTING A FOOTWEAR impression in the soft soil around the entrance to the altar building had been tricky. She'd mixed the standard 800gms of dental stone with 300mls of water, hoping the consistency wouldn't prove too thin. The liberal use of hairspray sealed the impression, preventing the casting material from damaging the finer details. It took half an hour in situ to set, then overnight air drying in the lab before she could begin to clean it.

Rhona moved the fine brush delicately over the surface. Too heavy a hand could remove the detail she needed to preserve.

She already had a test print from the small trainer found near the altar. A layer of water-based ink painted on the sole had produced an imprint in acetate. The child's partial print in blood from the kitchen and the dust one from the gate sat side by side with the imprint from the actual shoe. She had examined them in detail. Because her test impression hadn't been produced while being worn, it was lighter, but the random damage characteristics were identical.

The trainer belonged to Stephen.

She laid down the brush and fetched the scene of

crime prints for the adult shoe. The distinctive pattern of the sole identified by searching 3,500 sole patterns of 220 brands in the Solemate database, was the same. Of three areas of damage from casual wear on the waste-ground impression, two were visible in the same locations on the partial print from the kitchen.

The man entering the cylindrical building on the waste ground had walked through Carole's blood in the kitchen.

He had brought Stephen to that place and taken him away again. Whether Stephen was dead or alive, she couldn't tell.

Rhona had kept her mind solely on the job up to this point. As she wrote up her findings, the soft Irish voice of the previous evening crept back. She instinctively knew that Kitty Maguire was telling the truth. She was Sean's wife. A wife he had never alluded to in all the time they had known each other. Secrets. Secrets and lies. She silently admonished herself. She too held secrets. McNab was one of them. But you could not burden each new relationship with a confession of past failures.

Once, sitting in a restaurant, she had overheard a couple at the next table. A woman in her thirties spoke to an older man as a friend, perhaps even her father. 'I have sixteen years of failed relationships behind me,' she'd said.

It had been a startling admission, spoken in a resigned manner, with lost hope at its core.

An echo of her own personal life until she met Sean . . . or until last night, before the phone rang. Their

relationship had survived many things, including imagined and actual infidelity on both sides. It had never
had to face a wife.

'I love you.' The unexpected announcement had
stunned her. She had not reciprocated, thinking it
prompted by loss and alcohol.

Perhaps Sean had foreseen that his father's illness
would bring more than just death into their lives.

Death in many ways was her life. Violent death. It
was a morbid thought. She shivered, feeling a sudden
cold draught from nowhere.

Judy had returned the finger bones. 'They give me
the creeps,' she'd admitted, which was strange coming
from someone for whom the study of old bones was as
much a passion as a profession. Rhona ran her eyes
over the detailed report that had come back from
GUARD.

The bones were the answer to everything. Why
Carole and her mother were murdered, why Stephen
was taken, why Abel had been killed.

They had revealed their owner's age and gender and
where the eight-year-old boy had grown up.

That boy, according to GUARD, had been Abel.

The bones were defleshed using a knife, Judy wrote, *its
tiny surface cuts visible under a low-magnifying microscope. The same knife cut the three striations on each bone.
Imperfections along the blade left their identifying marks.
No peroxide was used to whiten them.*

The cross cut on Carole's back suggested the same
knife that killed her and her mother, had stripped the
bones clean. In Dr Sissons's opinion there had been

only one attacker. And he had taken his knife with him to use again.

Rhona's imagination was already generating the next scenario. The one that included Stephen.

A missing child was everyone's child.

A murdered child became your own.

The odds that Stephen was still alive had been falling with exponential speed. If only she had been faster about identifying the trichomes, swifter at finding the locations of viper's bugloss, searched the waste ground earlier, they might have found Stephen instead of his shoe.

If. Such a small word. Such big consequences.

The bones choose their next victim. That's what Sam's mother had written.

Judy was right. There was something creepy about the bones. Rhona pushed them away, disgusted and frightened by the images they conjured up.

She faxed her results to Bill, knowing she should have picked up the phone and called him, but they were somehow estranged from such familiarity, like a couple 'on a break'.

Both men in her life were keeping secrets from her.

An insistent pain had begun to throb at her right temple. She had tensed up and the muscle contraction in her neck had worked its painful way up the side of her face. She tried to relax, letting her shoulders sink and closing her eyes.

The funeral was tomorrow. She would have to decide soon.

'Dopehead,' Chrissy announced on entry.

'What?'

'Presumptive tests indicate the presence of cannabis in the urine on Enid's hair. Toxicology report confirms this.'

'Only cannabis?'

'No alcohol, no other drugs. But enough cannabis to make him pretty high.'

Cannabis, alcohol and other chosen drugs of abuse were a common mix in violent crime. Cannabis on its own wasn't particularly associated with violence. Although the drug was linked with paranoia, especially if there was evidence of mental illness.

Chrissy was examining her like a specimen. 'You look terrible.'

'Thanks.'

'Okay, what's up?'

'Nothing.' Her denial was too quick. Rhona could have kicked herself. Keeping things from Chrissy was an art form.

Chrissy glanced pointedly at the clock. 'Lunchtime. I'm starving.'

Chrissy was always starving. Where the food disappeared to was a mystery. The word *diet* didn't figure in her vocabulary and didn't have to. Chrissy ate anything and everything with relish and stayed the same weight.

'What about going out for lunch?' she suggested.

Going out for an interrogation more like.

'I'd be happy with a sandwich,' Rhona protested weakly. It was a forlorn hope.

'You need a walk in the fresh air.'

Chrissy was already pulling on her outdoor gear, a fitted furry jacket that conjured up an image of a wolf stalking its prey.

They walked down University Avenue to Di Maggios on Gibson Street, a Chrissy favourite with portions to match her appetite. It was lunchtime busy but Chrissy had a word with the waitress and they were quickly led to a secluded table. Rhona's forensic assistant was wasted in the lab. She should be in the CID, or MI5 for that matter.

Rhona glanced at the menu and ordered a hot sandwich. Chrissy went for a two-course menu.

Silence descended. 'The funeral is tomorrow,' Rhona began.

'And you're worried about going?'

This was too easy. 'We're . . .'

'So busy. Your favourite excuse.'

Rhona managed a guilty smile. It wasn't difficult.

'An early morning flight from Glasgow to Dublin. Come back the same day. But hey, it's the weekend. Come back Monday morning.' Chrissy was on a roll.

'Sean wants away as soon as possible,' Rhona explained.

'And *you* are the perfect excuse. *You* need to get back for work.' She was triumphant.

Rhona allowed Chrissy her moment.

'Okay, when we get back to the lab, you go online and book.' Chrissy wasn't taking no for an answer.

'Maybe.'

'Definitely.'

It was as though the decision had been taken out of

her hands. But she had forced fate to play the card she wanted. That was the truth.

Rhona's sandwich tasted like cardboard in her guilty mouth. On the other hand, Chrissy, the innocent, enjoyed the largest serving of Fettucine Di Maggio known to woman, followed by a mammoth helping of Hot Banana and Rum Pancakes.

24

VIOLENCE. A CANCER eating its way through the heart of his city. A city he loved, despite its tough reputation. Those who wrote about Glasgow often forgot it was also known as the friendliest city in the UK. The city where old ladies paid bus fares for tourists when they heard a story of exile. Bill knew, because it had happened to a Canadian nephew of his, who would never grow tired of telling the tale.

See Glasgow. The worst and the best. And the worst was exposing its racist underbelly. A black child was missing, a black child's torso found floating in the Kelvin. So it must be African voodoo. How the hell had the newspapers got hold of the voodoo angle? Not from him, that's for sure. Black immigrants mixed up in voodoo – a racist's dream ticket.

There had already been a flurry of incident reports from those brave enough to lodge them. It made a change from sectarian abuse. Dark skin was as much a marker as a Rangers or Celtic scarf. Only now both sides of the religious divide had a common enemy: anyone of a duskier hue than themselves. The continent of origin wasn't an issue. Africa, Asia, they didn't even know where they were on a map. Just as long as they could vent their self-righteous spleen on someone different.

Bill had taken Janice's phone call as a constable laid the report list in front of him. He was pleased DC Clark had a lead on the white van, yet the words *well done* stuck in his throat. Anger coloured everything. Made you spit when you should smile. What was the point of being nice, when shit kept coming anyway? Bill suddenly felt ashamed. If Margaret thought he was taking problems in his personal life out on his team, she would never forgive him. She wasn't taking it out on anyone. She had confessed to raging around the house, punching cushions and shouting her anger, but had waited until he left for work and the kids for school.

The buzz of conversation in the outer office faded to silence when he opened his door. Bill marshalled his expression into something resembling pleasure.

'DC Clark's got a number for the white van.'

There was a wave of excitement, almost a cheer.

Bill passed the number to the nearest officer. 'See if Traffic can tell us anything about the owner.' He paused. 'If anyone's looking for me, I'm at the Nigerian Church of God, Maryhill Road.'

The congregation met in an old Presbyterian hall. The neighbouring church building had been converted into a singles bar called the Dream Club. Bill had done a routine internet search and discovered the Nigerian Church of God had ministries in all West African countries, a strong presence in Europe and England,

150 churches in North America, and had recently purchased a multimillion-dollar property in Dallas, Texas. Apparently Glasgow was their first foray into Scotland.

Miracles were high on their agenda. That's what people wanted to believe in, why they paid their tithe. And judging by the rapid increase in membership from an initial half-dozen members meeting in a room in Lagos in 1957, to millions worldwide, the members thought they were getting what they paid for.

Bill checked himself, as he often did when his natural scepticism came into opposition with his wife's religion. Margaret was a believer; even her illness hadn't shaken her faith.

There was no sign of Janice when he drew up in front of the church hall. Bill trusted she would spot his parked car and went in alone.

The big oak door spoke of wealthier times. In the foyer a display of church dignitaries consisted of six colour photographs with names and positions below. All but one of the dignitaries were black and wore national dress. Pastor Achebe looked imposing and confident in his position and beliefs. Bill wished he felt the same. A list of activities included Daily Worship, Sunday School, House Fellowship and Internet Radio broadcasts. A special Miracle Service was scheduled for the last Sunday of every month. Members were requested to state the miracle they desired. As Bill ran his eye down the list, a distant murmur rose and fell like waves on a shore, audible through the half-open inner door.

Inside a large echoing room, ten people sat in a circle, heads bowed in prayer. In the centre was a table like a small altar on which six candles burnt. The room smelt warmly fragrant.

Bill waited as the tide of voices rose to a crescendo, finishing with a joyous chorus of 'Hallelujah', which sent an involuntary tingle up his spine. A belief in God had been the unspoken certainty of his childhood, along with a clear definition of right and wrong, and perhaps the greatest gift his mother could bestow: a respect for people whoever they were. Only the God bit had gone.

A tall man he recognised as Pastor Achebe came towards him, hand outstretched. First impressions could be wrong, but not often. The churchman's expression was open and welcoming. 'You must be Detective Inspector Wilson.'

Bill took the large firm hand in his. He had not warned the pastor of his intended visit, nor was he sure how he had been recognised. Either Sam Haruna had furnished a very good description, or the pastor had second sight as well as an ability to perform miracles.

'I do not perform miracles, only God can do that.'

'What?'

The pastor smiled, exposing two rows of perfect white teeth. 'I saw you reading the request list, Detective Inspector. If you ask God for help, I am sure he will answer.'

'I'll settle for your help, Pastor, for the moment.'

'Of course. Would you like to come through to my study?'

The candles had been blown out, the altar moved to

the wall. Six men and three women were donning coats and heading for the door, calling their goodbyes.

'Christ be with you.'

'And with you.'

Bill ran a swift eye over the worshippers. Mixed age group, two white faces among the black, both of them middle-aged women.

Pastor Achebe led him to an open door at the rear of the hall. The room was warmed by a gas fire and lit by a single window that looked out on a stone wall three feet away, which, judging by direction, belonged to the Dream Club. A simple wooden cross hung on the wall behind a desk that housed a pile of papers and an ultra-slim laptop. Beside the cross hung a map of the world, many of the countries marked by a small cross. The map reminded Bill of the one in his old schoolroom, but with the Nigerian Church of God replacing the pink expanse of the British Empire.

He took the seat the pastor indicated.

'I understand Carole Devlin and her son were members of your church?'

The pastor settled himself behind the desk. He was a broad man, his bulk more likely to be muscle than fat. 'Not *my* church,' he gently corrected. '*God*'s church. I am merely a member.'

'But you are in charge?'

'I have certain responsibilities, yes.'

His professions of modesty were beginning to irritate. 'Tell me about Carole.'

'She came with Stephen most Sundays. The boy

attended Sunday School while his mother worshipped in the main hall.'

'How well did you know her?'

'Not well, I'm ashamed to say. But I understand she attended one of our sister churches in Kano before returning to the UK. She did not mingle with the other worshippers here, merely arrived for the service and left swiftly afterwards.'

'Wasn't that strange?'

'Our church is our family, Detective Inspector. Yes, it is, was, unusual. What I can tell you is that Carole entered a request for a miracle last Sunday, the day before she died.'

He pushed a black diary across the desk and pointed at an entry which said simply *'Don Allah'*.

'What does it mean?'

'In the Hausa language it means "please" or, more precisely, "please, God".'

'That's all?'

'God knows everything. There was no need for her to write down the miracle she needed. It was enough to say please.'

'Do you know what she wanted?'

He shook his head. 'No. But I can surmise.'

'And?'

'In my experience women rarely ask anything for themselves. Whatever she wanted it would be for her child.'

Bill changed tack. 'And Carole Devlin's husband?'

'I never met him.' The pastor's tone of voice didn't change, but his answer was almost too swift.

Bill examined the eyes that stared unblinkingly into his. 'Do you know a Dr Olatunde?'

The pastor had no difficulty with that question. Practice was making his responses perfect. 'Not directly. Sam Haruna has mentioned the name to me. He works at the university, I believe.'

'He is not a member of your church?'

He shook his head sadly.

'But he is Nigerian?'

The pastor placed his hands together in a prayer-like gesture. 'Not all Nigerians are men of God.'

'There are elements of this case that suggest a link with voodoo.'

The pastor looked distressed. 'The African term is juju, Inspector. Yes, I am sorry to say some of my fellow Africans still run after fetish priests and other powers of darkness for assistance.'

'Like Dr Olatunde?'

'I cannot say that, for I do not know.'

Bill felt he was wading through treacle. Regardless of how accommodating Pastor Achebe appeared to be, he had told him nothing, except that Carole had asked for a miracle and her God had failed her. 'I will need contact details for all members of your church.'

Pastor Achebe opened his mouth to protest, but Bill went on regardless. 'I will also require every male over the age of sixteen to give a DNA sample to eliminate them from our enquiries.'

The pastor had regained his composure. He rose from the chair, with an accepting smile. 'Of course, Inspector. I understand. Although among the black community, might such a requirement be seen as police harassment?'

Bill was already rehearsing the conversation he would have with his superior officer over such a request. And sampling the male congregation depended entirely on Pastor Achebe persuading his flock to come forward. The Nigerian Church of God, he suspected, had members entirely unknown to the Home Office. Perhaps an admission of illegal status was as sacrosanct to Pastor Achebe as an admission in the confessional.

When they emerged from the office, Janice was in the foyer, reading the miracle list. She threw Bill a swift smile, before adjusting it to a nod. Obviously smiling had not been well received of late.

Bill introduced her to the pastor, who shook her hand.

'Pastor Achebe has kindly agreed to supply us with the names of males over sixteen in his congregation, for DNA testing. I want you to wait here until he puts this together.'

Janice's presence might encourage the pastor to give a more comprehensive list.

'In view of the nature of the case, I would also like the names of families with children under the age of sixteen.'

'Of course, Inspector. I will do everything I can.' The pastor's expression grew grim. 'Those who engage in witchcraft have great control over believers and a vested interest in keeping that control. For that reason alone, they are dangerous.'

It struck Bill as he walked to his car that had the pastor substituted 'religion' for 'witchcraft', his pronouncement would have held the same truth.

25

MALCHIE WAS WORRIED, although he was sure the story of the van and stolen goods had worked. Danny had played that detective along, even fooled his da into believing the shit-scared trick. A rare wee actor was Danny.

The charge of sexual assault had no hope either. The security cameras were too far from where they'd handled the woman. And anyway, the cameras had been smashed so often that if any of them worked it would be a miracle.

Malchie gnawed at his fingernail, biting it to the quick. But if HE thought for a minute they'd led the police to the site? He and Danny had been given the job of keeping folk away from that building, and they'd been paid well for it. Heavy-duty shit that blew your mind even without the drink.

Malchie ran a furred tongue over his lips, finding a sore at the corner of his mouth. He picked at it, tasting the salt of his own blood.

At least he didn't have the mobile on him when they took him to the police station. He'd managed to slip it down the side of the settee when it was obvious the pig would insist he go with them. If the fucking phone had gone off, he really would have shit himself.

To make himself feel better, Malchie imagined doing more than just sticking his hand between the woman's legs. He would fix her for reporting them. Fuck the bitch till she bled. A rush of pleasure filled his groin and he rubbed himself hard, imagining her frightened face, looking up at him, begging him to stop. When he was ready, he yanked down the tracksuit bottoms and let fly, shouting short staccato 'fucks' with each spurt.

Momentarily released from his anger, he slumped back in the chair. Whatever he did to the woman wouldn't bring his job back. Now that the police were swarming all over the site, that was gone, along with his supply. No shit, no fun and no cash.

He pulled out the phone. What if he was the one to make contact? Tell HIM what was going on here. Tell HIM about the woman.

Whatever fantasy he dreamt up to pay her back was nothing to what he might be told to do.

Malchie punched out the keys before he changed his mind, and waited for a connection. HE had never answered the phone, only a standard answer machine. This time there was nothing but a dead-end drone. Malchie tried again, cursing under his breath, already suspecting that any contact they'd had was at an end. His drug ticket was gone. He didn't know who HE was or where to find HIM. Their only contact had been the mobile.

He threw the phone on the bed, slammed the door

behind him and went downstairs to take it out on his mother.

She was in the kitchen, her hands in the sink. The radio was on, playing a stupid tune and she was humming. He stood at the door watching and waiting. He'd seen his dad do that lots of times. Wait till she looked happy before he moved in for the kill. Sometimes his father would go out of his way to make her happy. Her expression would slowly change from fear to hope, then pleasure. Malchie'd watched the performance as a child, still on her side, hoping when she hoped. Gradually he learned that hers was the losing side. Learned to hate her when she cowered like a frightened sheep. From then on he got what he wanted. He was his dad's partner in the game, a game that grew ever more cruel.

His mother turned, sensing his presence. For a moment she was his mum, the one who used to shield him from his father's rages. Malchie immediately dismissed the uncomfortable feeling that gave him.

'Food,' he demanded.

She pointed at a pot on the stove. 'There's mince.'

'Fuck mince.'

He snatched her purse from the table.

'Ah haven't . . .' she began, then stopped, drying her hands nervously on a tea towel as he rifled through the purse, taking the one note in there. She opened her mouth to protest, then rapidly shut it again.

The gesture of futility fanned Malchie's simmering resentment. He lifted the pot from the gas and threw it across the table at her. The boiling mince flew out, spraying the table, the floor and her outstretched hand.

She smothered a scream, clasping the burnt hand to her chest.

Malchie turned from her shocked face, enjoying the rush of adrenalin pumping through his veins. The money would buy him dope, drink and a pizza, in that order.

When she heard the slam of the front door, she turned on the cold tap and stuck her hand under the running water. The radio was playing a love song. She held the injured hand with the other to stop them both shaking. She was muttering, 'Malcolm, Malcolm,' under her breath as though to a child. Her eyes were dry as dust, red-hot from unshed tears. Her knees buckled slightly and she pressed them against the sink, forcing herself to stay upright. When the pain lessened, she wet the tea towel with cold water and wrapped it around the rising blisters.

She held the banister with her good hand as she climbed the stairs. When she pushed open the door of her son's bedroom, the smell of unwashed male rushed out. She walked to the window and opened it, then looked around the room.

The fancy mobile was lying on the bed. She picked it up, without looking at it. Downstairs again, she slipped on her coat and put the mobile in her handbag along with her purse, after checking she had enough change for the bus.

Malcolm hadn't told the police about the phone. But

she would. The phone had something to do with that place they'd found the wee boy's shoe.

There was a bus waiting at the terminus. She got on, paid and sat at the back, one hand still wrapped in the wet cloth. Her man would come home and find the mess. No tea either. The script was already written for what would happen next, but for once she would not be playing her part.

After the police station she would go to Karen's. She knew where her daughter lived; the men of the family didn't. Karen had wanted her mother to leave ever since she'd left home herself.

But she hadn't wanted to go until she was sure. She couldn't say 'sure that Malcolm was going to turn out like his father', not out loud, nor even silently in her head, because she knew that by staying and taking it for so long, she had probably made that happen.

The woman was sitting in reception when Bill got back to the police station. She wore the same resigned expression, her eyes somewhere else, far, he suspected, from the here and now.

The desk sergeant explained in a low voice, 'She wants to see Dr MacLeod. I told her she was forensic and not a policewoman. She was adamant. Dr MacLeod.'

The woman was probably here to plead her son's case. More fool her. Didn't she realise that the more she covered up for him, the worse he was likely to get?

'Mrs Menzies? Can I help?'

She turned a startled gaze on him. 'I need to speak to the woman, Dr MacLeod.'

'Sergeant MacVitie has explained. Dr MacLeod is a forensic scientist, not a police officer. She doesn't work here.'

'I have something to tell her.'

'Will I do?'

A flash of stubbornness crossed her face. Something had driven her to come here. It had taken courage. She wasn't going to give up now. 'I have to talk to the woman.'

She turned from him, settling back into her trance.

It was then he noticed her hand, wound around with what looked like a kitchen cloth.

'Have you hurt yourself?'

She glanced down. 'I burnt it on a pot.' She took a sharp breath that sounded like a sob.

'Sergeant, a cup of tea for Mrs Menzies. And bring the first-aid kit,' he ordered.

The sergeant raised an eyebrow, then dropped it when he saw Bill's expression.

'Right away, sir.'

Bill left her sitting there and went straight to his office.

The lab phone rang out half a dozen times before Chrissy picked up.

'She's here all right,' she answered Bill's swift enquiry. 'I'll get her for you.'

Bill had worked with Rhona MacLeod long enough both to respect and like her. But his current view on the world had made him feel estranged from everyone, including her. Despite his best efforts, his voice still sounded gruff. 'Malcolm Menzies's mother is here. She wants to speak to you. I've told her—'

Rhona interrupted him. 'I'll come.'

'I don't think she wants to plead his innocence.'

'I don't think she does, either. I'll be there in twenty minutes.'

The main incident room was ringing with phones, chatter and the relentless click of computer keys. McNab had caught Bill's eye and followed him to his office, waiting impatiently while he made the call to the lab.

McNab spoke as soon as the receiver went down. 'The van belongs to the Nigerian Church of God by way of a charity called One World.'

'Bastard!' Bill's fury caused McNab to take a step back. 'Call DC Clark. She's with the pastor now. Find out what he knows about that van.'

Bill was still seething when Rhona arrived fifteen minutes later. Her face was pale against the long slim-line black coat. He was struck by the purple shadows under her eyes.

Bill talked to cover the unease between them. 'Chrissy's lead to the Nigerian Church of God was a good one. Turns out the van is owned by a subsidiary charity of theirs.'

'Oh.' Rhona thought for a moment. 'If you suspect a member of the church might be involved—'

Bill cut in, his tone abrupt. 'I need a DNA check on all male church members over sixteen.'

She regarded him coolly, a questioning look in her eyes, then nodded. 'Of course.'

It would mean a massive effort on both their parts. But such a move had produced results before now.

However, if Stephen were still alive, it might put him in danger . . .

It seemed Rhona was reading his thoughts. 'I think Stephen's alive.' She seemed puzzled by her own certainty.

'Why?'

'I can't explain.' She shook her head. 'Is there any chance he's been smuggled out of the country?'

People were trafficked into the UK. Women and children mostly, to work in brothels and God knows where else. London was the most popular destination but Scotland was by no means free from the trade. With its extensive remote coastline and direct sea links to Northern Europe, it would take an army to watch every possible landing point. If someone brought illegals in, they could take them out as well.

'His mother requested a miracle before she died.' Bill felt embarrassed saying it. 'The church has a miracle service once a month. You put in your request and God answers, apparently.' He didn't like the sneer in his own voice.

'What did she ask for?' Rhona's voice was low, almost breathless.

'*Don Allah*. Please, God. That's all.'

Rhona thought about that. 'She was asking God to protect her son.'

'You think she knew her attacker?'

'Circumcision is personal. I think she was punished for bringing Stephen here, away from something or someone. I think whoever punished her wanted Stephen back.'

It made sense, but then many scenarios could be written to try to make sense of the few facts they had.

The next step was Customs and Immigration. To find out where, when and how illegals were arriving in Scotland.

'My biggest mistake was to let so-called Mr Devlin out of my sight.'

'We all make mistakes, Bill.' She looked tired. Tired but determined. 'Okay, where's Malchie's mum?'

26

WOMAN TO WOMAN with Dr MacLeod. That was Malchie's mother's request. Bill had agreed, on condition the interview was observed and taped. Mrs Menzies had something to say. If there was the slightest chance it concerned the murder investigation, then it had to be on record.

Rhona waited until the female constable had set the tape running, announced who was present, then exited, shutting the door. She didn't glance at the two-way glass, behind which Bill and McNab stood unobserved.

'Mrs Menzies,' she began.

'My name's Sara. Please call me Sara.'

'Mine's Rhona.'

They exchanged cautious smiles.

'I wanted to tell you I'm sorry.'

Rhona's heart sank. Was that the only reason Mrs Menzies had asked to speak to her?

'I needed to say that first.'

Rhona waited for her to go on.

A pulse beat rapidly at the side of the woman's thin neck. Small beads of perspiration clung to her pale forehead. She cleared her throat, then, as though making up her mind, she reached in her handbag and withdrew something.

Rhona caught a flash of black metal. Realising what it was, she raised her hand to indicate to the silent watchers that there was nothing to fear.

Sara laid the fancy black mobile phone on the table between them.

'He was using it to contact somebody about –' her voice caught in her throat – 'that place on the wasteland.'

Rhona could taste the woman's fear.

'Somebody was giving my son drugs to keep folk away from that building.' She wiped an eye with a shaking hand.

'How long for?'

'He's been smoking dope for months. That and drink. So he was getting money from somewhere. Today he took money from me.'

Rhona's eyes were drawn to the bandaged hand. 'The police can protect you.' The words sounded as feeble as the promise.

Sara made a small noise in her throat. 'Aye.' The acceptance was more for Rhona's peace of mind, than her own.

'What was Malcolm guarding?'

'I thought it was stolen stuff or drugs.' Her eyes reluctantly met Rhona's. 'Then I worried it might be something worse.'

'Why did you think that?'

'Malcolm was frightened. He used to be like that when he was a wee boy. Always frightened.'

Rhona recalled the sly face, the cruel twist to his mouth. Malchie had learned that the best way to handle fear was to dole it out.

Sara drew herself up. 'He came home one night really scared. I heard him being sick in the toilet. When he came out he had a towel wrapped around his hand. He wouldn't let me see it. I waited till he was asleep and looked. Someone had cut a cross there.' She pointed to the hollow next to her thumb. 'The inspector said there was one like it on the wall inside that building.'

Sara had run out of steam. She slumped, folding her body into itself.

'You did the right thing,' Rhona said.

Her eyes raised in despair. 'Betraying my son?'

'Protecting your son.'

Sara stared at the mobile as though it were a dangerous weapon. 'Can you find out who gave him that?'

'We'll try.'

Her bandaged hand lay on the table. Rhona reached out and touched it gently.

'Malcolm is safer if we catch this man.' Even as she said it she wondered how Sara could love a son who inflicted so much pain.

'Have you got any children?' Sara asked.

The age-old response of 'no' was primed and ready, but Rhona didn't use it. 'I have a son.'

'How old?'

'Eighteen.'

Sara gave her an appraising look. 'I have a daughter, Karen. I'm going to stay with her.'

So coming here meant leaving husband, son and home.

'Your husband . . .'

'He's a lorry driver. Away a lot.' She indicated the mobile. 'He knows nothing about this. He and Karen fell out. He doesn't know where she lives. She wants it like that.'

'Can we contact you there?'

A flash of concern crossed Sara's face. 'I'll give you the number.' She put her emphasis on 'you'.

'I'm not a police officer,' Rhona tried to explain.

'If he finds out he'll come for me.' It was a bald admission of terror. 'His' identity was left to supposition.

'I'll make sure he doesn't find out.' A big promise she would have to try to keep.

Sara seemed to take her at her word. She wrote a number on a piece of paper and passed it across. It was the 0141 prefix for Glasgow followed by a 946 code.

'Can I call your daughter? Get her to come for you?'

'No.' She was adamant. 'I'll get the bus.'

Rhona stood up, indicating to those on the other side of the glass that the interview was over. Bill wisely didn't come in. The woman had come of her own free will. They had no reason not to let her walk back out.

The door was opened by the female constable carrying an evidence bag. Rhona slipped the mobile inside and followed Mrs Menzies to the door. Now that the deed was done, the woman was anxious to leave. Rhona saw her through to reception.

'I hope you find the wee boy.'

'Thank you for your help, Sara.'

Sara looked down at the proffered hand. The gesture seemed inappropriate and oddly masculine, but she took it anyway. 'Don't phone unless you have to.'

With that she turned abruptly away.

Bill and McNab were waiting in Bill's office.

McNab looked pleased with the result. 'We'll dust the mobile for prints. Then the tech boys can take a look. The provider should have a record of the owner and any calls.'

It wouldn't be the first time a mobile phone had helped trace a criminal.

'How long will that take?' asked Rhona. How often had she fended off that selfsame question?

'They promised priority,' McNab assured her.

'Whoever gave him the phone was giving him money to keep people away from that building. The altar suggests some kind of juju worship was going on there. That could involve more than one person.'

'We'll bring Malchie in, find out what he really knows,' Bill said. 'Can we have the contact number his mum gave you?'

Rhona reluctantly reached in her pocket and retrieved the slip of paper.

McNab made a note of it. 'I know that 946 is the code for Maryhill. We'll get the address from BT.'

'If only we had a lead on Mr Devlin.' Rhona didn't like saying it, knowing how Bill felt. But if they only knew who Devlin really was . . .

McNab came to Bill's rescue. 'We have an enhanced image from the footage in the mortuary, although it's not great. We've contacted the main oil firms working in Nigeria to see if they have Devlin on their books.'

The Nigerian connection had to be important.

'I checked out the foreign office website,' Rhona told them. 'There're only four thousand UK citizens living in Nigeria. Most in Lagos, fewer in Kano. I bet the British consul in Kano knows every white face within a hundred miles, including Carole Devlin.'

Bill looked up. 'And the pastor said Carole attended one of their churches there.'

'Wasn't Kano where they had those big riots a couple of years back?' McNab asked.

'According to *onlinenigeria*, only one per cent of Kano residents are Christian and most of them live, or lived, before the riots, in the *Sabon Gari*. That was why it was so easy to find them. Over a hundred people died, Muslim against Christian.'

'*Sabon Gari*?'

'Hausa for foreigners' town, apparently.' Rhona thought for a moment. 'That's where the witch doctor advert came from, the one that Sam showed me.'

'In your report you said the mineral content of Abel's bones suggested he grew up near Rano,' Bill said. 'Is that near Kano?'

'Half an hour away, near Tiga Dam,' she told him. 'When's Olatunde due back?'

'University says he has compassionate leave, so no definite date,' McNab answered.

'What if Sam's right and Stephen's drawing is Olatunde?'

Bill threw Rhona a swift look. 'Right. We check out

the Olatunde home, forensics included.' He turned to McNab. 'Get back on to the university. Insist on a contact number or address for our doctor in Nigeria.'

The majority of murders were carried out by someone the victim knew, despite what the tabloids would have you believe. If Carole's circle in this country was as small as it seemed, Olatunde was one of the few members.

Rhona waited until the office door closed behind McNab. They had made some progress, in thought at least. Bill had slumped back into his chair. She had always thought of him as the captain of the *Starship Enterprise* when he sat in that chair. Not today.

'I should have searched Olatunde's house before now,' he muttered.

'On the strength of a child's drawing?'

'And Sam's identification.'

'Being a member of that church makes Sam a suspect too,' she countered.

They both digested that.

Bill snorted. 'I'm losing it.'

'Losing what?'

He indicated the noisy police office through the glass. 'Them. This case.'

His eyes were haunted.

'What's wrong, Bill?'

'Apart from three murders and a missing child, you mean?'

She ignored the sarcasm. 'I mean, with you?'

She watched his defences crumble. His voice when he finally spoke, was heavy with dread.

'Margaret's got a lump, probably cancer.'

Rhona suspected she was the first person he'd told. 'Where?'

'In her right breast.'

'How long has it been there?'

'A few weeks.'

'Have they done a biopsy?'

He nodded in slow motion. 'We're waiting for the results.'

'She'll be okay.'

She was saying this as much for herself as for him.

Hope sprang in his eyes. 'How can you know that?'

'The survival rate is good if caught early. Margaret is a fighter. And she's got you.'

The conviction in her voice made hope a brief reality for him. Rhona pushed her own problems to the back of her mind, and smiled encouragingly.

'Thanks.'

It was as though she had saved his life as well as Margaret's.

He stood up. 'Margaret wants me to find the boy. It's as important to her as what the doctors say.'

That fact had added to his despair. How could he tell Margaret that Stephen died before he got to him?

'Stephen left that building alive.' That much Rhona knew.

27

HE'D LEFT THE phone on the fucking bed!

Malchie threw the duvet up in the air, waiting for the thump as the metal hit the carpet. Nothing.

He searched the floor, tossing dirty underpants and socks to one side, muttering to himself all the time.

'I left it on the fucking bed.'

The combination of dope and drink in his bloodstream was still strong enough to dampen his growing anxiety, until he felt the draught on his face.

He spun around.

The window was open. His brain cells struggled frantically to function. Who the fuck opened the window?

Who else but his stupid mother. *Open the window, Malcolm. Let some air into the room.*

His father never came in here any more, not since the last attempt at a beating, when Malchie'd pulled out his knife to defend himself. His dad didn't like that. No fist was as quick as a chib.

Only his mother came in here now, even when he warned her not to.

Had she taken his phone?

His search became more desperate. He stripped the

bed and carefully checked inside the duvet cover, then pulled the bed away from the wall and lay across it, searching behind. More dirty clothes and a few empty beer cans. No phone.

Fear was threatening to swamp the pleasant fug of chemicals in his bloodstream as he took the stairs two at a time.

He didn't shout her name, not wanting to give any warning. When he threw open the kitchen door, the room was empty, the pot lying where he'd thrown it, its cold congealing contents a thin slick across the floor.

A sick apprehension flowed through him. Where had she gone? He recalled her gasp of pain as the boiling mince hit her hand. Had she gone to the hospital? He dismissed the thought almost immediately. She never went to the hospital, no matter how badly hurt she was. He checked the hook at the back door for her coat; the surfaces, for her handbag. Both were gone.

Malchie felt for the reassuring presence of his knife. The handle was cool to the touch. He pulled it out and set it on the table. His scarred hand had begun to throb. What if she gave the phone to the police? Malchie had no doubt what would happen next. The kitchen swam in front of him and he knew he was going to vomit.

A mess of semi-digested pizza and cider hit the stainless-steel sink. He heaved twice more, before his trembling legs allowed him to sit down at the table.

He wiped his mouth with the back of his hand.

They would come for him. He would end up like that kid.

His gaze flicked wildly around the room as the memory of the drums began a steady beat in his head. He could hear the chants again, see the kneeling figures as clearly as when it had happened.

The dog's eyes bulge in fear, its snapping muzzle bound with barbed wire, preventing it from biting its tormentors. Still it tries to escape, its head twisting wildly, mucus flying from bared teeth.

Its death is swift, a clean slice to the neck, muffled whines ending in silence as blood gushes into the waiting bowl. The hot salt smell of fresh blood sends a ripple of excitement through the kneeling group. Another swift cut and HE holds up the dog's testicles. The crowd groans in pleasure.

Malchie's own blood is beating furiously through his veins, bulging his temples, firing his heartbeat, hardening his prick. It's the same feeling he gets when he holds up his knife and watches the fear on his victim's face.

They bring the bowl to him and hold it under his nose. His eyes stream as he breathes in. The chanting begins again, rising steadily like his climax. They cut him as he drinks. A swift cross cut into his hand. There is no pain, even when they dribble the purple liquid into the wound.

Malchie swallows the last of the blood. Salt and metal. He feels it flow down his throat in a warm red stream. As it hits his stomach, he feels his prick spray inside his pants. An intense pleasure fills his body and he feels himself sway. Strong arms lift him then and drag him towards the door. Malchie doesn't want to go. His fear has dissolved. He is one of them now.

On the way out he sees the black kid, gagged and tied up

against the back wall. His head is tipped back, his eyes rolling white in his head.

When Malchie's head stopped swimming, he checked the couch in the living room in the vain hope the phone was down the back. Then he fetched a can of cider from his bedroom and sat down to wait for his mum to return. No point in telling Danny yet, until he was sure the mobile was really gone. Danny hadn't been at the initiation ceremony. Danny knew only what he told him and that wasn't much. And it meant Malchie could split the money and the drugs the way he liked, with plenty for himself. Danny was useful to cover for him, that was all.

He must have dozed off, because the rattle of the letter box woke him. He jumped up, convinced it was his mother. But the key didn't turn in the lock and the front door didn't open.

Malchie stood for a moment before walking through to the hall. At first glance there was nothing on the carpet. Then he saw the wizened shapes tied together with red thread near the foot of the door. Someone had posted them through the letter box.

Malchie ran panic-stricken to the kitchen for his knife. The weight of it in his hand gave him the courage to go through to the sitting room and look out of the window.

The street was empty. Grey rain splattered the pavements. The street lights had come on, throwing an eerie orange glow on the puddles.

Whoever had posted the dog's testicles through his letter box was long gone.

Back in the hall, Malchie slid down the wall and sat, knees up, the object of his terror a metre away. Adrenalin twitched his legs in a parody of running and he was a wee boy again, listening to his mother's screams, knowing he should go and help her, but choosing self-preservation instead.

He spat out his childhood disgust and guilt and wiped his mouth with a trembling hand. The stupid bitch never learned. In that moment Malchie knew the truth. She had taken the phone to the police. His mother was upset about that woman on the waste ground. His stupid mother had fucked him up because of that.

The object on the mat reminded him he had to get away from here, and quickly. He thought about calling Danny to warn him what had happened, then dismissed the idea. Danny would have to look out for himself.

Malchie stood up and slipped the knife out of sight, then went upstairs to collect his gear.

Day 5

Friday

28

BEING BACK IN church gave Chrissy a bad feeling. She didn't like to call it guilt, because it was much more complex than that. The Nigerian Church of God was nothing like a Catholic chapel. No statues of the Virgin Mary, no Jesus with sorrowful eyes and bleeding hands and feet. But they did have a miracle list. Chrissy eyed it with interest and a certain degree of anticipation, much as she read her stars in the newspapers, particularly the *Sunday Herald* magazine, which always guaranteed something nice was going to happen. She wasn't sure how she would have reacted had Sam's name appeared on the list. What would he have asked for?

She hadn't had the nerve to tell Sam to his face that she couldn't see him any more. She'd taken the cowardly text route: *V busy work cant see u fr a while.* Now that the Nigerian Church of God was part of the murder investigation, she couldn't see him at all.

DC Clark was with the pastor discussing the DNA testing. The rest of the team were due any minute. According to Janice, the pastor had given them the room normally used for the Sunday School. Chrissy picked up her forensic case and went to check it out.

Someone had already cleared the child-size tables and chairs to one side. The room was warm and carpeted, the walls decorated with brightly coloured crayoned posters. Jesus figured in a lot of them, telling stories, suffering the little children to come unto him. In the drawings Jesus was a black man, the children a mix of colours and creeds, which made a pleasant change. The words and music of a song sat on an upright piano. 'One More Step Along the World I Go'. Chrissy felt a lump rise in her throat. That had been one of her favourites in school. The tune came back into her head and she found herself singing the words quietly. As a child it had made her feel safe. A bit like 'The Lord's My Shepherd' did for adults. In both, the darkness of the world couldn't get to you. Not like in real life.

'It is a good song.' The male voice was deep and resonant. The man came towards her and extended his hand. 'I am Pastor Achebe.'

Her hand was encased in his large warm handshake.

'Chrissy McInsh, forensics.'

'At the forefront of science.' He smiled.

'We try.'

'I'm a *CSI* fan myself, although I set great store by human intuition.'

'Intuition is often at the heart of the investigation,' she agreed. 'Science provides the proof.'

'So you do not believe in blind faith?' His gaze was compelling and not a little scary.

'I prefer hard evidence.'

Pastor Achebe was a charismatic character. The

height, the voice, the eyes. His flock must love him. Probably do anything for him. The thought chilled her.

Her childhood priest, Father Riley, had many of the same characteristics. Crinkly smiling eyes and a persuasive way with words. She had escaped his sexual advances, being a girl. Her friend, Neil MacGregor, had not.

The remainder of the team had arrived. She heard McNab's voice in the main hall. He was asking Janice where Rhona was.

The pastor handed Chrissy a printed list of names. 'I have spoken to the men of my congregation and explained how important it is that they come here today.'

Chrissy glanced at the paper. It looked like at least fifty names.

'Many of them have come from countries where you cannot trust the police.'

She met his eye. 'If they are innocent they have nothing to worry about.'

He shrugged. 'Innocence has not protected them up to now.'

'No two people share the same DNA unless they are twins.'

'You and I know that, they don't. Many of these men are deeply superstitious as well as religious.'

Chrissy stopped herself from suggesting they were one and the same thing. 'We take a small scraping of cells from inside the mouth,' she explained. 'Painless and quick.'

McNab came in, preventing further discussion.

Chrissy wondered how diligent Pastor Achebe had been at persuading his flock to attend. And what about those who were here illegally? There were plenty of those, if you believed the tabloids. Would any of them turn up?

McNab took a good look around. 'Where's Dr MacLeod?' He tried to sound casual.

'Dublin.'

That floored him. 'Dublin?' he repeated.

'At a funeral. Sean's father died.'

A swift angry look crossed his face, before he managed to replace it with an attempt at compassion. 'She never said.'

'Well,' Chrissy met his eye, 'she wouldn't, would she?' She couldn't resist the jibe. Just in case McNab had any ideas about muscling back in. 'This is routine stuff,' she went on. 'Dr McLeod doesn't need to be here.'

She handed him the list.

'You can check off the names.' Whether he would be able to pronounce any of them was another matter.

'Have you organised an interpreter?' he asked.

'I would need several. Hausa, Yoruba, Ibo, and that's only the main Nigerian tribes. Pastor Achebe assures me they all speak English. It's the language of government and the school qualification system.'

McNab smiled. 'The good old British Empire.'

Kola Belgore looked as though he was wearing his entire wardrobe against the Scottish weather. He had at least three jumpers on under a padded jacket. His face was pinched with cold and fear, his eyes darting about, as though waiting for the devil himself to appear.

Sam had taught her some Hausa phrases. Basic polite greetings that should be answered in a certain way. Also a few general expressions and some sexual innuendoes. The basic Hausa greetings were proving very handy. Using them seemed significantly to reduce the terror in her victims, including Kola.

'*Sannu.*'

His face lit up. '*Yawa, sannu.*'

'*Lafiya?*'

He grinned, despite her strangled rendition of his language. '*Lafiya, lau. Da godiya.*'

She returned the smile. 'That's about all I can manage. Can we switch to English?'

'Of course.' His voice was solemn.

Chrissy showed him the cotton stick. 'I need to take a small sample of skin cells from inside your mouth. Is that okay?'

He nodded and opened wide. His teeth were a brilliant white. No Glasgow diet of sweets and ginger or stains from chewing kola nuts, despite his name.

She scraped the inside cheek and transferred the results to the waiting receptacle. All mouth scrapes from this morning's testing would be quickly frozen for later DNA extraction.

He sat waiting.

'That's it,' she assured him.

His relief was obvious.

'*Na gode,*' she added for good measure.

As he left, McNab popped his head around the door. 'One more.'

Forty-six at the last count. Chrissy looked longingly at the fast-cooling cup of coffee Janice had brought a few minutes previously.

'Send him in.'

Her preoccupation with the constant stream of frightened young men had made her forget the obvious. Sam.

He stood, hesitant, in the doorway.

Chrissy was filled with conflicting emotions at the sight of him. Delight at seeing him again, an intense longing to touch him, coupled with a desire to run.

'*Sannu.*'

'*Sannu da aiki.*'

'Don't know that one.'

'It means "greetings in your work".'

She gestured him to a seat. 'I'm going to take some cells from . . .'

'I am a medical student, remember. You don't have to explain.'

She felt a fool, although his words were light-hearted enough.

He opened his mouth to her, and in that moment she could taste him, his tongue meeting hers, the press of his lips.

She pulled herself together. This wasn't professional. Someone else had to take this sample. 'If you could wait a moment, please.'

She walked swiftly to the door. Janice was standing in the main hall, talking to McNab. Helen, the assistant who had been helping her, emerged from the toilet and Chrissy waved her over. 'I'd like you to take the last sample.'

McNab looked over, puzzled by her tone.

'Anything wrong?'

She shook her head. 'Nothing.'

Helen followed her into the room.

Sam sat where she had left him, his long slim hands clasped together in his lap.

Chrissy handed Helen the cotton stick.

Afterwards, she wrote on the sample container that it had been taken by Helen White.

'Thank you, Mr Haruna,' she said for Helen's benefit. 'You can go now.'

'*Sai da yamma?*' His eyes met hers, willing her to understand.

'*Yauwa, sai da yamma.*'

Sam bowed graciously and left.

Helen was impressed. 'I didn't know you could speak the lingo.'

McNab was watching from the door. 'Where did you learn that?'

'I've just sampled nearly fifty men, most of whom speak Hausa. I asked how to say the greetings. It made them more relaxed.'

Helen bought her story; McNab she wasn't so sure about. He didn't go to the jazz club, as far as she knew, and he hadn't shown any recognition when Sam came in. Chrissy would explain to DI Wilson what she had done. There was no need to expose her private life to McNab.

Until tonight, Sam had said. He wanted to see her and she had indicated he would. Speaking to him at the jazz club wasn't breaking any rules. Whether she was strong enough not to go home with him was another matter.

29

WHEN BILL DECIDED to examine the Olatunde home forensically, Rhona knew it provided a perfect excuse not to go to Dublin.

Immersion in work was infinitely preferable to checking up on Sean. Her initial dismay at Kitty's phone call had been followed by anger, then an overwhelming suspicion that threatened to cloud her judgement. Eventually the rule by which she lived had reasserted itself. She was first and foremost a forensic scientist.

She made arrangements to meet Bill at the Olatunde flat early on Friday morning, about the time she should have been boarding the plane.

University Avenue was quiet; it was too early for either staff or students. When she was a student here, her maths lecture had been scheduled for nine o'clock. An unholy hour to contemplate set theory or the delights of integral calculus, however much you enjoyed the subject.

She had lived then in a tiny two-room flat in Partick. The flat just off Dunbarton Road had been left to a friend's mother on the death of an elderly relative. It had been as basic as they come, a two-bar electric fire, an ancient gas cooker and no shower or hot water. She'd loved it despite its lack of home comforts. A twenty-minute walk or a couple of stops on the underground took her to the university campus.

Today she brought the car and parked near the lab, grateful not to meet Chrissy, who wouldn't have bought her story. It wasn't as if she was the only member of the forensic team equipped to examine the Olatunde residence.

The doctor had rented an upstairs flat in Ashton Road, where University Avenue met Byres Road. The row of renovated Victorian properties was a perfect example of style-conscious Glasgow, lights at the various windows illuminating a selection of classy interiors.

Bill was sitting in his car. He didn't see her approach but continued to stare straight ahead, his face haggard and lost in thought. When she knocked on the window, he got out and joined her on the pavement. At her questioning look, he shook his head, indicating silently that there was no further news on Margaret's tests.

'The university authorities gave me a contact mobile number for Olatunde in Nigeria,' Bill said. 'His home address there is the *Sabon Gari*, Kano.'

'Any luck contacting him?'

'No connection.'

'Maybe he put a spell on it.'

Bill pulled a wry face. 'I'm beginning to think we need a witch doctor on our side for a change.'

Rhona had spent the previous evening researching African juju practices via the internet. The search had thrown up a variety of links, including newspaper articles on the torso in the Thames and their own gruesome discovery in the Kelvin. Most tabloid articles had the UK overrun by immigrants from the dark continent who brought their evil practices with them.

Anything she read only served to reinforce what she knew already. Children were killed to provide potions for a variety of purposes, which included increasing sexual prowess, curing AIDS and ending infertility. The biggest horror was that people believed what the witch doctor told them was true.

'Okay,' Bill said, 'what are we looking for?'

'I'd like some of Olatunde's DNA. Then anything that suggests Stephen or his mother visited here.'

When Bill rang the doorbell, the owner of the flat opened the door almost immediately.

'Mr Kirk?'

'That's right.'

Mr Kirk, Rhona guessed, was in his forties, but trying to look younger. His head was shaven to a stubble, echoed by a carefully tended designer-stubble chin, and he smelt of expensive cologne.

He examined the identification Bill produced, then gave a cautious smile. His voice was cultured and a little higher than your average tenor. He looked and sounded embarrassed by this interest from the police force. 'Dr Olatunde was recommended by the university authorities. I don't just take anyone as a tenant, you know.'

'When is Dr Olatunde due back from Nigeria?'

'Nigeria?' Mr Kirk pulled a face. 'He didn't tell me

he was going to Nigeria.' He made it sound like another planet.

'The university gave him compassionate leave to go home to Kano.'

'I had no idea.'

'He didn't tell you?'

Mr Kirk shook his head adamantly. 'He told me he had bought a flat in Athole Gardens and was moving in immediately. I was quite angry. It takes time to advertise for a new tenant.'

'When did he leave?'

'A week ago.'

Bill glanced up the wrought-iron staircase. 'Has anyone been up there since?'

'I've been away at a conference. I flew back late last night. I've not had time—'

'We'd like to take a look.'

They followed him up the staircase. He was making small irritated noises in his throat, intimating his displeasure at the world in general and his absent tenant in particular.

He paused on the halfway landing. 'I've forgotten the key.' He tutted as though it was their fault. 'I'll have to go back down for it.'

Bill stepped to one side to let him pass, then went on climbing. At the top was another landing. A well-built and tasteful extension created a single-door entrance to what had originally been the upper rooms of the two-storey house.

Mr Kirk came bustling up to join them. 'Of course, he forgot to leave his set of keys, which means I'll have to have the locks changed.' He threw his glance ceiling-wards in disgust.

Bill held out his hand for the key. 'If you don't mind, Mr Kirk, it would be better if you waited downstairs.'

The man looked as though he might argue, then shrugged his shoulders. 'I have to leave for work in an hour,' he warned them.

They waited for his footsteps to descend then Bill turned the key in the lock.

The scent of fresh blood and body waste was obvious.

'Bloody hell,' Bill muttered.

Rhona pulled the door shut. The last thing they wanted was Mr Kirk catching a whiff of what was in here and coming up to investigate.

'We'd better dress up before we go in,' she advised.

She handed Bill a forensic suit.

The hall floor was sanded wood with multiple layers of varnish, glinting like honey in the soft glow of half a dozen embedded ceiling lights. A blue runner carpet ran up the centre. Bill followed the smell to a part-open door.

He was as tense as Rhona was, his neck beating a raised pulse to match her own. Her imagination was working overtime, creating a series of pictures, most of them involving the inert body of a mutilated child.

The door swung open on a sitting room. Morning light rimmed the closed wooden shutters. Bill felt for a light switch and she heard him draw a deep breath against what was coming.

Malcolm Menzies lay curled in a pool of blood and

urine, tracksuit bottoms at his ankles, his hands clutching his scrotum, like a footballer in a defence wall. Blood was sprayed widely over the surrounding surfaces. But the worst thing of all was the look on his face.

Shock and pity flooded Rhona's senses, followed by guilt. When Malchie'd licked his lips and pointedly looked at her crotch, Rhona had wanted him dead. Now he was, she wished she'd never harboured such thoughts.

Bill's voice betrayed a similar frame of mind. 'They got to him before we did. We'd better get a pathologist out and inform the fiscal office. This is turning into an episode of *Taggart*,' he said grimly. 'We poke our noses in and the body count doubles.'

Bill went to inform Mr Kirk he had a dead body on the premises. The resulting wail was loud enough to carry upstairs and through two doors. Five minutes ago, all Mr Kirk had to worry about was changing the locks.

Rhona undid the catch on the shutters and folded them back on their hinges, letting a wash of grey light fill the room. Beyond the glass, Byres Road was nose to tail in traffic, the pavements a stream of people walking to work. A vision of normality in stark contrast to the contents of the room.

Malchie had been last seen by his mother the previous day, when he assaulted her and took her money. Rhona knelt in the rigid curve of the body. Rigor mortis invariably began in the jaw and neck muscles, then worked its way downwards to affect the arms, trunk and legs within twelve to eighteen hours of death. But it was highly unreliable in timing death.

She studied the face. The look of terror was straight out of a horror movie, an impression accentuated by the opaque quality of the staring eyes and the stiff set of the jaw. In rare instances, cadaveric spasm occurred immediately after death, mimicking the onset of early rigor mortis. No one knew why it happened, except that it was linked to extreme fear.

The reason for Malchie's terror was displayed on the makeshift altar. His genitals had been cut off, tied together and placed in front of the skull of what looked to be a small mammal, wrapped in barbed wire – an offering to whatever hellish deity the murderer worshipped.

The act of mutilation and its associated shock may have killed him, but the killer had made absolutely sure.

A knife had been thrust up and under the lower back rib and into the kidney. Quick and efficient. But you needed strength and accuracy to do it properly. Hit a rib and the force would come back at you with the recoil of a gun. Whoever knifed Malchie was a skilled killer.

In death, Malcolm looked his real age. Sara had said her son was frightened. *He used to be like that when he was a wee boy. Always frightened.*

And he had certainly had something to be frightened of.

Rhona began to process the body, taking as many samples in situ as possible. There were no obvious defence marks on Malcolm's hands or arms, suggesting he hadn't put up much of a fight. The furniture wasn't disturbed either. Which might mean he had been knifed in the back first and then mutilated.

She tried a closer look at the knife wound, but it was impossible without moving the body. Rhona sat back on her ankles. Sissons would have to deal with that.

It was then she noticed something small wedged between the upper arm and the floor. Rhona extracted it with her gloved hand. The object was the size and shape of a large clove of garlic, but brownish-red in colour.

It was a nut of some kind. She sniffed it. She had never seen one in real life, but it looked like pictures she'd seen of a kola nut. The end had been chewed to release the juice rich in caffeine and other stimulants. Her Nigerian research had been peppered with references to the kola nut, its associations with religion, social etiquette, health and sexuality.

She was pretty sure Malchie hadn't been the one chewing the kola nut, and saliva was a great source of DNA.

Rhona sampled the end of the nut and bagged it, then went back to study the tale told by the trail of blood.

30

IN OTHER CIRCUMSTANCES, Chrissy's expression might have made Rhona laugh. 'Don't say, "What are you doing here?"' she begged.

'I'll keep that for later,' Chrissy warned her, running a practised eye around the room.

The body had already been taken to the mortuary. Rhona had watched it pass Mr Kirk's horrified eyes. Renting again would likely be impossible after the story hit the papers. On the other hand, he could be bombarded with weirdos who wanted to live in a flat where a murder had taken place.

Needless to say, Mr Kirk had not left for work as intended. Instead, he was holed up in his flat with a male friend, who was there either to help soothe his nerves, or else hear all the gory details.

Chrissy had appeared at Ashton Road shortly after Rhona called her. The church samples were on their way to the lab and Helen had been left at the church to catch any late arrivals.

McNab followed Chrissy into the room. Judging by their reaction to one another, Rhona suspected they had shared transport. She wondered how McNab had dealt with Chrissy's acid tongue and frosty demeanour.

Forgiving and forgetting were not Chrissy's strong points. Loyalty to her friends was.

'How did he die?' Chrissy asked.

'Fright, by the look on his face.'

Chrissy glanced at the altar.

'Someone cut off his penis and testicles and laid them there,' Rhona explained.

'Ouch!' Chrissy watched McNab flinch at that bit of news. He didn't move to shield his vital parts, but he looked like he wanted to.

'They made sure he was dead by knifing him in the kidney.'

Chrissy shook her head in disbelief. 'He was a wee shite, but I wouldn't have wished that on him.'

'Me neither,' Rhona said fervently.

'Now we know that Malchie was mixed up in some way with the murderer.'

'Or murderers,' Rhona corrected her. 'If Olatunde is involved and he left for Nigeria a week ago, he didn't kill Malchie.'

'This case is doing my head in,' said Chrissy.

'Fortunately you and I just do the forensics, so we don't have to solve it,' Rhona reminded her.

'Don't forensics always solve it?' said Chrissy sweetly, for McNab's benefit.

He looked set to argue, but thought the better of it. 'Where's the boss?' he asked instead.

'He left with the body,' said Rhona.

Chrissy waited until McNab had departed, before she spoke. 'Sam turned up for a DNA test.'

'And?'

'I got Helen to do it.'

Rhona caught the worry in Chrissy's voice. 'That was the right thing to do,' she assured her.

A flicker of worry crossed Chrissy's face. 'What if Sam is involved?'

'Do you have any reason to think he is?'

Chrissy shook her head. 'It's this church thing. I'm not sure about the pastor.' She struggled to find words to explain why and finally settled for, 'He's too sincere.'

'Sincere?'

She frowned. 'You know, like Tony Blair.'

Rhona laughed. 'Now you have got me worried.' But she took Chrissy's words seriously. Chrissy was a good judge of character. If she didn't trust Pastor Achebe, there was a reason for it, even if it was subconscious. 'What does Sam think about him?'

'Sam says the pastor teaches that love is greater than hate.'

'You can't fault that.'

Curiosity, Rhona told Chrissy, had taken her through the entire flat while she waited for the crime scene personnel to arrive. The rooms were all spacious, tastefully decorated and furnished. Mr Kirk was a landlord who took his role seriously. The kitchen was well equipped and looked recently installed with oak cupboards and marble worktops.

None of the rooms gave the impression that a family with a six-year-old child had lived there. Rhona spent some time in the smaller bedroom, looking for evidence of Yana. The only result of her thorough search was a white ankle sock with a pink frill jammed between the bed and the wall.

All bedding and towels had been removed, denying her a good source of DNA. The dishwasher had also been run, removing any human imprint from the dishes and cutlery. When she checked with Mr Kirk, he told her he'd arranged for his cleaning lady, Mrs Wright, to come in while he was away.

'She always cleans thoroughly between tenants,' he assured her. 'No one wants someone else's hair in their bath,' he added with a grimace.

The linen had been sent to the laundrette. The place swept, hoovered and dusted. The scent of bleach still lingered in the kitchen and bathroom. All evidence of the Olatunde family had been wiped away.

Rhona left Mr Kirk on the phone to his insurance company, trying to find out if they would cover the cost of a new sitting-room carpet. She didn't envy him the task of describing what had happened to the current one.

Mr Kirk was correct. Mrs Wright was thorough. There were no hairs in the bath. The plughole of the shower cubicle was another matter.

With a pair of tweezers, Rhona carefully extracted a long thin string of soapy hairs and bagged them. They might help produce a DNA profile for the members of the Olatunde family.

Her next bit of luck was the toilet seat. Someone had lifted the lid and left a print. If Mrs Wright was as meticulous as she appeared to be, she would surely have wiped the toilet seat. Which meant the print was put there after the big clean-up.

Sara Menzies stood among the crowd outside the police cordon. Rhona was unrecognisable in the white suit and mask as she exited the building, but something drew their eyes together and she knew that Sara was aware that it was her. She pulled off her hood and slipped down the mask.

Sara's terrified expression eerily mirrored her son's.

Rhona spoke to a nearby constable and asked him to let the woman through the cordon. 'It's the boy's mother,' she said.

He glanced over at the tragic figure in the crowd. 'Jesus,' he said.

Sara walked towards her like a robot. 'I saw the news. It's Malcolm, isn't it?'

Rhona took the woman's arm as her legs buckled under her. 'Help me get her inside,' she told the constable.

The sight of grief is compelling, sweeping other emotions aside. Mr Kirk let them into his flat without question.

'This is the victim's mother,' Rhona explained. 'She's just found out her son is dead.'

He led them past his open-mouthed friend into a small sitting room that looked out on a back garden. A bird table piled with seed was being guarded by a belligerent robin, keeping chaffinches and tits at bay. The robin's breast was the blood-red of winter, his warning chirp unnaturally loud in the tense silence.

Rhona helped Sara to a chair and watched as she collapsed into it.

She crouched in front of Mrs Menzies, whose blank eyes and ashen face made her look suddenly ten years older. 'I'm so sorry, Sara.' The only words we can use in these situations, but they sounded bland and inadequate.

'How did he die?'

Rhona kept it simple. 'A stab wound.'

'Can I see him?'

'He's at the mortuary. I'll take you there.'

Sara was shredding a paper hanky on her lap. 'I should never have gone to the police.'

She met Rhona's eye. They were complicit in this, both of them. She wasn't blaming Rhona, but she wanted an acknowledgement of that fact.

'We didn't kill Malcolm,' Rhona said. 'We were trying to save him.'

Sara touched Rhona's head, like a mother would a child who simply didn't understand what the world was really like.

'They found out about the phone,' she said.

It was a bald statement of fact. Malcolm was dead because the police had the mobile.

'We'll get them, Sara.' Rhona said it as much for her benefit as Sara's. In a moment of time, her life had become entwined with this woman's. She had gone to the waste ground alone, against Bill's orders. Her meeting with Malchie and Danny had been the catalyst for what happened afterwards.

The door opened and a nervous Mr Kirk appeared

carrying a tray with two mugs and a china teapot. He sat it on a nearby table and left without speaking.

Rhona poured the tea and added two sugar cubes and milk. Sara took a mug in blue-tinged hands, with a murmured thanks.

'Does your daughter know?'

Sara shook her head. 'She's at work. She's a cancer nurse at the Beatson. The centre in the Western Infirmary.'

'Would you like me to call her? We could pick her up on the way to the mortuary?'

'I can't remember the number.'

'That's no problem. Tell me your daughter's name.'

'Karen. Staff Nurse Karen Menzies.'

The centre was a stone's throw from where they were now, but Rhona didn't want to leave Sara, nor did she want to send a policeman to break the news.

When she explained to the switchboard that she was from Strathclyde Police Force, she was put through immediately.

Karen sounded like a younger version of her mother, without the stuffing knocked out. Rhona explained who she was. You could tell from the silence at the other end, that Karen was expecting the worst.

'Your brother has been found dead in a flat in Ashton Road.'

Karen's relief was palpable. 'I thought you were going to tell me my mother was dead.'

Whatever she'd experienced in that household hadn't endeared Karen to her younger brother.

'Mum will blame herself, whatever happened,' she announced. There was a catch in her throat as she went on, 'Stupid wee bugger. He never had any sense. You could never tell him. Wanted to be a hard man. Like my dad.'

'Can you come over? Your mum wants to go to the mortuary.'

'I'll be there in ten minutes.'

As a nurse, Karen must deal with death all the time. She ended the call with the detached professional air Rhona recognised in her own tone.

Sara was still nursing the mug. She looked up as Rhona came in.

'Karen's on her way.'

'She always said this would happen.' Sara gave a weak smile. 'Karen's been grown up since the day she was born. More sense than the rest of us put together.' Her voice broke and she turned her attention to the film forming on top of the cold tea.

'Do you want me to get you a fresh cup?'

Sara shook her head. 'No. I'd just nurse it until it got cold anyway.'

McNab put his face around the door. 'Can I have a quick word?'

They walked outside, away from Mr Kirk's satellite ears.

'I need a car to take her to the mortuary,' Rhona told him.

'The DI's been trying to contact her at her daughter's number.'

'Karen will be here any minute. She works at the Western Infirmary.'

'How did Mrs Menzies hear about . . .' He nodded at the upstairs window.

'There was a report on the news. She decided it was Malcolm. A mix of guilt and intuition.'

He was standing close to her, keeping their words for them alone. A flash of a camera in the distance suggested they might be featured in tomorrow's paper. *Forensic officers at satanic crime scene.*

'The Super pulled in the boss,' he said. 'One murder too many.'

'It's not Bill's fault.'

'The DS is muttering words like Taggart and body count.'

'Bill was joking about that earlier.'

'The DS doesn't think it's funny.'

She met his look. 'Neither do I.'

'There're moves afoot to send a team to Kano.'

'Oh,' she said cautiously.

'Passport control came back with the news that three days ago a Dr Olatunde departed from London Heathrow for Kano with, wait for it, his wife and two children.'

'*Two* children?'

'A girl and a boy, separate passports.'

'I thought he only had Yana.'

'Mr Kirk says only one child stayed in the flat. He doesn't normally take kids, made an exception on the doctor's part. But one quiet girl only. So who was the boy?'

'Stephen,' she said, and his face told her he had reached the same conclusion.

31

BILL FELT CURSED. Despite countless years on the job, this time his ability to separate private life and work had evaporated. DS Sutherland said as much when Bill explained about Margaret.

'You should have told me sooner.' He made it sound easy. 'Who else knows?'

'Dr MacLeod. That's it.'

'Your children?'

'Margaret wants to wait until it's definite, one way or the other.'

A look of sympathy crossed the DS's face. Bill didn't want sympathy, he just wanted to get on with the job.

'I think we need to send a team out to Kano,' Bill said. 'If the boy travelling with Olatunde is Stephen then the sooner we get to him the better.'

'I agree. But not you, Bill.'

The use of his first name brought down the professional barrier between them, disconcerting him. There were many things about the Super that both frustrated and irritated Bill. His use of his position in the police force to infiltrate the upper echelons of Glasgow society for one. The Super saw a gong on the horizon for himself and was already building the trappings to go with it. Bill had watched the DS rise swiftly through the ranks. He wasn't envious, knowing the higher you went, the less you dealt with real crime. It was the difference between being a classroom teacher and being a headteacher. Margaret had always wanted to stay in the classroom. He wanted to stay with his team.

'Then I suggest DS McNab and a forensic,' Bill went on, trying to focus solely on the task in hand. 'Abel's torso suggested he came from the Kano area. Forensic can confirm this once they're out there.'

'Dr MacLeod is the most experienced.' The DS was thinking aloud.

Bill wanted to steer him away from that line of thought, but how could he explain that McNab and Rhona were not a combination she would relish? Some more private business the DS knew nothing about.

'Okay. Set it up,' DS Sutherland said firmly. 'As soon as possible. And can we go light to the press on the ritual aspects of the latest death? Talk only of a stabbing?'

'The stab wound killed him. That's what we're saying.'

'You're certain the death is linked to Stephen's abduction?'

'Malcolm Menzies was guarding the building on the waste ground. His mother brought in a mobile he'd been using to keep contact with whoever was paying him to keep people away from there.'

The DS nodded, acknowledging the connection. He shuffled some papers. The perfect cue for Bill's exit.

'And let me know what happens on the home front.'

Bill gave an almost imperceptible nod. Like hell he would.

There was a strained atmosphere in the team office and not just because of the latest death. The police station was like a tiny village where gossip was as swift moving as a westerly breeze. As soon as Bill was called in front of the Super, the world and his granny knew about it.

The faces were half turned towards him, not staring, but indicating that if he wanted their attention, he could have it pronto.

Bill stopped in front of the wallboards that held the photos of all the victims. The beaten slumped body of the old woman; her daughter splayed out like a mutilated carcass; the boy, sweet and innocent in school uniform. A constructed image of what the computer department thought Abel would have looked like. And now Malcolm Menzies. A victim of his own stupidity and the evil that surrounded this case.

Bill outlined the information from passport control to the waiting group. When he mentioned a boy and a girl had flown to Kano with the Olatundes, there was a collective gasp. Everyone in that room made up their mind that the child must be Stephen – the alternative was unthinkable.

'We're sending out a team to locate and hopefully bring back Olatunde and the man who professed to be Carole Devlin's husband.'

'Who's going, sir?' an unidentified voice called from the back.

'Not sure yet,' he lied. He wouldn't be short of volunteers, but the boss had spoken and his will must be done. 'Okay, we need everything possible on Malcolm Menzies. School, friends. Bring in his mate Danny Boy again. And in particular we need to know who he was getting his gear from.'

'Can I speak to you, sir?' Janice asked. 'It's about the white van.'

He motioned her into his office.

The van had been spotted after hours of trawling through transport video recordings of the motorway system that riddled the centre of Glasgow and its surrounds. A van with the number plate supplied by Mr Martin, S 064 OXO.

The vehicle, according to Pastor Achebe, was not used directly by his church. It did a variety of charity work, having been made available to cancer charity shops, housing the homeless, helping the aged, and anyone else that needed something shifted – household articles, clothing and occasionally people.

'He sounded genuine,' she told Bill.

He grunted but kept his mouth shut and let her go on.

'He had a list of all users of the van. The arrangement is pretty flexible. The church pays for its upkeep, insurance, tax, repairs and so on. The other charities supply the drivers.'

'So what was on the tape?'

'The van was recorded heading south via the M74 on Tuesday morning at six o'clock.'

'And, let me guess. None of the charities have seen it since?'

'We're working our way through the list.'

'Who used it last?'

'We don't know that yet. Sorry, sir.'

Her apology was unnecessary. DC Clark had been working harder than he had, and with more focus and dedication.

'There's one more thing.'

He waited, sensing how important this might be from the look on her face.

'Vice called when you were at the mortuary. They raided a sauna reported as working illegal immigrants. A Nigerian girl, in her early teens, said she'd been brought here by force from Lagos.'

Vice had taken the girl to the safe suite. She sat hunched in the corner of a sofa. When she saw Bill, she visibly retreated, her expression one of terror. Bill had interviewed countless victims in his many years as a police officer, but he had never seen such abject fear in a woman's eyes. He was shocked.

The female officer in charge of the unit suggested he retreat and leave DC Clark to observe. He could watch from behind the glass screen.

Bill took her advice and went next door. A vice squad detective, Andy Davies, was waiting for him there.

'We found her in a room in the basement,' Andy told him. 'The girls on duty upstairs denied all knowledge of her. We would have missed her except one of our bright new recruits, a structural engineer in his former life, insisted there had to be another level to the building. The entrance was behind a cupboard.'

They had brought in an interpreter, a tall ebony-coloured woman, her long hair braided with small gold coins. She was sitting on the sofa, an arm's length from the girl. Her voice was soothing and the tension in the girl's body had lessened.

Davies explained who she was. 'Larai is Fulani, from Northern Nigeria. A professor, no less, of African and Oriental studies.'

Davies's sarcasm couldn't quite disguise his awe at the beautiful and commanding woman in the next room. Under her gentle encouragement, the girl began to talk, gradually increasing in speed, as though she had to get it over with.

DC Clark sat opposite, her expression strained, particularly when Larai translated for her benefit, and theirs.

Her name was Adeela. A thirteen-year-old Hausa girl from Bauchi State. She was captured in the bush when fetching water from the river. She was taken to Lagos where she was made to service men, including *Baturi* – Europeans – from the oil rigs. She tried to run away twice and was beaten. The woman in charge told her if she tried again she would become a juju sacrifice and her mother declared a witch. One night, she was taken to a rig and from there to a ship. She was on the ship a long time. They drugged her before they took her off. She woke up in the cellar.

When Larai joined Bill and Andy in the side room she was visibly angry.

'She is sure there are others,' she told them. 'She heard crying on the ship. A boy's voice called to her. He said his name was Sanni.' She turned to Bill. 'The girl has been circumcised. It is not a tradition practised by my tribe, the Fulani, but it is common in other Nigerian tribes. The Hausa method is the most severe form. All external genitalia are removed and the vagina sewn up to make entry more difficult. For white men this is a novelty they will pay for.'

Beside him, Davies made a small noise in his throat, a mixture of anger and disbelief. Bill had a daughter of seventeen, but he well remembered her at thirteen. Then he had never wanted her to grow up.

'I read in the paper that the woman, Carole Devlin, had been circumcised by her attacker?' Larai asked.

Bill nodded. There had been no point hiding the fact, however gruesome it might be to the general public.

'Some tribes believe that if a male child's head touches the clitoris during birth, he will die,' she told him. 'Others that lying with an uncircumcised woman can make a man impotent, destroy his fertility and make him go mad.'

Larai, wittingly or not, had given Bill the first tangible explanation for Carole Devlin's mutilation.

32

STEPHEN TRIED TO sit up, but each time he raised his head he felt sick. The small dark space was going up and down and his stomach with it. He wanted to be asleep again. In his dreams everything was all right. He was back in the garden in Kano, before he and his mum ran away.

He lifted the plastic bottle of water. It tasted funny, but he drank it anyway. Almost immediately he felt himself sink back into an oblivion filled with dreams of the past.

Boniface was hanging out the washing on the line between the two acacia trees. The heavy wet clothes made the rope sag in the middle. Water dripped onto the dry soil, throwing up little puffs of dust.

Stephen was watching a column of big black ants, using the rope as a walkway between the two trees. Then he spotted the red velvet spiders. They were crossing the narrow path that snaked through the tall stalks of dry elephant grass. Boniface made him wait until he checked the spiders out, then smiled an okay, his teeth orange from chewing kola nuts, and told him the swarming spiders meant the rains were on their way.

Boniface pointed at the sky where thick dark clouds threatened on the horizon.

'Ruwa.' Boniface grinned. 'Ruwa!'

Stephen knelt and carefully picked up a spider, cupping it in his hand. It played dead, while he stroked its soft velvety surface.

The rain came that night. He sat on the verandah seat beside his mum and watched lightning dance in the sky. The wind blew into their faces, bringing the first smell of rain for seven months. Then the wind suddenly changed direction and the first big drops began to fall. Soon a wall of water was falling from the overhang, digging a trench through his mum's zinnia patch. Stephen ran down the steps onto the drive, screaming and laughing, to dance in the muddy puddles.

When he eventually looked back, his mum was talking to a man with scars on his face. Stephen stood perfectly still, feeling the rain drum on his head and run down his chest. He shivered, his temperature dropping with the watery onslaught and his growing fear.

33

RHONA HAD DRUNK three glasses of wine one after the other. She didn't seek oblivion, only to take the edge off the memory of her time in the mortuary with Sara Menzies.

A parent should never bury a child, no matter what that child has done. It is an aberration of nature.

Sara had stood, her hand in Karen's, as the cover was pulled back. Thankfully, she never saw below Malcolm's neckline. As rigor had eased, his face had assumed a less tortured look. His eyes had been closed. He had been made pretty in death. His smooth skin betrayed his youth, and the angry young man was gone. Sara's child, the son she loved, had been returned to her in death. Sara had looked down on the boy she had set out, in vain, to save.

Karen had displayed the stoic stance of someone who knew the truth. Bad memories had replaced any that were good, yet even she had buckled at the sight of her dead brother.

They had held one another up, these two women, without the man who had made the child in his own image. Rhona wondered if Sara had even informed him. He was somewhere on the road, oblivious to what had happened to his family.

Rhona took up her favourite place at the kitchen window. The convent garden was in darkness, apart from the spotlight illuminating the Virgin Mary, blessing the world and all its sinners.

Where was Malcolm now, apart from a drawer in the mortuary? Was he at heaven's gate, being turned away? Or was he apologising for his sins and being forgiven?

The wine was her refuge from the questions her brain couldn't answer. In the space of five days, her world had changed. But she was alive and privileged and anything that happened to her was insignificant in comparison to what had happened to others. She thought of Bill, tortured by the thought of the illness and death of the woman who was his life. Sean, his father's demise both a release and a curse. Stephen, alone and in danger, knowing his mother had been murdered. And Sara Menzies, living with the knowledge that her dead son was complicit in the death or torture of others.

Having a child meant carrying its sins on your shoulders along with your own.

Rhona didn't hear the buzzer at first, lost as she was in her own troubled thoughts. When she did answer, McNab's voice on the intercom was not one she anticipated or wanted to hear.

'We need to talk,' he said.

'No we don't.'

Rhona didn't need to talk to anyone. She preferred

to stay mildly drunk and alone with her morbid thoughts.

McNab spoke again, more insistent this time. 'The DS wants us to be the team sent to Kano.'

She buzzed him in, hearing the front door bang shut below.

He stood in her hall, hiding a smile at its familiarity.

Rhona led him through to the kitchen. He glanced at the open wine bottle on the table, but she didn't offer him any.

'I came to check if you were okay about us travelling together. If not, I'll find some personal reason not to go.'

He was challenging her. If she said she didn't like the idea, he would withdraw, but she would never hear the end of it. It was not in McNab's nature to be magnanimous.

'I have no problems with that.' Rhona met him eye to eye.

'Good. I'll tell the DI.'

'Bill sent you here?' Now she was surprised, and not a little annoyed.

'Not exactly.' Even McNab wouldn't be daft enough to lie about that. 'But I had to be sure.'

They had reached a compromise. She sat down at the kitchen table, indicating that he should do the same. 'I've whisky,' she offered, 'if you don't like wine.'

She knew he didn't drink wine and he knew she knew. A memory of a sex game they'd played involving whisky brought colour to her cheeks.

'I'll have a whisky,' he said, pretending not to notice.

'It's next door.' She stood, turning her back on him, glad of a moment to regain her composure.

There was a bottle of Bushmills Malt in the cabinet for special occasions. She fetched it with a suitable glass.

'It's Irish,' she said unnecessarily.

McNab gave a wry smile. It should have annoyed her, but she felt herself soften. He had been ousted by an Irishman and was not about to complain about it.

She poured him a decent shot.

He raised his glass. 'To past and future endeavours.'

It seemed churlish not to chink her glass to his.

They spoke of the case. McNab related what had happened with Larai, the interpreter. Rhona listened carefully, realising the importance of the woman's knowledge.

'If Carole's husband decided she should be circumcised and she refused—' Rhona said.

'It would make her run, and take the boy with her.'

The thought of it horrified Rhona. 'I don't understand . . .' she began.

'What?'

'Why men hate women so much.'

'Well, if they're not circumcised, they make a man impotent, scupper his chances of being a father and their clitoris can kill a baby boy if it touches his head during his birth.'

Rhona looked at McNab aghast.

'So Larai told us. Or, to be more exact, so the Hausa tribe believes.'

'How on earth did such an idea begin?'

He smiled wryly. 'Fear of women and all they can do and all they are.'

His green eyes locked with hers. Rhona felt her stomach contract. He looked younger than Sean, his deep auburn hair cropped close to his head, a day's stubble on his chin. There was a tense energy about him, like a tiger waiting to spring.

She stood up. 'When do we leave?'

'Tomorrow. Evening flight to Heathrow. Stay over in the airport hotel. Kano flight leaves early Sunday morning.'

'It's short notice.'

'As far as Stephen's life is concerned, not short enough.'

McNab had stayed no longer than it took to drink his whisky. When Rhona showed him out, he was cool and contained, but underneath, she knew, he was relishing the fact that they would be alone together, strangers in a strange land, with no one but themselves to rely on.

He handed her a pack of anti-malarial tablets.

'One a day, starting tonight.'

'I've been to Africa before,' she said.

He raised an eyebrow. 'Good. You'll know what to do when we get there. Apparently it's the beginning of the wet season, so pack for hot and humid.'

He stopped short of suggesting what forensic equipment she should take. Their African adventure had already captured McNab's imagination.

Rhona's sleep was disturbed by alcohol and vivid dreams, in which all her frantic efforts to get to the airport were constantly thwarted. She dreamt of Liam, his Nigerian village always hidden despite her constant attempts to find it.

She was woken around midnight by the sound of Sean's key in the lock. She heard the suitcase hit the hall floor and a strangled curse. He was home and tipsy, if not drunk.

Rhona waited in silence, incapable of facing him. Then she heard him whistling softly as he moved about the kitchen. The bottle of Bushmills and two glasses sat on the table and if he wasn't too drunk he was bound to notice. She sat up, cursing herself silently for not clearing up after McNab's departure.

Sean went on whistling. The tune was unfamiliar and sad.

Her need for him at that moment was as strong and painful as a kick in the groin. But she couldn't go through.

He opened the bedroom door and stood, illuminated by the hall light.

Her eyes were half closed, but she saw him smile.

'Beautiful one,' he whispered.

She heard the shower come on and his gasp as the water hit his nakedness. When he finally crawled in beside her, his body was ice-cold.

'I am cold but sober,' he offered. 'And I dearly want to fuck you.'

He slid downwards, licking her body in small gasps. He laid his face in her groin and breathed her in. When she did not open her legs, he pushed them apart, then lifted them up.

He played with her then, his entry a promise but not a reality until she begged him with a whispered please.

Afterwards he lay, his head on her stomach, nursing her feet as though they were his child. 'I want to make a baby.'

His voice was muffled by her flesh but she had heard him. Rhona lay silent and apprehensive in the dark.

His voice slurred, 'I want to have a child.'

She let him sleep, rising before dawn to look for her passport and start packing. He woke around lunchtime, finding her in the kitchen preparing some food.

He was naked, rubbing his hand through his hair, bemused by waking up at home again. He stood behind, pressing himself against her, his penis rising in expectation, his breath warming her neck.

It was not the right time, but she said it anyway: 'How's your wife?'

His body tensed. Rhona waited for shock to soften his prick.

'What?'

'Kitty Maguire. Your wife.'

It was a bad scene from a TV drama. Naked man, loving and aroused, confronted with the other woman.

Sean turned her around to face him. His cock, whether through anger or confusion, refused to give in and droop.

'She called the flat to let me know you were married.'

Rhona wanted him to deny it, tell her it was lies. He didn't.

'Kitty always hopes we will get back together.' He sounded both sad and sorry.

It wasn't what Rhona expected or wanted. 'So it's true?'

Sean gave a small laugh. 'It's true.'

'You never told me you were married.'

He came back right away. 'You never told me you had a child. Not until you had to.'

Rhona wanted him to cover his nakedness, but he made no move to.

'Kitty and I were married at seventeen. We were fucking one another and she was ashamed. She decided she was pregnant and, like any good Catholic boy, I married her. Except there wasn't a baby, only a ring and a priest.'

'So she trapped you?'

He shook his head. 'I trapped her. I fucked her when I should have kept my cock in my pants, like my granny told me. Twenty years ago, where I come from, that was the crime.'

Rhona could think of nothing to say.

In awkward silence they moved separately around the flat, she packing and he unpacking, each thinking their own thoughts.

34

CHRISSY HESITATED ON the steps. By nature, she made up her mind quickly and didn't prevaricate. Not tonight. She wanted to see Sam, to at least try to explain her recent behaviour, but avoidance seemed the easier option. If Sam had given her the brush-off, she would have been insulted and hurt. Nothing in his treatment of her had been unkind or untrustworthy. He deserved the same.

This little internal speech sent her down the steps and into the club. Rhona had declined her offer of a drink to end a difficult day. A visit to the mortuary with Malchie's mother had rendered Rhona incapable of being in any way sociable. She had gone home to take refuge in silence and a glass of wine, depriving Chrissy of an ally.

Chrissy stood at the inner door, listening for Sam's piano. There was music playing, but it wasn't Sam. A wave of disappointment swept over her. She had moved from thinking about seeing him to wanting to, and the realisation that he might not be there was suddenly painful.

A jolt of pleasure hit her when she spotted his dark head at the bar. He turned, sensing her presence, and smiled. The smile was one of relief. He had expected her not to turn up. Chrissy felt saddened by the thought and not a little guilty.

Sam stood to welcome her, suddenly shy in her presence. Not for the first time, Chrissy realised how strange she must seem to him: strong willed, opinionated, sexually overt. Were there women like her in his culture?

Chrissy asked the barman for her usual, and Sam waited while she took a drink.

'I did not think you would come,' he said gently.

'I said I would.'

'I asked in Hausa.'

'You're a good teacher.'

The exchange was flirtatious, as though they had just met, never kissed and knew little about one another. Sam understood the game she was playing, distancing herself from the closeness they had enjoyed. At the point of breaking up, the last thing you want is to remember moments of intimacy.

'It would have been unprofessional,' she began, 'for me to take a sample from you.'

'I know.' The tone of his voice suggested he was puzzled that she felt the need to explain. 'I am a suspect.'

Chrissy avoided his gaze. 'Everyone connected with the case is a suspect. That is the law.'

'Ah, English law.'

She corrected him. 'Scottish law. It's different. We're different.'

He smiled. 'That, I do know.'

They lapsed into a more comfortable silence.

'The death in Ashton Road?' A shadow crossed his face. 'It was something to do with . . .'

'They cut off his genitals.' The tabloids would eventually find out anyway. 'There was an altar with an animal's skull.'

Sam flinched and Chrissy was sorry she had been so blunt.

'He betrayed them.' His voice was low and fearful, and a shiver ran up Chrissy's spine.

'You're afraid.' It had not occurred to her before now, that she should fear the perpetrator of these crimes. They were remote from her, part of her job. If she was afraid every time there was a murder in Glasgow, she would never go outside the door, let alone sleep. 'You said you didn't believe in witchcraft,' she accused him.

'You said you didn't believe in God.'

They acknowledged each other's lies. Saying such words was easy. Believing them was not.

'Give me the boy until he is seven, and I will give you the man.' Chrissy smiled cynically. 'The Jesuit brothers said that. I expect it works for Catholic girls too, but they didn't think we were important enough to mention.'

On an empty stomach, the drink had gone straight to her head. She liked the feeling. It took away the stress of talking to Sam and made the decision to leave less important. She nodded at the barman to give her another.

'So what are women allowed to do in your culture?'

She was goading him. Wanting him to say something she could disagree with. If she fell out with him, everything would be easier.

'We are Fulani. In our culture, it is the young men who wear make-up and jewellery and hold hands until they are married.'

Her jaw dropped. 'You're making that up.'

Sam shook his head. 'Young men wear kohl around their eyes and henna on their lips until they are chosen by a woman. Our women are very beautiful. They are tall, with long necks and high cheekbones. Like Egyptian princesses.'

'Wow! Why aren't you married?'

'I will be after I get my degree.'

'You're already betrothed?' Why did that suddenly matter to her?

'No. My mother wished it, but no.'

'What about sex before marriage?'

'It is forbidden.'

'You must be glad you came here.'

He winced at the sharpness of her tone. 'That doesn't mean it doesn't happen.'

Chrissy thought of his hand on her skin. The knowledge he had of a woman's body. Sam was either well practised or a natural.

He was also fending off her attack with dignity. 'You think we are different,' he said. 'But I think there is more about us that is the same.'

'Let's see. You get an education, have lots of sex without commitment, then settle down.'

'As I said, we are not so different.'

She wanted to say that women pay a bigger price for their freedom. That sex, for most of them, needs an element of love, or caring at least.

'Chrissy.' His voice was thick with emotion.

She turned to meet his eye.

'*Labarin zuciya a tambayi fuska,*' he said softly.

'What does that mean?'

'One's face shows what is in one's heart.'

He had set up an altar of his own. A simple wooden cross on a white cloth. The candles on either side were burnt down halfway. A small black bible sat between them. Chrissy kept her glance averted as she walked past and into the bedroom.

This would be the last time. A farewell fuck, she told herself crudely. She already knew it was a mistake, but it seemed inevitable. Like a smoker reaching for the next cigarette, promising it would be their last.

There was an urgency about their actions, as though each of them expected the other to vanish suddenly into thin air. Gone was the gentle approach, the delicate play of senses. All she wanted was him inside her as soon as possible.

Chrissy felt reality seep back as the pleasure retreated. Her body felt slick and heavy and not her own. She slid away from Sam and his encircling arm gave up its struggle to keep her close.

'Don't go.'

She sat up. 'It's late. I have to get home.'

'Stay, until morning.'

She had never stayed until morning, but his words weren't an accusation.

Chrissy lay back down beside him. 'I can't see you again.' The words were out and they hung like sharp points in the darkness. She tried to soften them. 'Not until the case is over. I shouldn't be with you now.'

'I have done nothing wrong.'

She touched the back of his head, fingering the stiff tight curls. 'I know.'

Chrissy left at dawn. Sam was sound asleep as she crept from the bed. Or he was pretending to be, to make it easier for her.

In the sitting room, she stopped in front of the altar. She hadn't spotted the photo last night. A newspaper cutting of Stephen in school uniform was slipped inside the small bible. Sam had been praying for the missing boy.

Day 6

Saturday

35

'I HAVE A strategy meeting about Kano.'

'That's fine.'

The f-word. So overused, often in direct opposition to its true meaning.

'When do you fly out?'

'I'm on an evening flight to Heathrow. The Kano flight's tomorrow morning.'

'I'll take you to the airport.'

'McNab— A car is picking me up.'

'We have to talk before you go, Rhona.' Sean always tagged on her name like that when he was upset or agitated. 'I want to tell you the whole story.'

'There's more than a wife?' Her shock wasn't just for show.

'That's not what I meant.'

'Tell me something, Sean. If Kitty hadn't phoned here, would you ever have said you were married?'

Anger played around his mouth.

'Tell *me* something, Rhona. If I asked you to marry me, would you say yes?'

She couldn't answer him, but the implication was clear. The only time having a wife made a difference was if, or when, he wanted to get married again. Maybe

Kitty had served as a good excuse not to get too involved. Maybe he had used her as an excuse in previous relationships. Not with Rhona, but perhaps with others?

She asked the obvious question. 'Why didn't you get a divorce?'

'Kitty is a practising Catholic.'

'And she's waiting for you to come home and make Catholic babies with her?'

After his drunken revelation the previous night, it was a cruel thing to say. Rhona watched his face as her words hit home. It didn't stop her carrying on. 'When did you last sleep with her?'

'What?' Sean sounded genuinely perplexed.

'That's why she called me, wasn't it? You slept with her when you were there.'

Rhona had never seen Sean so angry. His hands were fists by his side, the muscles of his upper arms clenched tight. She wanted to scream and cry herself. She had run down a dark alleyway, with no way back.

He took a deep breath and unclenched his fingers. 'My father thought I should have stayed in Dublin, had kids. Instead, I ran away, from him, Ma, my sisters and Kitty.'

'And now you regret it?'

'Kitty and I would have killed each other, slowly and painfully over the years.'

'But you would have had kids.'

'I never wanted them . . .'

'Until now,' she accused.

He read the hurt in her eyes. 'The Irish are always maudlin in drink. Take no notice.'

He had regained his composure. Sean did not do scenes. His anger dissipated as quickly as it rose. The fuss was over. He didn't want to talk about it any more.

She, on the other hand, would worry at it, if not for ever, then for too long. It was as well she was going to Kano. It would be easier falling out with McNab.

She was going to Africa with an old lover, one who – like Kitty – had taken a long time to let go. If indeed he ever had. She should tell Sean this, talk it through with him. But she'd never mentioned McNab before now. Just as he had never mentioned Kitty. She and Sean were more alike than Rhona cared to admit. But in an argument, it was always better to occupy the moral high ground.

Sean left for the club shortly after the skirmish, promising to be back before Rhona departed for Kano. She secretly wished he wouldn't. There was nothing else to say, and once her mind was focused on the trip and its possible outcome, there was no room left for personal turmoil.

They were all there when she arrived, even though she was early. A tray with coffee and cups sat in the middle of the table, but no one had poured. Rhona wondered if they were waiting for her to do the honours.

It was Superintendent Sutherland who spoke first. 'Ah, Dr MacLeod. Please join us.'

Rhona chose the empty chair on Bill's right. McNab was on Bill's other side. He wore an expression that could be described as smug, but that may have been paranoia on her part. Bill gave her a quick hello. He looked no better than the last time she'd seen him. Superintendent Sutherland sat at the head of the table, like the host at a dinner party. He had the air of someone who had set the ball rolling and was pleased with the outcome.

'The Passport Office have coordinated with the Nigerian embassy to issue visas,' he addressed her and McNab. 'Your passports will be stamped with these at Heathrow. On arrival in Kano a representative of the British consul will take you to your hotel. Meetings have been arranged with the honorary consul and with your police liaison officer. They are both keen to cooperate.'

High-powered, international organisation suited DS Sutherland. He was pleased with his endeavours on their behalf. But Rhona suspected he had no real idea what they would face in Nigeria.

Rhona stole a glance at McNab, wondering if he had either. She was not unfamiliar with Africa. Two trips to Zimbabwe, before Mugabe had moved further into dictatorship, had made her fall in love with the dark continent. But Zimbabwe was not Nigeria. West Africa hadn't been dubbed 'the white man's graveyard' for nothing. The west's climate was more extreme than the east. At this time of year, Kano would be in its wet season, which brought more than just rains. The damp humidity encouraged disease: meningitis, malaria, plus a current outbreak of polio. Not to mention endemic HIV and AIDS. And that wasn't all. There were frequent riots for and against the Sharia law imposed on Kano State by a Muslim-led state government. It made Pitt Street Police Station on a Friday night sound like fun.

'There are a number of warnings for travellers on the British High Commission website,' said Bill, addressing Sutherland. 'Including ones about indiscriminate attacks against foreigners.' Rhona listened, feeling fearful for Liam, wherever he was.

The DS looked suitably concerned. 'I am assured the team will be under Nigerian police protection at all times.'

'What about bringing Stephen back?'

'Stephen has a UK passport.' DS Sutherland implied by this that there would be no problem. 'As to Dr Olatunde and possibly Mr Devlin, we are in discussion with the appropriate authorities regarding such a possibility.'

No one mentioned that they had to find these people first.

'I need to take a variety of samples, including soil from the surrounding countryside, meat and vegetables from the local markets, to establish mineral content,' Rhona told him.

'I've read the Met report on the Adam torso,' the DS assured her. 'You will be taken where you need to go.'

'The Met sent a team of three,' Bill reminded him.

By rights Bill should be going with them. Rhona wondered if he had pulled out, or the DS did it for him.

'With the ongoing investigation here, two is all we can spare.'

DS Sutherland was right. There was nothing to suggest that Malcolm Menzies's death would be the last one in the case. Bill was needed here, in more ways than one.

'How long have we got?' Rhona asked.

'A week, initially.'

Long enough to get the samples and judge if they were on a wild goose chase.

When the meeting ended, Rhona called Chrissy on her mobile and found she was at the lab. 'Working on a Saturday?'

'My boss is off to Nigeria,' Chrissy said in mock accusation. 'Someone has to do it.'

'I'll be with you in half an hour.'

'Good.' Now her voice was serious. 'I need to talk to you.'

McNab was hanging around the entrance, as though waiting for her.

'All set?' He said it as if they were off on holiday together.

Rhona kept her voice cool. 'I'm packed, if that's what you mean.'

'Nigeria is a cash economy. No credit cards. No cheques.'

'So it's a suitcase full of money?'

'Looks like it.'

McNab's enthusiasm was catching. Rhona relented and returned his smile. Being back in Africa was something she was looking forward to, whatever the circumstances.

'You're in for a big culture shock,' she warned.
'With you by my side, I'll cope.'

Chrissy was usually the one arguing for a clear division between work and play. A Jiminy Cricket at Rhona's shoulder, reminding her that life was about more than DNA samples and forensic evidence. It was strange to observe their roles reversed.

Just short of fifty saliva tests to process, added to the evidence collected at the more recent murder scene, made for a substantial workload even though Chrissy wasn't responsible for all of it. But the extra work wasn't why Chrissy had turned up at the lab today. The laboratory was a great place to hide from the outside world. Rhona had used it often that way herself. The certainty of science replacing the uncertainty of life.

'I slept with Sam last night.'

It hadn't been a wise move, but Chrissy didn't need to be told that.

'He had an altar in his room—'

'What?' Rhona interrupted her.

'The Christian version, complete with candles, bible and a newspaper cutting of Stephen.'

'He was praying for him?'

'That's what it looked like. I didn't ask,' she added.

The act of unburdening takes time. Rhona kept quiet.

'I should have kept away from him as soon as the church became involved.'

'True, but he works in the jazz club. I also have contact with him.'

Lin Anderson

'But you don't exchange bodily fluids.'

'I take it neither will you after last night?'

'That's what I wanted to tell you.'

'And Sam knows that?'

'I said it, loud and clear.'

'Well, that's all right then.' Even as she uttered the words, Rhona wondered if that was true. If she were Chrissy, she would want to prove Sam's innocence, for her own sake as well as his.

'You have Sam's sample?'

'Helen did it.'

'And?'

'It's being checked against the database.'

Rhona changed the subject. 'The Velcro fastener on Stephen's trainer was a rich source of DNA. We need to check my results on that against the samples from the church.'

'Will do.'

The small trainer was a timely reminder of what this was all about. The scuff marks, the torn stitching, the worn sole, told the story of a small boy's life. A boy who was afraid of the dark. A boy who saw his mother die.

Rhona spent an hour putting together notes for Chrissy and filing her results. A week was a long time away from a case. She had to keep reminding herself that the Kano trip was just as important as the work going on here. At the moment it felt like running away.

36

RHONA HEARD THE miaow when she opened the door. The kitten came skidding across the polished wood towards her. It was the colour of a tiny wildcat. When she picked it up, it wrapped itself around her neck in a gesture of violent affection.

She waited for Sean to appear and explain, not keen to let down her guard and seek him out. Eventually she wandered into the kitchen to find a litter tray, cat food and a note.

I phoned the cat refuge and they said they had a motherless kitten. If you don't like him, they'll take him back. He's called Tom.

Have to cover at the club for Sam. Won't manage to get back before you leave.

Sean

Rhona wanted to be irritated by Sean's interference but didn't have the heart. He knew how much she missed her cat and had been encouraging her to get another one for months. She had finally decided to replace Chance but the pressure of work had conspired against her. He had simply saved her the bother.

If it was a peace offering, it had worked. But a break in hostilities didn't mean the end of the war.

She had left herself little time to finish her preparations before McNab arrived to pick her up. If she was honest she had delayed coming home. Sean was astute enough to sense her mood and make himself scarce, leaving behind a surrogate object of affection.

Psychologically, a good move.

The kitten watched her with interest from the bed as she closed the suitcase and put on clothes suitable for travelling. The weather in Kano was currently hot and humid, and she had packed accordingly. Despite the seriousness of the trip it felt like going on a summer holiday.

She wasn't a great flier, but did it from necessity. Despite being a scientist, Rhona could never really accept the physics of flying and always needed a stiff drink beforehand. Flying with McNab would either make things much better or a hundred times worse.

McNab was bang on time. Rhona was ready for him, having bolstered herself with a glass of wine. She lifted the sleeping kitten from her knee, laid him on the couch and went to answer the buzzer. She told McNab she was on her way down.

McNab met her halfway and offered to carry her case. It seemed churlish to refuse. Rhona followed behind, thinking that if they were going to be thrown together for a week she would have to make an effort.

He loaded her suitcase into the boot of the police car alongside a large leather holdall, which she assumed was his. Rhona slipped her forensic case on top.

McNab offered her the front passenger seat beside the plain-clothes driver but she declined. 'I'm happy in the back.'

Rhona slipped in and fastened her seat belt. For some reason she felt more comfortable with McNab in front rather than behind her.

'The hotel's booked. We should get there in time to eat.'

Rhona acknowledged this, then lapsed into silence as the car approached Charing Cross and negotiated its way through the Saturday city traffic and onto the M8 motorway, heading west.

The sky over the airport was a flat grey, weighted down with impending rain. A few spots dotted the windscreen as they drew up in front of the main entrance. This time Rhona wouldn't let McNab take her case. She pulled it along behind, the forensic bag hooked over the handle.

They waited silently in the queue for Heathrow. Now that they were completely alone, without the structure of their profession, Rhona could see how difficult this was going to be. She should have asked not to go. Made some excuse about Sean's father's funeral. Anything not to be standing alone with Michael McNab on her way to Nigeria.

McNab's expression reflected her own discomfort covered with a thin veneer of bravado. Any thought that he might have engineered this trip together evaporated. McNab was as awkward about this as she was. The realisation made Rhona relax a little. After they'd handed over their luggage, McNab suggested coffee or a drink.

'A drink. I don't like flying.'

'I remember.' He looked annoyed at his quick answer, realising it might irritate.

'We can't go on like this,' she told him firmly.

'No.'

'So what do we do?'

'You could start by calling me Michael?' He smiled.

As always, it was difficult to tell when McNab was coming on to her. Rhona had avoided using his name at all, had to acknowledge silently that she had been thinking *McNab* in her head. His surname had a distance to it she was happier with.

'Okay,' she conceded.

'I take it I can call you Rhona?' He raised an eyebrow.

'That's my name,' she said in a neutral fashion.

'I also propose we forget the past.'

'Agreed.'

Easier said than done, but worth a try.

She settled for a gin and tonic. McNab ordered a pint of lager, which gave Rhona another pang of familiarity. They discussed the plan for Kano. Rhona was impressed by how organised McNab was.

'Apparently our man in Kano is the remarkable and charming Henry Boswell OBE, who has been there for ever. He's a true Brit, tea in the afternoon and cucumber sandwiches.'

'Gin and tonic sundowners on the verandah?'

'You wish.'

'I know,' Rhona replied firmly. 'I've been to Africa before, remember?'

Discussing the case and the arrangements brought

them back on neutral ground. They could even afford to smile and joke with each other.

'We're staying at the Prince Hotel, just across the road from the consulate,' McNab went on. 'It's modern, clean and secure. We meet the police liaison officer as soon as it can be arranged.'

'Sounds like you've thought of everything.'

He accepted her praise with a wry smile. 'Both the police and the consul know about Stephen. Let's hope there's some news by the time we get there.'

They lapsed into silence, reminded of the reason for their journey.

Heathrow was a madhouse, as usual, with armed police officers everywhere. The contrast with a relatively sedate Glasgow was marked.

A bus took them straight to their hotel. Rhona was hungry and quickly agreed when McNab suggested they eat as soon as they got there. They met in the lobby ten minutes later, just enough time to wash her face and compose herself. She was hoping for a meal and bed and no long chats in the bar.

She checked her mobile before ordering but there was nothing from Chrissy or from Sean. Relief must have shown on her face.

'Everything all right?'

'Looks like life goes on without me.'

It was meant to be flippant, but in retrospect took on more meaning. McNab busied himself with his bread roll. 'I'm seeing someone,' he said.

Rhona looked up, trying not to appear curious. It didn't work.

'It's Janice Clark.'

Now she was surprised. She'd seen nothing to suggest they were an item. 'I didn't know,' she stammered.

'We've kept it quiet.'

They had also kept it quiet. Three months and no one but Bill knew, and only when she had to tell him. There was Chrissy, of course, but despite her love of gossip her assistant was the soul of discretion where friends were concerned. She might give you a mouthful about it, but she would fight your corner to the death.

McNab had told her about Janice to make her more at ease. Rhona had a fleeting thought that he might be making it up. After all, she could hardly ask Janice. And Chrissy obviously didn't know about it, the way she'd gone on about McNab's return. And Janice didn't even seem his type.

Rhona was glad when the main course arrived and she could concentrate on her food.

The rest of the meal passed in relative silence. Afterwards she declined coffee and declared herself ready for bed. It meant she went up in the lift alone.

She checked her phone before she went to bed, but there was nothing from Sean. Through the sealed windows she looked out on greater London, a myriad of lights on a flat plain that seemed to go on for ever.

Her sleep was punctuated with vivid and grotesque dreams. A maze of rooms, each one more dark and claustrophobic than the one before, and always the wrong one no matter how carefully she followed the child's high, frightened voice.

Day 7

Sunday

37

MARGARET WAS AT church. The silence suggested both his kids were still asleep.

Normally Bill liked a Sunday morning. Alone, but not really alone. Margaret's warm presence a part of the surrounding silence, even though he'd heard the click of the front door and knew she had already left.

It was the only day in the week he lay in bed longer than necessary, putting off the moment he had to engage with the day.

The bedroom was their place, shared for all of their married life. They had created two children in this bed, loved, laughed and cried. He sat up, watching pale morning light stretch across the covers. He lay his hand on Margaret's side and imagined he could still feel her warmth. The scent of her lingered and he breathed it in.

When their son, Robbie, was born, he wanted to buy Margaret a present. She asked for perfume, L'Air du Temps. He remembered her sitting up in bed, the baby in the cot beside her, dabbing the scent on her neck.

She'd worn that perfume ever since. It had become part of her. She laughingly said she couldn't smell it any more, but he could.

The normal comfort of a Sunday morning was gone, replaced by a creeping fear that it could never be recaptured. The time of certainty was past and Bill wondered if he had ever really appreciated it when it was there. What if the empty space beside him was to become the norm?

He rose, refusing to let his mind answer the question. He too was going to church this morning: the Nigerian Church of God.

Church attendance wasn't high in Scotland, but on a Sunday morning it looked that way. There were few cars on the road and no one was up and about, apart from groups around church doors. When questioned, most folk said they believed in a god, they just weren't church regulars. Like Bill, they had too many questions and not enough answers.

The sky above Glasgow was a clear blue. The air was crisp, the pavements dry with a light silver frosting. He left the car a hundred yards from the church hall and walked along, enjoying the spring sunshine.

Outside the Dream Club, someone had sprayed the contents of their stomach over the pavement. A man with a bucket approached from the church hall as Bill passed, sloshing soapy water over the offending mess.

Pastor Achebe was greeting his flock at the front door. When he caught sight of Bill, he beamed, as though the prodigal son had returned. 'Detective Inspector, I am glad you have come.' He offered his big hand.

'Strictly business,' Bill told him.

'All business is God's business.'

The man could always turn the subject back to God. It was called living the faith.

'Today is our miracle service.'

'That's why I'm here.'

'You wish to ask for a miracle?'

Bill shook his head. 'I would like to observe.'

The pastor shrugged his shoulders. 'God's door is always open.'

'I'd also like to speak to the Sunday School teacher who taught Stephen.'

It was Pastor Achebe's turn to look serious. 'Of course. Sunday School today follows the miracle service, so the children can be with us during the requests.'

As it turned out, the experience reminded Bill of an AIDS service he'd attended with Margaret at Christmas. Victims' names read out and lovingly remembered by friends. A candle lit for each one. Here, the names weren't those of the dead, but those who feared death. A prayer was sung for each name and a candle lit. The voices of the congregation rose and fell in a harmonious wave, resonating deep in Bill's chest, as though warm hands had been placed there.

When the voices went silent he felt suddenly bereft.

The children, about twenty of them, began to file out, followed by a young man and woman, both black. Bill followed them into the side room.

Small blue plastic chairs were placed in two circles, an adult-size chair alongside. The young woman looked up enquiringly as Bill entered.

The young man came towards him and offered his hand. 'May we help you?'

Bill showed his ID card and asked who taught Stephen. The two exchanged glances before the man answered, 'Stephen is in my class, with the younger ones.'

A circle of children aged between six and nine stared solemnly up at Bill.

'Can I have a brief word with you about Stephen?'

The man nodded. 'Of course. We will go to the storeroom.'

The storeroom was little more than a cupboard, walls shelved and filled with books, paper and boxes of crayons. From beyond the closed door, Bill heard children begin to sing in high piping voices. It was a song Lisa had learned at Sunday School and insisted on singing to him at every available opportunity.

'My name is Isa,' the young man said formally. 'I gave a DNA sample yesterday.'

His skin was blue-black, the whites of his eyes a creamy yellow and a little bloodshot at the corners. His wrists were thin and bony inside the frayed but clean shirt cuffs.

'How well do you know Stephen?'

Isa thought for a moment. 'Not well. He has not been coming to church for long. He likes to sing that song.' He inclined his head towards the door. 'He told me his granny liked to hear it.' He thought again. 'He draws well. Lots of pictures of his life in Kano. A garden with acacia trees and bananas. And drawings of insects. He said he had a collection. Red velvet spiders are his favourite.'

It was the most Bill had ever learned about Stephen. Despite the child's colouring, Bill had always imagined him as Scottish. He hadn't really registered that Stephen had spent his entire childhood in Nigeria.

'He speaks English with a Glasgow accent,' Isa smiled. 'He is fluent in Hausa.'

'Is Stephen afraid of anyone?'

Isa considered this before he answered. 'He drew a picture once of a man with tribal scars on his face. When I asked him who the man was, he said it was the devil.'

God could not exist without the devil. Every force in the universe has an opposing force. As a child, Bill had been as frightened by the Old Testament God as by the devil. Vengeful and ever watchful. The stuff of nightmares. He wondered if they still frightened kids at Sunday School.

'Have you any idea if the man is real?'

'All fears are real when you are six years old.' Isa spoke as though he understood fear and had lived it himself. 'I am a refugee,' he explained, reading Bill's expression. 'I was a boy soldier in Niger.'

Bill tried not to show his thoughts. Not sympathy, but the realisation that Isa probably knew how to kill, swiftly and skilfully.

'Would you be willing to come to the police station and make a formal statement?'

'But I've told you all I know.'

Bill tried to look encouraging. 'Sometimes giving a

proper statement reminds us of things we've forgotten.'

Isa struggled for a moment, then looked resigned. 'I would be happy to cooperate.'

The main church hall was hushed when he re-entered. The pastor stood on the dais, his hand raised over a sea of bowed heads.

'Luke 21:36 says: Watch ye therefore, and pray always, that ye may be accounted worthy to escape all these things that shall come to pass, and to stand before the Son of Man.'

A murmur of 'Amen' rippled among the bowed heads like a breeze over a barley field. Bill muttered his own 'Amen'.

The pastor walked with Bill to the door. 'You spoke to Isa?'

'He's agreed to come to the station for further questioning.'

A flicker of worry shone in the pastor's liquid brown eyes. 'Isa was eight when he was captured by rebels and forced to become a soldier.'

'So he knows how to kill?'

'We all know how to kill, Inspector. That doesn't make us murderers.'

Bill acknowledged this in silence.

'Isa is frightened of the past and of the future,' the pastor said.

'Is he here legally?'

'The Home Office is considering his case. If they send him back he will be killed.'

Going to a police station was like a death sentence for Isa. No wonder he looked scared.

'Tell Isa I'll be in touch if I need to talk to him again.'

Pastor Achebe looked satisfied with this small concession.

'Have my team sampled every adult male in your congregation?'

'All, Inspector, including myself.' The pastor smiled as though he had made a joke.

Every time Pastor Achebe looked pleased with himself, Bill felt he had been fooled in some way. Weren't men of God supposed to tell the truth?

He left the pastor at the door, saying goodbye to his flock. Bill drove to Pitt Street instead of heading home. A murder enquiry continued whatever day of the week it was.

The office was quieter than on a weekday but those on overtime were working just as hard as usual.

DC Clark looked up with relief when Bill came in. 'I tried your mobile, but it was switched off.'

'I was at church,' Bill told her.

'Mr Devlin's dead.'

'What?'

'Carole's husband died five years ago. He was a British engineer working in the oil business in Nigeria. He was killed when an oil rig was taken over by rebels. His family was originally from Nigeria but he was born in London.'

'Then who the hell was our Devlin?'

'That I don't know yet.'

The imposter had Devlin's passport. It was his

photograph inside. And he'd believed the guy, even allowed him to be alone with the body. Once again Bill wondered if he was losing it because of his worry over Margaret.

'Passports are stolen all the time,' Janice said, sensing his anger. 'You weren't to know.'

Her reassurance only made Bill feel worse.

'The fake Devlin took photos of Carole's injuries. Why?' he said. 'If he was the murderer he already knew what he'd done.'

To walk into a police station like that, he'd have to be either completely innocent or a very cool customer; or thought he was above the law.

Bill turned to Janice, who was watching him expectantly. 'Check with the Foreign Office,' he said. 'I want the names, addresses and photographs of all Nigerians with diplomatic immunity currently in the UK.'

'Yes, sir.' Janice realised where that line of thought had originated.

There had been an incident two weeks earlier. A posh flat in Glasgow's west end, where the tenant had complained of harassment by a landlord. He'd come to his neighbours for help after the landlord had gripped him around the neck. The neighbours had encouraged him to call the police. He had, but then chickened out. When Janice checked up, the landlord turned out to have diplomatic immunity, which meant the police couldn't prosecute without the permission of the UK Crown Prosecution Service and the Foreign Office. In most cases this resulted in nothing more than a warning issued by the Head of Mission of the foreign country involved.

Bill went to his office and sat back in his favourite chair. Through the window Glasgow was still enjoying its Sunday morning slumber, with only the occasional pedestrian or car going past. He let his thoughts run free. The fake Devlin had been courteous, but there was an underlying arrogance in his manner. Bill had the impression Devlin viewed him as a lackey whom he would rather not deal with. But the big question was why did the false Devlin want to see the body?

Because he wanted to be sure that Carole was dead?

Because he wanted to be sure she had been circumcised?

That was why he came to the police station, why he pretended to be her husband. And he didn't care about Stephen, because he already knew where he was.

Bill carefully examined his hypothesis. It was a leap of faith, based on intuition and simple logical deduction. He had no concrete proof, yet instinctively he knew he was on the right track.

If they found the fake Devlin, he would lead them to the killer, because he had organised the kill.

38

CHRISSY STARED AT the text message. Just two words. 'I'm sorry.' She checked the time of arrival: 2.30 a.m. The middle of the night. Why had Sam needed to apologise in the middle of the night? She was the one who had dumped him. But she hadn't dumped him. She had told him she couldn't see him while the investigation involved his church and everyone in it, the pastor included.

A strange sense of unease lifted the hair on her forearms. Was Sam in trouble? She texted back: 'don't b. r u ok?' The resulting image suggested the text had gone, but then a message appeared telling her it had failed to deliver.

Chrissy frowned at the screen. This had never happened before. Sam was obsessed with his phone. He always answered text messages right away. She used to joke with him about it. How could he play jazz piano and answer texts at the same time?

Chrissy rang the number this time. She wanted to hear Sam's voice. Only that would convince her he was okay.

The unfamiliar tone that resulted prompted her to phone the provider, who told her that the phone must be out of range of European transmitters.

But Sam was in Glasgow. She had been with him on Friday night, all night. Her continuing sense of unease made her phone the jazz club number, but no one was about at this time on a Sunday morning. Her last port of call was Sean. Chrissy knew she had woken him by the sleepy tone of his voice. She explained she was trying to contact Sam but there was something wrong with his phone.

'That's funny,' Sean replied. 'He didn't turn up last night and I couldn't reach him either.'

'But he always answers his phone.'

They both fell silent.

'Maybe he's ill,' Chrissy suggested.

'He usually phones in. He's very reliable.' Chrissy sensed the growing worry in Sean's voice.

'I'll try the church first. He goes there every Sunday. Then I'll try his flat.'

'Good idea. When you find him, tell him we could use him tonight.'

Chrissy said goodbye, aware that Sean was almost as concerned as she was. He was right. Reliable was Sam's middle name. He wouldn't leave Sean in the lurch.

She made herself a coffee and moped about the flat for a while. The last thing she wanted was to phone the Nigerian Church of God during the Sunday service.

When she finally reached Pastor Achebe, he was decidedly unhelpful.

'Sam was not at this morning's service.' He made it sound as though it was Chrissy's fault.

'There seems to be something wrong with his mobile.'

The pastor didn't offer an explanation or sym-
pathise with her dilemma. 'May I ask who's calling?'
His tone was nippy.

'Chrissy McInsh. I'm a friend of Sam's. We met
when I came with the forensic team.'

Silence. Then, 'I'm sorry, I can't help you.'

The phone clicked down. Chrissy muttered a curse
under her breath. The pastor either didn't like her or
didn't like her connection with the police. What happened to his philosophy that love was greater than
hate?

The next-door tenement to Sam's was in the process of
renovation and covered in scaffolding. A chute for
broken stone ran the height of the building into a
waiting skip. Someone had decided the skip was for
general use and had thrown in old pieces of fitted
kitchen cupboards.

Chrissy glanced up at Sam's window. The curtains
were drawn. She checked her watch. Three o'clock.
Maybe Sam was ill and staying in bed? If so, should she
disturb him?

She'd told him she didn't want to see him until
after the investigation was complete. Now she was
back here on his doorstep. This was madness.
Chrissy turned to walk away, then something caught
her eye.

The bag of clothes was wedged in the skip between a
chipboard door and a crumbling block of stone.
Chrissy reached in and pulled out Sam's jumper.
The one he wore against the vagaries of the Scottish

weather. He'd bought it in a Cancer Research shop. It was dark-blue heavy-knit wool. Thick and warm. His favourite.

Her worry was fast changing to fear.

Sam wouldn't throw his favourite jumper away.

Chrissy made for the front door and pressed the buzzer for his flat. She waited, instinct telling her there would be no answer, wishing she'd accepted the spare key Sam had offered.

She rang the buzzer for five minutes until an irate neighbour pushed up his window and told her to 'Fuck off!'

Chrissy returned the compliment.

When he slammed down the window, she buzzed one more time in defiance, then left, still clutching the jumper.

The lab was eerily silent, but going home didn't seem an option when she was this worried. It was better to have something to do. Rhona had left a detailed list. It read like a guilt trip. Leaving an investigation as difficult and emotive as this one wasn't something she'd done by choice. Chrissy set to work on the Velcro from the child's shoe.

General skin cells found at a crime scene were not great sources of DNA for routine analysis. Skin cells rubbed off in sweat were better. The DNA material they got from urine, blood and semen richer still. But Velcro had a habit of removing skin cells, microscopic but plentiful.

The Velcro fastener was rich in DNA. Chrissy

eventually identified Stephen's own pattern, his mother's, his granny's and someone else's.

When she checked against the database, the search threw up a match from the samples she'd taken at the Nigerian Church of God. Stephen had been there more than once. He was a Sunday School pupil. It was highly probable that a member of the church had helped Stephen fasten his shoes. Most likely his Sunday School teacher, Isa. But the DNA profile was not a match for Isa.

According to the results, Sam had touched the Velcro on Stephen's trainer, even though he'd told Chrissy he'd never met either the missing boy or his mother.

39

THEY ARRIVED IN the late afternoon to find the city shrouded in red dust. Rhona only realised they'd landed when they thumped down on the tarmac. She'd tried to watch their descent, mesmerised and frightened at the same time, but the dust cloud that engulfed the runway was too thick.

The jolt when the wheels hit the runway jerked her against McNab. The roar of the backward-thrusting engines drowned out her apology.

They taxied towards a white two-storey building fronted by a row of pink oleander bushes. A large sign announced their arrival at Mallam Aminu Kano Airport. McNab was already unfastening his seat belt.

Rhona must have looked relieved they were down, because he gave her a quick quizzical 'Okay?'

She answered by undoing her own belt and standing up to retrieve her forensic case from the overhead compartment.

Then the door opened and the overwhelming smell of heat and dust swept in.

They were met in the luggage retrieval section by a smartly dressed man who told them his name was Abdul Bunda. He showed them a card with the insignia of the British High Commission. His intervention began the quick movement of their bags through customs via a firm handshake between Abdul and a custom's officer. If money changed hands, it was too quick and discreet even for Rhona's sharp eye.

Abdul showed them to a white car waiting under the spreading branches of a tall mango tree, its doors standing open. The driver lay across the front seat, snoring softly, his head in the fresh air. Abdul shouted something in Hausa, waking him so swiftly that he hit his head on the doorframe. Rhona had to smother a laugh. Abdul gave her a smile in return, his teeth blinding white.

He indicated that she and McNab should sit in the back, while he sat beside the driver and issued brisk instructions.

As they left the airport, the sun was setting on the horizon, its red rays diffused in the lingering dust cloud.

They said nothing as the car negotiated the packed streets of honking horns, weaving people and roadside vendors. Every time the vehicle slowed down, a woman or child appeared at the window, a tray balanced on their head, offering nuts or fruit for sale.

Rhona stole a quick glance at McNab. She had seen this before, and remembered quite vividly her first reaction to Africa. Sweat was trickling down the side of his face, rolling under his shirt collar. The air was clammy, like red soup. They were breathing in the Sahara Desert.

'Harmattan dust,' Abdul explained. 'It should have

gone with the rains.' He shook his head, annoyed by nature's trick on them.

The honorary consulate was in a leafy cul-de-sac, magically quiet after the madness of the teeming streets. They drew up in front of a wide verandah festooned with white and blue blossoms, the cooling air thick with their scent.

A man and woman rose from easy chairs to greet them. Henry Boswell OBE and his wife, Karen, were the epitome of charm. Everything Rhona had heard about 'our man in Kano' proved to be true. When he offered them a gin and tonic sundowner, she couldn't resist throwing McNab a 'told you so' look.

Sitting on the verandah with her drink, the remains of an African sunset streaking the sky, Rhona wished she were here for reasons other than the murder and abduction of minors. But after the niceties of hospitality, their host brought them swiftly to the task in hand. Abdul had been offered a seat beside them. The consul spoke intermittently to him in Hausa as he discussed with Rhona and McNab the details of the trip.

'First of all, your accommodation. The Prince Hotel is directly across the road. It is surprisingly good.' He didn't say 'for Nigeria'. That was implied in his wry smile. 'I have set up a meeting with John Adamu. He is your contact with the police force. Abdul will take you to meet him tomorrow.'

'Did you know Carole Devlin?' Rhona asked.

The consul glanced briefly at his wife. It was she who answered. 'I met her about six years ago. Her husband was an engineer. She was pregnant at the time.'

'That must have been Stephen,' Rhona said. 'And you never met her again?'

'She moved to Lagos before the child was born.'

'But she was living in Kano before she returned to Scotland?'

'When she came back from Lagos she was with another man, a Nigerian, I believe. She no longer mixed with expats.' Karen seemed embarrassed. 'This is a divided society,' she explained. 'The British are tolerated, but we are no longer a sizeable minority. If a British woman forms a relationship with a Nigerian, she joins their society. Carole never kept up with any of her friends here and most of them have left Nigeria now.'

'She apparently attended church here. The Nigerian Church of God.'

Abdul came in at this point, muttering quietly to Boswell in Hausa. When the conversation was over, the consul told them, 'Kano State is predominantly Muslim and currently under Sharia law. The Christian church is tolerated but its members keep a low profile. The leader of that particular church is Pastor Oye-kunde.'

'We'd like to speak to him.'

'Of course. Abdul will arrange this.'

Rhona outlined the investigation and the urgency of their hunt for Stephen. Henry told them that the search for the boy had already begun. Abdul was known in all the local communities. Henry was convinced they stood a better chance of locating the boy via him, than through the police force.

'Ordinary Nigerian citizens don't trust the police,' he told them. 'Until recently their anti-crime campaign was called "Operation Fire with Fire". Confrontation rather than protection. The fallout, I'm afraid, from the many military regimes. The new motto is "Serving with integrity and honour". Nice words but not much to back them up yet. Unfortunately the force is poorly paid. They make up their wages by demanding money from the public at checkpoints. One out of twenty stopped is shot, by accident of course.'

McNab was finding this hard to believe. 'There's plenty at home don't like us either.'

'Mostly criminals, I suspect,' Karen said. 'Here it's the innocent.'

'What chance do we have with the investigation, then?' Rhona asked.

'There are good policemen who are trying to make a difference. John Adamu, your liaison officer, is one.'

'Is a week here long enough?'

'We'll do what we can.' Henry sounded nervous, but determined.

Rhona's limbs felt like lead as she stood up. The journey and the heat were taking their toll. If she stayed awake long enough to eat, it would be a miracle.

'We would have offered you dinner,' the consul said, 'but unfortunately Karen and I are out on official business tonight. A meal has been booked for you at the hotel. I recommend the Lebanese dishes. They are excellent.'

They strolled across the road to the Prince Hotel.

According to Abdul, the driver had already delivered their luggage and it would be in their rooms. The dust had cleared and above them the night sky was alive with stars. The evening air was scented by cooking fires mixed with dust and oranges – the smell of Africa.

Rhona felt lethargic, as though the rhythm of the dark continent had entered her soul. '*Master must learn patience,*' Henry had told them before they left. 'You'll hear that said a lot.'

The Prince Hotel was cool and quiet, an oasis of white walls and greenery. Abdul escorted them to the dining room and helped them order. McNab fancied a beer, but didn't think it would be allowed under Sharia law. He was wrong. Cold African beer arrived in a large teapot with two china cups, so as not to offend any Muslim guests eating in the restaurant.

It felt like an illicit tea party. The sweet African beer quickly went to Rhona's head. A fan whirred above them as they ate, while outside a million insects sang.

She was too tired to care what her bedroom looked like, and got the haziest impression of white walls and African print curtains before exhaustion claimed her. The hum of an air conditioner rendered the temperature almost European. Rhona slipped between cool white sheets and was asleep in seconds.

Day 8

Monday

40

RHONA WOKE NEXT morning to a room filled with sunlight. A distant splash suggested someone was already up and using the swimming pool. She lay absolutely still, unable to believe she was here in Africa.

She finally rose, switched off the air conditioner and threw open the window. The white patterned security grille was locked and she had to be content with the view it afforded.

The air was clear, with no evidence of yesterday's harmattan. It smelt hot and damp and pungent. Through the leafy branches of a flame tree she could see the pool, a dark head moving through the blue water. Rhona wondered if it was McNab, but dismissed the thought. She didn't remember him as a fitness fanatic. Then she recalled how he'd run across the waste ground towards her. He'd got in shape since they were together. He obviously now relied on more than just sex for exercise.

The swimmer was McNab. Rhona watched as he pulled himself from the pool and began to towel dry. He turned, sensing someone watching, and Rhona slipped out of view, feeling foolish and embarrassed at the same time.

She decided against joining him and chose to shower instead. According to the information leaflet, breakfast was served between seven and nine. It was just before seven now.

McNab rang the room phone as she got out of the shower. 'Breakfast?'

'I'll be down in five minutes.'

'See you in the dining room.'

Rhona noticed the bones as she hung up. They were lying on the bedside table, tucked behind the lamp.

For a second, it was as though she were back in the tiny front garden, with the murdered bodies of the two women in the house behind.

Only now she knew what she was looking at. Now she knew what the fetish meant.

The bones choose their next victim.

She withdrew her trembling hand from the receiver and willed her shallow breaths into longer, deeper ones. Only when she felt in control, did she take a closer look.

As before, they appeared to be children's forefinger bones, tied with red thread in the shape of a diagonal cross. Each bone had three striations. There was no mistaking the pattern.

Water from the shower trickled down her body mixing with beads of perspiration. The realisation that she'd slept all night with the cross beside her made her heart take off again. If this was a threat, it was working. It had scared her half to death already. She forced herself into motion. Dried her body. Put on clothes. She had told McNab five minutes. He would come looking if she did not appear.

Once dressed, she fetched her forensic case, donned latex gloves, picked up the cross and dropped it into an evidence bag, taking time to write the place and time on the label.

The phone rang as she finished.

'Are you coming?' McNab sounded worried.

'On my way.'

He was seated at a table by an open French window leading to the pool. He looked up as she entered and Rhona readjusted her expression. She would have to tell him about the bones, but she didn't want to look frightened when she did it.

She fetched fresh fruit and yoghurt from the buffet table. McNab was already tucking into a cooked breakfast. The big overhead fans were working hard, moving the moist air of the dining room in an effort to cool it. McNab was wearing a khaki shirt and trousers and looked comfortable despite the heat.

'I spoke to Abdul. He says to walk across when we've eaten. He'll take us to the police station.'

Rhona took a sip of coffee before speaking.

'I found a set of crossed bones by my bed this morning.'

'What?' McNab almost dropped his fork.

Rhona produced the evidence and handed it to him.

He glanced inside the bag and his face blanched. He was interpreting the find just as she had.

'They weren't there last night?'

'I don't know,' she answered truthfully.

'You heard nothing during the night?'

'I don't think anything would have woken me.'

'Were there any signs of a break-in?'

'I haven't had time to look. We can check the room after breakfast.'

They sat in silence, food now untouched. Rhona assumed they had reached the same conclusion: somebody associated with Stephen's case knew they were in Kano. That wasn't surprising since Abdul had already been out asking about Stephen. But whoever knew didn't like the fact.

'I don't like being threatened.' McNab's expression was grim.

'Neither do I.'

When they opened the door, her bedroom had assumed an ominous air.

'Did you see anything unusual as you undressed for bed?' asked McNab.

'I only had the light on briefly,' she answered.

She ran through the previous night in her mind. Briefly admiring the African print curtains, the snowy walls. Noting the security grille outside the window. Listening for mosquitoes and hearing only the satisfying hum of the air conditioner.

McNab was thorough in his search. Rhona tried not to mind his presence in what was effectively her bedroom, with her clothes, including underwear, scattered about. Her forbearance was rewarded with a partial footprint below the window. A large bare foot had rested briefly on the tiles, leaving its imprint in red harmattan dust.

'It could have been left by a member of staff,' McNab suggested.

'I haven't seen one with bare feet.'

He nodded in agreement. 'Even the gardener wears flip-flops. Whoever got in didn't use the window.'

He echoed her thoughts entirely. McNab had tried hard to open the security grille, to no avail. 'Let's hope there isn't a fire while we're here,' he said cynically.

They decided against questioning the management themselves. According to the consul, it was better if Abdul did the talking.

A call for Rhona came through to reception as they were leaving. Her mobile was useless here, as was McNab's. Henry had promised them handsets that would work in Kano, but there was little chance of reception outside the city. The lack of contact from home was a serious problem.

'Rhona?'

'Chrissy! It's great to hear your voice.'

There was a short silence as though the phone had cut out.

'Chrissy, are you still there?'

'Yes.' There was a catch in her throat.

Rhona's heart sank. 'What's wrong?'

'Sam's disappeared.'

'What?'

It came tumbling out. 'He sent me a strange text. It just said, "I'm sorry." I went round to his flat, because he hadn't turned up for work at the club. Some of his clothes were in a skip outside. Then –' she paused and cleared her throat – 'his DNA was on the Velcro of Stephen's shoe.'

'He went to church with Stephen,' she tried. 'Maybe he helped him put on his shoe.'

'Sam told me he'd never met Stephen or Carole.'

Nothing Rhona could think of offered an explanation. 'Have they searched his flat?'

'There's nothing there. It's as though he never existed.'

'There must be something,' Rhona insisted. 'What about his laptop?'

'No sign of it. Bill thinks Sam's left the country. They're checking the airports.'

'His mother lives in Kano. We'll find her. Maybe she knows where he is.'

Sam had disappeared either because he had something to hide, or because someone wanted him out of the way. An image of Malcolm Menzies's tortured body flashed through Rhona's mind. Sam guilty or Sam dead? Neither was a prospect she wanted to consider.

'What if Sam's involved in this?' Chrissy voiced her fears.

'No!' Rhona was adamant. 'I don't believe that.'

When she rang off, McNab was waiting. From his expression it was obvious he had been trying to interpret the one-sided conversation.

'What don't you believe?'

Rhona looked at his worried face. 'I'll tell you on the way.'

41

CHRISSY REPLACED THE receiver, her hand shaking. Rhona's words had done little to ease her worries. It was easy enough to say that Sam wasn't involved, but the evidence pointed to the opposite. She kept remembering things he'd said, things she'd seen. Innocent words and actions began to take on new meaning. His words, 'I have done nothing wrong.' And what about the picture of Stephen in the bible? A chill ran down her spine. She thought of the times they had slept in the same bed, how they had made love. It filled her with horror. What if Sam was involved in juju or, worse still, a killer?

She crossed herself, an involuntary motion that both surprised and comforted her. One thing was certain: Sam had touched Stephen's shoe. Why, only Sam could answer.

She tried to get back to work. She hadn't finished processing all the DNA samples from the church. The pastor had listed fifty names. Forty-seven had turned up and Sam was the last. She made a note to speak to Bill about the missing three. Despite her best efforts, her mind continually returned to Sam. Her gut instinct told her he was alive. He had sent the message in the early hours of Sunday morning. Surely Bill could discover where the message had been sent from? The more she thought of his phrase 'I'm sorry', the more she knew it meant he was going away. Sam couldn't leave without saying something. But where had he gone?

Somewhere he didn't need warm clothes.

Home? Could he have gone home to Nigeria?

The more she thought about it, the more Chrissy suspected and hoped it was true. Sam threw the jumper away because he didn't need it any more. Not in a country where it was hot even when it rained.

Bill glanced through the pathology report one more time. Malchie had been high when he died. The report showed similar toxic levels to those found in the urine of the murderer, suggesting they were smoking the same dope. Why Malchie was at the Olatundes' flat, Bill had no idea. Had he gone there of his own free will? What connection was there between Olatunde and Malcolm Menzies?

One thing he was sure of: Malchie had died because he knew too much, or had met the murderer and could identify him. This probably meant his mate Danny was in danger too. Bill had already sent a constable to the Fergus home, where Danny Fergus Senior had given him extensive grief. He'd point-blank refused to say where Danny was and wouldn't believe that his son was in danger, even when the constable told him about Malchie's murder. They were trying to locate Danny. He could only hope the murderer didn't get to him first. Bill didn't want another dead teenager on his conscience.

They hadn't discovered yet who the extra child was who had travelled with the Olatundes to Nigeria. Bill had spoken briefly to Henry Boswell, the honorary consul in Kano. Apparently the Olatundes had left Kano almost immediately and gone to their rural home outside the city. The local police were checking.

The consul didn't sound too hopeful. 'The extended family system considers many members to be brothers or sisters. They don't need the same mother.'

'But he had only one child here.'

'Maybe the boy was staying with a relative, going to a different school. Boys are special in this culture.'

Didn't Bill know it? Two women and one young man lay dead in the mortuary, waiting for the murderer to be caught before they could be buried. They'd been killed because someone wanted Stephen, because he was a boy and special.

And what would happen to Stephen if they found him alive? Correction. When they found him alive. Who would take care of the boy now that his mother and grandmother were dead?

Bill wouldn't let himself think that way. That was the job of Social Services.

'Sir?'

Bill swivelled around to face Janice.

'Peter Niven on the phone.'

'Niven?' Bill dragged his mind back to the present. 'Operation Pentameter.'

'Right. Put him through.'

He picked up the receiver.

Operation Pentameter had been set up to monitor the increase in human trafficking into the UK, both adult and child. Fifty-five police forces were involved. North of the border it was coordinated by the SDEA, the Scottish Drug Enforcement Agency.

'DI Wilson?'

'Speaking.'

'Can you come down here? I have some info you should see.'

Bill hesitated before answering.

Niven spoke again. 'It's very important.'

'I'll be there in half an hour.'

The SDEA was based a short drive away on the M8, not far from Glasgow Airport. He left Janice and the team working on tracing Sam's last call, finding Danny Fergus, interviewing the sauna owner and trying to establish if Sam had left the country. And that was only the half of it. The deeper they went into this case, the more complex it became. Bill was beginning to wonder whether there was black magic working against them.

The run out to the Osprey House complex was easy now the morning rush-hour traffic had cleared. In the near distance, planes lifted from the airport runway into a cloudy sky, spelling escape. Bill wished he was on one, heading off on holiday, Margaret by his side. He made a mental note to book some leave for the summer. He would take Margaret and the kids away for a fortnight. They hadn't done that in years. Better still, him and Margaret alone for two weeks. No teenagers, no work, no dead bodies. He knew that any plans for the summer depended on the results of the biopsy, but he felt better making them anyway.

Margaret still hadn't heard from the hospital. A week she'd said. Every day felt like a fortnight. She had remained calm, but Bill knew when he woke in the night that she lay awake beside him. When he did hear the soft sound of her sleeping breath, he felt relief he could hardly describe even to himself.

The news that they thought Stephen had been taken to Nigeria had lifted her spirits. Bill didn't want to get her hopes up, yet he still coloured the story in a positive light just to watch her reaction.

'Child Slaves Trafficked to Scotland for Sex Industry' was the headline.

Niveh laid the newspaper cutting on the table. 'What he says is all true. It's the tip of the iceberg. They arrive with adults by sea or air via London. Their stories lack credibility, but we don't have the time or resources to investigate further.'

'How does this help us to find Stephen?' Bill didn't mean to sound so short, but he didn't want to find he had been brought here to listen to what he already knew.

'We think there is a group taking the children back out of the country.'

That he didn't know. 'Where?'

'Back to West Africa.'

Bill tried to digest this. 'Someone's bringing them here . . . and someone's taking them back?' He couldn't disguise his confusion. 'I don't understand.'

'It's not the same group. The girl you found in the sauna – Adeela – says *Jarumai* rescue them and take them home.'

'*Jarumai?*'

'It translates as "brave people".'

'Brave people take them home? Why not take them to us or you?'

'We suspect those involved are illegals themselves. Adeela says the boy on the ship with her was rescued by the *Jamurai.*'

'How does she know?'

'Word filters through. Whether it's true or not, I don't know.'

'Olatunde took a boy and a girl back to Nigeria. According to the passports, they were both his children, although we believe he only has a daughter.'

'And you thought the boy might be Stephen?'

It was a hope they'd clung to. Bill realised with sickening certainty now how slim the chance had been. Olatunde took a boy to Nigeria who wasn't his child. Bill had no idea what his motives might be.

'We're dealing with a culture we don't understand,' Niven went on.

'You don't have to go to West Africa to see child abuse.'

Niven acknowledged that with a nod. 'One more thing,' he said. 'There's a strong link between the Nigerian oil industry and child trafficking. Europeans get a taste for the girls they're offered. They want the same when they get home.'

*   *   *

On the way back Bill took a detour via Maryhill Road. The main church door was closed and locked. Bill rang the bell continuously until he heard footsteps.

The pastor's face was grey when he opened the door. He looked like a sick man or a very worried one.

'Detective Inspector!' He was clearly trying to summon his usual lofty manner, but failed.

Bill almost felt sorry for him. It looked like God had deserted the pastor in his hour of need. Bill knew what that felt like. 'Can I come in?'

Bill waited for 'the house of God is always open'. It didn't come. The pastor held the door wide for Bill to enter. The entrance hall didn't seem to have changed since the last time Bill had visited. The miracle list had at least a dozen names on it.

Achebe led him through to his study. He sank into the seat behind his desk like a man whose legs would no longer support his weight.

'What do you know of the *Jarumai*?'

The pastor's face was a study in blankness.

'The *Jarumai*,' Bill repeated. 'The brave ones.'

'I know what it means,' he replied sharply.

Bill waited. The pastor said nothing further.

'You have illegals attending this church. We will prosecute you and send them back where they came from.'

'Then you will send many to their deaths.'

'I have one dead child already and one missing. Two women mutilated and a daft punk with his testicles offered on a plate to some African deity.'

'The devil is not just African.'

'Where is Sam Haruna?'

'I don't know.' The pastor said it as though he meant it.

'Is Stephen Devlin still alive?'

A spasm of pain crossed the man's face. 'I pray he is.'

'Praying isn't enough. I'd like you to come down to the station with me.'

The pastor sighed as though he had been waiting for this moment and was relieved it had finally come.

42

THE SAUNA OWNER, Ted Mundell, denied all knowledge of illegal immigrants in his establishment.

'I have three saunas and two betting shops. I don't have time to run them myself. I have managers to do that. If there's anything illegal going on, it's their fault.'

Mundell wore a smart suit that screamed 'money', a silk tie and shirt that didn't come from a high street retail outfit. When the man spoke, Bill felt like lice were crawling over his skin.

'It doesn't matter. We'll prosecute you anyway.'

Mundell thought about that for a moment. 'I don't think so.'

He was contemplating his client list. No doubt there were one or two he hoped would help get him off in exchange for anonymity.

'The girl was thirteen years old.'

From his look, Mundell couldn't care less. 'I know nothing about the dusky Abdula ... .'

'Her name is Adeela.'

Mundell shrugged. He couldn't give a monkey's what her name was.

'I want the names of the men who paid to use her.'

'Speak to my manager.'

'We can't. He disappeared when we raided the place.'

Mundell didn't look surprised. 'Because he knew he would get it in the neck from me when I found him running this girl as a sideline.'

He examined his manicured nails.

The smell of aftershave wafted Bill's way. It turned his stomach.

Mundell glanced pointedly at his Rolex. 'My lawyer should be here by now.'

Bill left him sitting in the interview room and went for a coffee to settle his stomach. Mundell had all the appearance of money – the clothes, the manicure, the expensive watch – but he was still a slug.

Mundell's lawyer was at the desk, talking his way past the sergeant. Bill ushered him through the incident room and into his office.

'Where's my client?'

'There's something I think you should see first.'

Bill pushed a photo of Adeela across the desk.

The lawyer didn't look down.

'She's thirteen years old. Someone sewed her vagina shut, so men had a hard time getting their pricks in. They pay more for that.'

The man's face flamed. 'I don't see—'

'Your client runs a brothel he calls a sauna. This child was in the basement. The doctor examining her found recent traces of at least six types of semen in her body, mixed, of course, with blood from the difficult entry.'

The lawyer rose. 'I want to see my client now.'

Bill opened the door. 'Fine. When you look at him, remember what I just said.'

Bill knew he was way out of line, but anger was getting the better of him. He longed for a murder that was just two drunks knocking hell out of one another on a Friday night.

He sent another member of the team with the lawyer. He couldn't look at Mundell's smug face again. Mundell would give a statement and be released pending further enquiries. And they would be no nearer finding who supplied the girl, or who the murderer was. Mundell, he suspected, knew nothing. Had chosen not to know, but was raking in the profits anyway. One man, Bill was sure, knew a lot more than he was saying. Pastor Achebe.

The pastor's imposing frame seemed to fill the interview room. His skin had lost its grey colour and was restored to shiny black. He looked like a man who had fought his demons and won. He held a simple wooden cross in his hands, worn smooth by touch. A full glass of water stood on the table, a film of dust on its surface.

He looked up as Bill entered with Janice. When they locked eyes, Bill realised that this time there would be no pretence between them. He felt exposed and vulnerable as though his own truth would be revealed along with that of the pastor.

He asked Janice to bring him a coffee and the pastor a fresh glass of water. He wanted to be alone with Achebe for a few moments.

'I will tell you what I know.'

'All of it?'

'Everything.'

43

ABDUL WAS WAITING for them on the verandah. The consul's car, complete with alert driver, stood in the shade of a neem tree. A gardener was watering the plants with a hose, filling the small moats that encircled a variety of shrubs. Rhona recognised hibiscus and oleander among them. The scent of cooking fires hung in the air.

Henry appeared at the sound of their voices.

The formality of morning greetings and enquiries over, he told them that, according to the principal of Bayero University, Dr Olatunde had left Kano for his rural home.

'He couldn't tell us anything about the boy who travelled here with him.'

'We also need to find a Mrs Haruna. Her son Sam was studying medicine at Glasgow University,' Rhona said.

Henry and Abdul exchanged looks.

'She helped us with our enquiries about a fetish found at the scene of crime.'

Rhona produced a photograph of the original bones and passed it to him.

'What about—' McNab began.

Rhona cut him off, knowing what he was going to say. 'Mrs Haruna suggested the bones were juju and not to be touched. She said the bones choose their next victim.'

She studied both men's reactions to the image of the crossed bones. Henry was circumspect. Years in Nigeria had seasoned him to its ways, but he was an Englishman and did not believe. Abdul, in contrast, was clearly frightened, although he was trying to appear calm for their sakes.

Henry looked quizzically at Abdul.

'Mrs Haruna is correct. The bones, to those who believe, symbolise death.'

'Rhona found a similar set of bones in her room this morning.'

Rhona was irritated by McNab's intervention. She'd asked him to say nothing about her find yet. McNab ignored her glare and addressed Abdul.

'Was that a threat?'

When he didn't answer, Henry intervened. 'Abdul?'

Abdul chose his words carefully. 'These people are stupid. They do not realise *Baturi* are not frightened by such things.' He gave Rhona an encouraging look.

'Still,' Henry said thoughtfully, 'I think John Adamu should be told. It might be wise for you to have a guard.'

Rhona brought the subject back to Sam and his mother.

'I do not know Mrs Haruna,' Abdul said. 'But I can find her for you.'

*   *   *

The Police Headquarters was fronted by an open area of ground with a dry dusty football pitch alongside. A few men stood or sat about outside in the shade, dressed in dark uniforms with guns slung over their shoulders. Abdul addressed one, who stared at them intently then ushered them through the open door.

It was cooler inside, though just as dusty. Rhona tasted fine grit on her tongue, felt it settle on her skin. Abdul had explained that the wet season wasn't fully here yet. By August and September the ground would be saturated, the wetlands of the Hadejia river basin flooded.

'Plenty water then.'

Now the air was thick with gritty red dust.

Their liaison officer, John Adamu, was a tall handsome man in his mid-thirties. His English was that of someone who had spent time in the UK. He spoke partly in rapid Hausa to Abdul and addressed a junior member of his staff in another language which he told them was Yoruba.

'Nigeria was created by the British. In reality it is many nations. Yoruba, Ibo, Hausa . . .'

'And Fulani?' Rhona asked.

He looked impressed. 'You've done your homework.'

'A little, but I'm sure not enough.'

'I realise your priority is to find Stephen Devlin. My sources tell me Carole Devlin had a relationship with a member of the Suleiman family, the chief's son called Naseem. She left him and went to live in a house outside Kano, before she took the boy back to the UK.'

This had to be the man Carole was running from.
Adamu agreed. 'The Suleiman family is powerful,
with strong but well-hidden links with juju culture.'

'Can we speak to him?'

'He is currently out of the country, according to his
family.'

'Are they lying?'

'Probably.'

By the end of their conversation, the air conditioner
had spluttered to a halt. Adamu opened the louvred
slats of the window and a hot humid breeze swept into
the room, bringing more dust to dance in the air.

It was McNab who brought up the subject of the
fetish in Rhona's room. Adamu reacted as Henry had
done.

'These things only frighten those who believe.'

Abdul didn't look convinced, his earlier show of
confidence gone. Rhona wondered if his disquiet
had come with the mention of the name *Naseem*.

'Two of my men will accompany you.' Adamu
didn't say 'for your protection', but it was clear from
Abdul's reaction that he was relieved.

Carole Devlin's house lay in the direction of Rano, the
area from which Rhona was to collect samples. When
she asked to visit the house first, Adamu readily agreed.

'We checked the house when we got the call from
Glasgow. It was deserted apart from her *ma'gaadii*,
Boniface. He said he was waiting for his madam to
return.'

'*Ma'gaadii*?' Rhona asked.

'Her guard. It's common to have a security guard here. He also helped in the house and the garden. We told him about Carole. He was very upset.'

The consulate car was a white air-conditioned Peugeot estate. In a cocoon of chilled air they travelled south along dusty roads initially teeming with people and cars, the numbers dwindling as they reached the less-populated outskirts of the city. Mud-hutted villages flew past, neolithic images of compounds and cooking fires, naked or semi-clothed children waving or offering bananas, oranges and mangoes.

They negotiated a bridge over the river, behind a mammy wagon piled twice its height with goods and people. The laws of gravity suggested it should tip over. Many of them did, their driver told them. The guards led the way in a police vehicle. Now and again a local would raise his fist and shake it at the jeep.

'The people do not like the police.' Their driver was stating the obvious. Rhona wondered how it was possible to conduct an investigation here, if ordinary decent citizens didn't trust or like you.

McNab was silent, and seemed to be suffering from culture shock. Rhona recognised it, having experienced it herself. In the consul's residence and at the hotel, you could almost believe yourself in an exotic southern European country. Out here, in the African bush, it was for real.

Carole's house sat at the end of an avenue of tall flowering flame trees. The whitewashed mud bungalow stood on an escarpment. At its back, the land fell towards a meandering tributary of the Kano river. A washing rope hung between two acacia trees, and the breeze rising from the river was flapping two pairs of khaki shorts and a bright red T-shirt. To the left of the bungalow was a roundhouse with a thatched roof, its walls painted in patterns of ochre and dark blue. A man emerged at the sound of the cars' approach. When he saw the police jeep he looked as though he might bolt, then their driver called to him in Hausa and the fear on his face lessened.

Boniface's English was good. He told Rhona he had learned it from a priest at a nearby mission, then his madam had helped. He was happy to speak to Rhona, but less keen on McNab. He only relaxed when the two policemen moved away to sit under the shade of the flame trees.

'Who was Stephen frightened of?'

'The man with . . .' He ran his fingers down his cheeks three times. 'He came and made madam cry. She said, "No!" When he left, she packed her suitcase.'

'Can I look inside the house?'

He thought for a moment, then led her towards the verandah. The plants were watered, the steps swept clean. Rhona wondered how much he had been told. Did he know that Stephen was missing?

He was reading her face.

'Stephen is not dead,' he told her. He touched his heart. 'I wait here for him.'

He unlocked the glass door. It led into a rectangular tiled hall, empty of furniture. A door on the right gave onto a living room with a grey-painted concrete floor, a settee, two chairs and a wooden coffee table. Two windows looked in opposite directions, towards the avenue and the river. A door in the far wall led to a small kitchen, hot in the midday sun.

Rhona followed Boniface back through the hall to a tiny passageway with two doors. He opened one on a room with a double bed, spread with an African-patterned cover. A built-in cupboard held a variety of summer clothes and shoes. Carole had taken none of them with her. She knew the Scottish weather too well.

Stephen's room brought tears to Rhona's eyes. There was a small desk, a bed spread with a *Star Wars* cover. A selection of books and a jar with a pierced lid. Inside three spiders with soft velvety-red bodies sat on a stone.

All the rooms were tidy and clean. She suspected that Boniface continued to act out his role despite the death of his employer.

'Has anyone been here apart from the police?'

Boniface looked anxious. 'I have seen no one.'

McNab had followed them around the bungalow, lingering in each room and letting them go on ahead. He caught up with them in Stephen's room. Rhona heard his intake of breath behind her. Here in this room, she understood Boniface's conviction that Stephen was alive. It felt as though the child could walk in at any moment.

'We'd like to take a look ourselves now,' she told Boniface.

They waited until they heard the front door close.

'The place's been cleaned pretty thoroughly,' McNab echoed her own thoughts.

If someone had been here after Carole, all trace of them was gone.

McNab went back through the house for another look while Rhona stayed in the child's room. She donned gloves then carefully opened the desk. Inside was a muddle of drawings, pencils and notebooks. She leafed through the drawings. Done in a childish hand, they consisted mostly of pictures of insects, including a red spider like the ones in the jar. There was no drawing of a man with three scars on his face.

The *Star Wars* bedcover was a thin cotton, faded in parts. A small lump in the surface caught Rhona's eye. She ran her hand over it. It felt firm.

Rhona edged back the cover.

The lump was a small curled snake, bright green in colour. Her startled exclamation brought McNab running.

'What?'

He followed her gaze to the bed.

Her initial surprise gone, Rhona took a closer look. Red thread had been wound tightly around the dead body just below the head. A sharp thorn pierced the snake's skull between the eyes.

Boniface's fear was so strong she could almost taste it. He had retreated to his own hut to crouch under the overhang. He had come back to the room as they examined the snake, shouted, '*Macifi*,' and then run out.

McNab had brought one of their guards inside, but he was as useless as Boniface under their questioning.

They did establish that all Nigerians feared snakes and would kill them at any opportunity. Why this particular snake had been mutilated in this manner, the guard couldn't or wouldn't say. He was in agitated discussion with his colleague, interspersed with dark glances towards the house. Rhona was sure she heard the word *tsafi* in their mutterings.

Boniface was rocking backwards and forwards on his ankles, his arms wrapped about his body, his breath coming in small tortured gasps.

'What does it mean?' asked Rhona.

He looked up at her with bloodshot eyes. 'They will kill him now.'

44

THE PASTOR'S BULKY body had shrunk inside his clothes. Bill preferred this version of the man. He seemed more human, less confident. Now he and Bill had something in common.

'And Sam didn't know?'

'Sam came to church on Sundays. He was not part of the *Jamurai*.'

'His DNA was on Stephen's shoe.'

The pastor looked perturbed by this. 'He did not meet Stephen as far as I know. Or his mother.'

'And Olatunde?'

'There was a boy, Sanni Atta. He was snatched near Kano. I asked Dr Olatunde to take him home.'

'That was the boy who flew with him to Kano?'

'Dr Olatunde has a stepson. He is at boarding school here. Sanni fitted his description for the passport.'

'Why not come to us?'

The pastor was silent. They both knew the answer to that.

The interview lasted an hour. By the end, Bill had established that four children had been smuggled back to Nigeria.

'And none of them was Stephen?'

'Stephen was taken back, but not by us.'

'You know that for sure?'

'My sources in our sister church in Kano say Naseem's family were involved. He had an affair with Carole strictly against his father's wishes. He then married, but there are no children. The witch doctor says this is because Naseem slept with an uncircumcised woman, a woman who had a boy child by another man.'

'And that's why Carole was killed?'

'I believe so.'

'But why take Stephen?'

'They plan to use him in the cleansing ceremony.'

'What the hell's that?'

'It will make Naseem father a son.'

When Bill finally got through to the consulate, Henry Boswell sounded perturbed. He told Bill that Dr MacLeod and DC McNab had left early for the police headquarters in Bompai.

'Dr MacLeod asked to speak with a Mrs Haruna. Abdul, my aide, has gone to try to locate the woman. I've heard nothing back from either party.'

'Is that unusual?'

'No.' The consul weighed his words. 'It's just that Dr MacLeod found a fetish in her room this morning.'

'What?' Bill exploded.

'A cross of bones. She said it was similar to one found at the scene of crime.'

Bill swore under his breath.

'Ritualism is common here.'

'Well, it isn't common here.' Bill regretted his harsh tone as soon as he uttered the words. It wasn't the consul's fault.

'I told them to inform Adamu, their liaison officer. He will provide security.'

Somehow, that didn't make Bill feel any better.

'We have information that Stephen is in the Kano area,' he told the consul, 'possibly with Naseem's family. We believe his life is in danger.'

'I'll do what I can.'

They had been sitting at the police roadblock for half an hour. Their escort jeep had driven to the front of the queue of vehicles and never returned.

McNab had waited long enough. 'I'll go and see what's happening.'

The driver had given up running the engine and taken refuge under a roadside acacia bush. Even with all the doors open, the car was like a furnace. McNab and Rhona had deserted it and were standing in the shadow of a big truck whose driver was deep in conversation with theirs.

'We've been warned about police roadblocks,' Rhona said. 'Leave it to the guards.'

'The guards are shite. The first sign of trouble and they'll run.'

Rhona peered up the row of traffic, shimmering in the noonday heat.

'There's a hut on the other side of the road a bit further up. It looks like it's selling soft drinks.'

'Okay, you go buy us a hot Fanta. I'll check out the front of the queue.'

Rhona gave in. Preventing McNab doing what he wanted was never an easy option.

Women and children from the nearby villages had taken advantage of the blocked road and were wandering up and down with trays piled with overripe bananas and mangoes. Rhona bought a couple of mangoes and paid too much for them, much to the delight of the seller.

She crossed the dusty road and walked towards the hut. It was set back from the carriageway with a large mango tree out front. Crates of soft drinks, Coca-Cola and Fanta among them, were propped up in the shade. Rhona gestured to the crates, trying out the elementary Hausa phrases she'd studied on the plane. '*Biyu Fanta, don Alla.*'

The man gave her a grin that suggested her Hausa wasn't up to much and fetched two bottles. When she asked, 'How much?' he thought for a moment then suggested a price at the top of the range. Rhona paid it without arguing. He looked disappointed. Haggling was half the fun of selling. He flipped off the bottle caps for her with studied expertise and gestured at a rough wooden bench in the nearby shade.

Rhona sat down and took a sip of hot Fanta.

The sweltering heat enveloped her like a heavy blanket, sweat trickling down her body under her clothes. Despite her fears for Stephen, the heat had made her thought processes sluggish and laborious.

She longed for a cold shower or, even better, a face full of the cold wind that gusted up University Avenue.

She turned, hearing a vehicle behind her, and saw a black four-by-four pulling up on the dusty ground to the rear of the shack.

Two men climbed out, one glancing over at her. There was something in that look that perturbed Rhona. Sly, and calculating, at the same time. The other man was in conversation with the vendor, who also threw a quick look over his shoulder at her.

She stood up, attempting to maintain an air of nonchalance. Hers was the only white face in the vicinity, which could explain their interest, but she wasn't taking any chances.

She was only metres away when she registered the roar of the engine as the wheels skidded in reverse. When the vehicle swung alongside, she had almost reached the road.

Her brisk forward movement slammed her into its side. The collision sent the open bottles to the ground, the orange liquid spraying out. Rhona swung around, stunned, not sure whether to run forward or back.

Before she could regain her wits, the man on the passenger side was out and had a hold of her. Her screams were drowned out by the roar of the engine. If the stall owner saw her being dragged into the vehicle, he wasn't about to intervene.

The four-by-four sprang forward, swerved around the shack and took off across country, bumping wildly on the rock-hard rutted ground.

As she was pushed down onto the car's back seat, a sweaty hand clamped over her mouth, Rhona caught a last glimpse of the queue of cars beginning to move forward.

45

MCNAB'S MOUTH DROPPED open. It was a scene he couldn't have made up.

The three roadblock policemen, plus his own two security guards, were trying on sunglasses. The makeshift chair and table at the side of the road held a box filled to the brim with imitation Raybans. The lorry whose cargo it was, stood alongside, back open, the first in the queue of at least half a mile of backed-up vehicles.

McNab's stupefaction quickly turned to anger.

'What the hell do you think you're doing?'

The *Baturi* voice brought all five heads around. Recognising him, the two guards looked surprised then awkward, but not, he thought, embarrassed. The other three glared at him with something resembling contempt.

The guards came swiftly towards him, their faces angry, and one shouted something in Hausa. Roughly translated McNab guessed it meant, 'Shut the fuck up!'

They began bundling him towards the jeep. The sharp revving of an engine stopped them all in their tracks. A powerful black off-roader was crashing off into the bush. At least someone had the sense to get off this baking road, McNab thought. The image of the escaping vehicle seemed to propel the roadblock policemen into action. The one in charge barked an order. The sunglasses were loaded on the truck, the barrier pulled up and the vehicles waved on.

The fashion show was over.

McNab strode back towards the car, seething with anger. He would lodge a complaint with John Adamu regarding his officers. He would ask the consul to complain to the head of police. He would . . .

He stopped short of his own vehicle, suddenly remembering Rhona. The driver was back inside the car. He'd drawn it onto the verge to allow the queue to pass. The doors were closed, the air conditioner back on. Rhona wasn't inside.

McNab opened the front passenger door.

'Where is madam?'

The driver shook his head. 'I do not know.'

McNab glanced over at the shack. The brisk business it had done during the roadblock had dispersed. He could see one figure and it wasn't Rhona.

'Did she come back?'

'No, sir.'

Where the hell did she go? Maybe she needed the toilet? McNab imagined Rhona heading for a clump of bushes. She wouldn't want him searching there for her.

He walked slowly towards the shack. The owner, seeing him approach, began walking in the direction of the village compound a short distance into the bush.

'Hey!' McNab called.

The shout only made the man walk faster until the walk became a run. McNab took off after him, his heart thumping, sweat coursing down his face and chest. When he reached the compound, the opening in the high mud wall had been sealed with a thorny gate. Peering over, he saw only a couple of goats.

McNab was beside himself with anger and it wasn't helping. Being a Glasgow detective held no sway here. The guard's blank look spelt that out.

He tried again, keeping his tone even. 'The man ran away from me. He knows something about Dr Mac-Leod.'

'We have searched the compound. She is not there.'

'I didn't say she was. I said he knows what happened to her.'

'He knows nothing.'

'Then why did he run away?'

'These are peasants, they are frightened of everything, especially *Baturi* who threaten them.'

McNab's voice rose in exasperation. 'I did not threaten him.'

The guard looked at him stonily. 'We must report to our superior.'

McNab felt desperate. He couldn't just drive away. 'I will stay here and look.'

'As you wish.'

The guard walked back to his jeep, where his colleague sat behind the wheel.

'Who was in that black vehicle that drove away from the roadblock?' McNab called.

But the jeep was already pulling away.

'The black four-by-four!' McNab shouted at their retreating backs.

The consulate car was parked at the deserted shack. The driver had taken up his favourite position, along the front seat. McNab didn't have the Hausa words to rouse him into action. He sat down on a rough wooden bench nearby. The sweltering heat was crippling his thought processes. All around him the caked earth simmered. The incessant chirping of crickets had increased in frequency the hotter it got. The sound filled his head, adding to his inability to think.

He fetched a Fanta from the crate and snapped the lid off on the corner of the bench. It tasted like nothing he'd ever drunk before. Sickly sweet and hot. He gulped half the bottle before the sugar rush kicked in.

Fanta! She'd gone to buy Fanta. He stood up and tried to focus in the fierce rays of the sun. Assuming she had bought the bottles. What next?

He took his time, peering at the ground, looking for some mark of her presence. He walked towards where the car had been parked, then he saw the chink of reflected light.

The two open Fanta bottles lay close to the roadside. They were half empty, the spilt liquid soaked into the parched ground. He touched the rapidly drying damp spot with his finger.

She'd dropped both bottles here. Why?

The dry soil was churned up. There had been a struggle here. Big tyres had stamped their pattern in the dust.

The four-by-four!

He remembered the vehicle's mad dash across country, then the sudden spring into action of the roadblock police when they saw it make off.

Whoever was in that vehicle took Rhona.

That's what the roadblock was there for. To capture her. And the police had helped.

46

THE TWO-ROOMED BUNGALOW was built with concrete blocks, painted white. It had window openings on all sides, shutters fastened back, the constant breeze from the reservoir blowing through. The two men who'd deposited her there hadn't tied her up or locked her in. There was no reason to. The bungalow stood on a tiny island in the middle of a large expanse of water. The only way off was by boat or a very long swim.

After the men left, she'd raged around the house, then walked the short shoreline. Calmer, she'd eaten something and had a long drink of cool water from a hollowed-out gourd, but not before she smelt and tasted a little of the liquid in case they planned to drug her.

Flanked by two of her captors in the back of the vehicle, she'd tried to follow their route. After miles of open bush and numerous identical compounds of mud huts and staring locals, Rhona had practically given up.

Then she saw the long expanse of the grassy embankment of the dam, rising maybe forty metres above the river bed.

The vehicle had travelled downstream from it,

through acres of irrigated fields filled with maize tall enough to swallow them. When they reached the road atop the embankment, Rhona was stunned by the size and strange beauty of this artificial lake. She'd read about Tiga Dam in her rapid attempt at research before her journey here. The few pages of information on the internet spoke of drowned farmland and villages. No trees had been felled before the river valley was flooded, leaving strange skeletal limbs to rise from the water like white spectres, their underwater tangle a haven for breeding fish. And so, she'd read, the displaced farmers had become fishermen.

Concentrating on what little she knew about the place helped control the intermittent surges of fear and disorientation that threatened to swamp her. Her life had been threatened before now, but to be catapulted from her world into this, where none of the normal rules applied, had left her feeling more alone and out of her depth than ever before.

There seemed no point in struggling as she was transferred to the small motor boat. Any argument would have resulted in a beating. That had been made clear in the only English spoken on the journey. If she was going to have her wits about her, it was better to conserve her strength.

Standing outside the bungalow, her eyes shaded, she thought she could make out the line of the distant shore and the white shape of an occasional building. If there was a house on the island, it stood to reason there might be similar constructions on the shore. This bungalow wasn't owned by local people. It must be a weekend retreat for a well-to-do Kano resident. Someone who wanted her out of the way.

And they'd succeeded. There was nothing she could do on the tiny island but think. And it didn't take Rhona long to work out how she'd ended up here. The roadblock had been a set-up. She had been kept there until the four-by-four turned up to collect her. And she could only assume that Adamu's men were in on it.

Rhona pictured McNab's return to the Peugeot. His concern when she wasn't there. His search for her at the shack. She remembered the fear in the owner's eyes. He had been warned to say nothing. If McNab hadn't spotted the four-by-four taking off, then all he would find were the discarded Fanta bottles. Even if he had seen the black vehicle drive across the bush, he could hardly follow it over rough ground in the Peugeot estate. And something told her the police jeep would not take up that challenge.

McNab was already struggling with the heat and the culture shock. His temper would be even shorter when he realised how little influence he had here, despite being a policeman. What chance would he have of finding her?

The reservoir was the colour of sand, its surface smooth as silk. She contemplated a long swim to shore through the silt-laden waters, weaving between the dead arms of the trees. She was a good swimmer, having learned the hard way in the peat-brown lochs of her home island of Skye. Cold and murky water didn't scare her, and neither did the fish lurking in Tiga Dam. She would doubtless catch a parasitical infection from the water. Probably bilharzia, like Abel. Unpleasant but curable.

It was the possibility of water snakes that worried her.

The sun went down swiftly. To someone used to the twilight of a northern land, its descent was frighteningly fast. The island was soon enveloped in a suffocating darkness as though a thick blanket had been thrown over it.

Rhona had checked earlier for candles and found a ready supply, but the only box of matches she located was damp and useless. In the dark she couldn't see the mosquitoes although she could hear them. The anti-malarial tablets were back at the hotel, so anything that bit her would have a field day.

Now the cool water looked like a refuge from the biting insects. The faint wavering glow of cooking fires picked out the distant shore. In the deceptive darkness the land didn't look so far away after all.

If she stayed here, what would happen? The sudden shocking image of Carole's bloodied body spread out on the kitchen floor sprang to mind.

The two men expected her to remain in the bungalow. No one, they thought, would be foolish enough to swim Tiga Dam at night. Especially not a lone *Baturi* woman. She wouldn't wait around for them to do to her what they had done to Carole.

Rhona took off her shoes and walked into the water.

47

'DANNY FERGUS IS here, sir.'

It was the best bit of news Bill had had in the last week.

'Where?'

'With the desk sergeant.'

'Get down there. And Janice, for God's sake don't scare him away.'

By the time Bill arrived, Danny was in an interview room. When Bill walked in he was shocked at the change in the teenager. He'd seen kids in Danny's state before. It was usually when the duty doctor was signing the piece of paper that would commit them to an emergency mental ward. The result of too many drugs taken too often, or in too many combinations.

Danny might have looked psychotic, but what Bill smelt was fear. Danny reeked of it. It was fear that made his teeth grind, his hands twitch and his blood-shot eyes roll.

At first Danny kept repeating the same sentence over and over. 'HE's coming to get me.'

They found the cross of bones in his pocket. Taking it away from him didn't calm him down. He'd been frightened before, but now that he knew the bones had been secreted on his person, he was terrified.

'Danny, listen to me. We can get him if you tell us who he is. Then you'll be safe.'

Danny looked at Bill, wanting to believe.

'He can't get you in here,' said Bill.

Danny looked around the bare walls, the heavy door.

'An officer will stay with you all the time.'

Danny's hunched shoulders slowly straightened. He breathed in. 'I want my ma here. Not my dad.' He shook his head. 'Not him.'

'Of course.' Bill gave Janice a nod. 'Get his mother here, pronto, and someone from Social Services.'

When Janice left, Danny began to crumble. Tears squeezed out of his eyes and ran down his cheeks. The big man act was gone. Danny Fergus was a fifteen-year-old boy who wanted his mother.

'Okay, I'll tell you.' Saying the words seemed to unnerve him again. His teeth rattled together in his clenched jaw. 'It's her fault, that woman forensic. If she hadn't turned up on the waste ground everything would be all right. HE's going to get her too.' Danny checked Bill's reaction to that.

'HE is getting no one,' Bill told him. 'We're getting HIM.'

It had started so easily. Malchie had seen a black guy at the building on the waste ground.

'He thought he was one of those illegal immigrants, sleeping in there.'

They'd watched at night, seen others coming and going. 'Not all black,' said Danny. 'Malchie figured they were illegal workers. He said we could make some cash.' Danny chewed his lip. 'He spoke to the black guy. They did a deal. All the dope we wanted, to keep folk away.'

A dream ticket for the pair of them. Act like the punks they were and get paid for it in cannabis.

'Malchie wanted more. I told him to leave it alone . . .' Danny stumbled. 'He went to one of their ceremonies. Initiation, that's what he called it.' The boy's face flushed. 'They cut off a dog's testicles and drank its blood. Malchie said it gave him a hard-on.' Despite his fear, he looked slyly at Janice.

'A name, Danny? A name to keep you safe.'

'Malchie said you couldn't touch the guy in charge. That he was immune.'

'Immune?' What the hell was he talking about? 'I need a name, Danny.'

Janice came in. 'Immunity, sir. Diplomatic immunity?'

'Did you see this black man?'

'I followed Malchie once. I saw him then. He was tall, black. That's all.'

'Great.'

Danny looked worried that he wasn't giving enough. Not enough to be safe.

'There was a white guy too. I saw him with a black lassie. Young, maybe twelve or thirteen. He put her in a car and took her away.'

That was more like it. 'Tell me about him.'

The description seemed to fit Mundell, but that may have been wishful thinking. Then Danny came out with another gem: 'He had a fancy watch. Malchie said he looked at it all the time. A Rolex.'

Bill tried not to smile. 'Would you recognise this man if you saw him again?'

'Aye, I would.'

'Good boy, Danny.'

Danny sat back relieved. Safe for the moment. Bill and Janice rose to leave.

'You won't leave me alone, will you?'

'There's a constable standing outside the door. Your mother'll be here shortly.'

'You promised I'd be safe.'

'We'll lock the door when we go out. No one can get in except us.'

Danny didn't look convinced. Bill couldn't blame him. Everyone connected with this case ended up dead.

'Bring in Mundell. Let's set up an identity parade.'

'Do they all have to wear Rolexes, sir?'

The attempt at a joke brought a half smile to Bill's face. He would dearly love to nail Mundell. Abusing a minor would be a start.

The Home Office had not been prepared to release a list of those with diplomatic immunity. It was up to him to submit the name and offence to them, he'd been politely informed. Eventually common sense, or a little arm-twisting from the Procurator Fiscal's Office, had produced a list of a dozen people currently resident in Scotland. One name interested Bill the most. Prince Kabiru Suleiman, who gave his Nigerian address as *Sabon Gari, Kano*.

48

KANO WAS IN semi-darkness. Those with standby generators had switched them on, the patches of light delineating the well-to-do from the poorer areas of the city.

The consul's driver had been sympathetic but not much else. He had talked to the owner of the soft-drinks stall at McNab's orders. The madam had got into a large black vehicle. That's all the man would say. *No. He had never seen the men before.* He didn't think the madam looked frightened. McNab knew he was lying. His eyes were wide with worry. From the compound behind, women watched, babies slung on their backs. All of them seemed nervous.

When the driver mentioned the British consul, there was a slight release of tension. McNab jumped on the opportunity. 'Ask him which direction the vehicle went.'

The rapid exchange elicited the word *north.*

'What's up there?'

The driver thought for a moment. 'Tiga.'

'What's Tiga?'

The driver threw his arms wide. 'A big dam.'

'Can we go there?'

'Not this way.' The driver shook his head. 'We go back to the consulate.'

The driver was right. They couldn't go across the bush in this vehicle. The best bet was to speak to the consul. McNab had never felt so useless in his life. This was one crime scene he couldn't manage. Everything he knew, everything he'd learned, was futile here.

On the way back to town, he stared at the unremitting barren terrain that rushed past his window, as though he might spot Rhona or the black vehicle moving among the endless scrub and low bushes. When he'd heard about the decision to send a team to Nigeria, he'd done everything he could to make sure he went with Rhona. He wanted to be alone with her. He wanted to show her that there was still something between them. Something that they both needed and wanted, despite the Irish guy, despite Janice. His hunger to be with her had put Rhona in danger. As the sun went down and darkness fell, McNab's mood was as black as the night that surrounded him.

Henry Boswell paced the tiled floor. In his long white socks and big baggy khaki shorts he looked every inch the colonial. He might have resembled a relic of the past but his brain was sharp enough.

'And you're convinced Adamu's men were involved?'

'It was too much of a coincidence. They were at the front of the queue with the others. When the vehicle took off into the bush with Rhona, the policemen dismantled the roadblock.'

'How did your guards react when you found Dr MacLeod gone?'

McNab thought for a moment. 'Worried.'

'Surprised?'

He had to admit they had been. Then when he started shouting at them, the shutters came down.

'I have reason to thank John Adamu for my life. I trust him implicitly. But he cannot vouch for all his men, which makes his job even harder.' Henry paused. 'Naseem's family are conspicuously absent. His father, the chief, is in Lagos overseeing his oil interests in the Delta.'

'Oil interests?'

'He owns a major Nigerian oil company. It employs a number of Europeans.'

The large puzzle was beginning to come together.

'John has been in contact with the family. They deny all knowledge of Stephen and his mother. He knows they are lying, but the family are very powerful in Kano State.

'So what do we do?'

'Dr MacLeod is in danger. I have no doubt of that. But we can do little in the dark.'

The lights flickered as the generator stalled, then brightened as it kicked back into action.

'If she was taken in the direction of Tiga Dam . . .' He paused again. 'I have a house there. So too do a number of expats and wealthy Kano residents. We can search the area at sunrise.'

'What about Sam's mother?'

'Abdul went to her home. Her houseboy has not seen her for several days.'

'She's missing?'

'According to Abdul, the man was terrified. He says a black vehicle took the madam away. He tried to report this to the police and was beaten for his trouble. He only told Abdul because he knew he worked for me.'

'I think we should speak to him.'

They were on their way to the car, when Henry's mobile rang. As Henry answered, McNab could just make out Bill's voice on the other end, tinny but clear. When Henry filled him in on Rhona's abduction, there was an explosion of furious expletives.

Henry handed the mobile to McNab. 'It's DI Wilson. He wants to speak to you.'

McNab told Bill the whole sorry story.

'Find Rhona. Get her out of there.' Bill's voice was thick with anxiety.

'There may be a ritual planned for Stephen. From what Danny Fergus said, Rhona could be in danger. It looks as though they might involve her. Go to the Nigerian Church of God. It was the pastor there who told Achebe about the ritual . . .'

The mobile cut out before Bill could finish.

Henry directed the driver to head for the Nigerian Church of God.

'Pastor Oyekunde is a good man. He'll help us all he can.'

The *Sabon Gari* was bustling despite the blackout. Every shop and stall had its own paraffin lamp, and was doing business in its circle of light. The Peugeot estate had been exchanged for a Land Rover. Abdul sat in front with the driver. Following his directions, they weaved their way around the potholes, horn honking, the mass of humanity that thronged the shadowy, rubbish-strewn streets giving way before them.

Pastor Oyekunde was in his candlelit church, a low red-mud building with a tin roof and a small bell tower. The church was surrounded by a high wire fence, a guard at the gate. When the guard saw the consul in the Land Rover, he pulled the gate back to let them in.

'The Christians feel under threat here since the riots. Although one guard won't keep out a mob,' Henry explained.

McNab was inclined to agree. The gate was a token gesture, nothing more.

The pastor, a small round man, robed in black, welcomed the consul as though he expected him. They exchanged a series of greetings in a language McNab didn't recognise. Once these were complete, the consul introduced McNab in English.

Oyekunde held out his hand. 'I am sorry for what has happened.'

When they were seated, he told them what he knew.

'The practice of Ritualism, as Mr Boswell is aware, is a continuing problem among both Christians and Muslims. Even those educated in the West are not free of its influence.'

The talk wasn't moving fast enough for McNab. He butted in. 'Do you know where this ceremony will be held?'

The pastor indicated he did not. 'However, the ceremony mirrors baptism, so it should be held near water. A river or lake.'

'Tiga Dam,' McNab muttered.

The consul explained. 'Dr MacLeod was taken from the Rano road across country, we think towards Tiga.'

'The Suleiman family have a small house on an island in the lake,' said the pastor.

49

RHONA VEERED LEFT at the hum of the motor boat's engines. A powerful light on the bow illuminated the small bungalow. She heard the backwash slap the boat's side as it turned and one of the two men jumped into the water, heading for the house.

She was barely twenty yards from shore. A short distance away, the white spectre of a drowned tree reflected the light of a pale white moon. She kicked out smoothly towards it, trying not to splash. It would only take a few seconds for the men to realise she wasn't on the island. Maybe if she hid in among the submerged trees they wouldn't find her.

Rhona felt a sharp jab of pain in her foot. She trod water for a moment, feeling gingerly with her hands and feet, trying to judge how far she could swim into the tangle of branches. A loud plopping sound beside her told her she had disturbed something big, causing it to surface.

There was a shout from the shore. Then the light swung over the water. Rhona took a gulp of air and sank.

Her eyes were open, yet she could see nothing. The water lapped over her head. Her shirt billowed in descent, snagging on a twig. She struggled, panic-stricken, imagining herself trapped for ever in this watery coffin. The twig snapped, freeing her. She rose against her will, broke the surface and gasped for air.

The motor boat was inching towards her, the head-lamp slowly turning this way and that, searching.

Rhona filled her lungs and sank again.

She had no idea how many times she did that. Up for air briefly, then down again. The men were frustrated and angry. She heard the rapid Hausa, sometimes English, as they called for her across the water. Eventually the motor boat gave up and headed for shore.

She waited until she was sure, before she dared leave her thorny refuge. Then she trod water, wondering which way to swim, her limbs heavy, her muscles aching from tension and exhaustion.

Could she reach the shore or should she return to the bungalow, safe now in the knowledge that they thought her gone?

She had no idea how long she had been swimming. Her world had turned into the swish of water, the plop of fish, the moon on the surface of the lake, the ever-distant lights. If she ceased her stroke she knew she would sink like a stone. At first she counted using Hausa numbers to keep her awake. *D'aya, biyu, uku, hud'u, biyar, shida, bakwai, takwas, tara, goma.* She only knew up to ten and repeated them endlessly until she remembered them too easily, and started to nod off. She switched to Gaelic, then French.

She was in her fourth group of ten in French when her hand hit the side of a dugout canoe.

The panic she caused the occupant was almost as bad as her own. The night fisherman dropped his net mid-cast, startled out of his wits. He grabbed for his paddle.

Rhona clung desperately to the side, her body exhausted, her sodden clothes dragging her downwards.

'*Don Allah*,' she shouted. 'Please, God. Help me.'

The compound consisted of two roundhouses, a grain store sitting on misshapen wooden stilts nearby.

Her rescuer, who said his name was Joshua, brought her to a central fire, kept alive and banked up overnight. Rhona was shivering now, in rapid juddering waves. He gave her a blanket that smelt of dust and smoke. She wrapped it around her and huddled close to the glow.

At a shout from Joshua, two women appeared from one of the houses. One was elderly and walked with a pronounced limp. The other was a young woman, a baby suckling one breast.

From the door of the roundhouse, three sets of eyes stared at Rhona with more curiosity than fear.

Joshua had displayed some knowledge of English in the boat as he paddled her to shore. Rhona had tried to explain that her boat had sunk in the lake. He'd accepted this without question and did not ask why she was alone.

The younger woman put some water to boil in a black kettle over the fire. When it began to simmer, she threw in a pinch of tea from a leather pouch at her waist. The result was a hot sweet concoction of boiled tea, goat's milk and lots of sugar, which tasted delicious. Rhona drank it all down and was offered another.

When she tried – with her few words of Hausa and his halting English – to explain that she needed to get to Kano, Joshua looked baffled. He understood the urgency of her request from her tone, but how was she to get there? He only had his canoe.

'*Baturi*?' she asked. 'Are there any *Baturi*?'

Joshua nodded, understanding.

'Yes – *Baturi* houses, lake. We go?' he said, pointing back towards the island.

She had no way of telling him that she wanted to know about houses on the shore of the mainland, and the thought of being transported back to where she had come from was too much to bear.

She fell asleep at the fire, the hum of a motor boat engine punctuating her dreams, transforming them into nightmares. When she woke, it was still dark, the night lit only by a white moon and surrounding stars. The fire had burnt to a glow and its lingering smoke hung in the air, mingling with the mist that clouded the lake.

Joshua and his family were nowhere to be seen. She had grown used to the rustlings and mutterings of the family and the silence of the compound was unnatural.

Rhona tried to stand, her body stiff with exhaustion. 'Joshua!'

She let the blanket fall. The air was warm and sultry, yet she shivered as though drenched in cold water.

'Joshua!' she called again, willing him to walk into the fire circle or emerge from a roundhouse.

The figure that did appear, came from the direction of the rocks behind. At first alone, then followed by two men.

He was dressed like a *Baturi*, but moved with the graceful ease of an African. As he drew closer, Rhona saw the three tribal scars scored across each cheek.

The two men behind were halted in their approach by his raised hand. The scarred man stood still, taking time to appraise Rhona. His glance passed from her feet upwards, paused briefly at her breasts, then rose more slowly until his eyes met hers. Rhona was transfixed like a small mammal waiting for a snake to strike.

Her instinct was to break that locked gaze, yet she could not. Both fear and fascination kept her eyes on his. This was the man who terrified Stephen so much he drew pictures of him and scribbled them out. This was the man who had made Carole run across continents to escape him. This was the man responsible for her mutilation and death.

The words were gently spoken, his English perfect, with no hint of his African origin.

'You are far from home, Dr MacLeod.'

The words were gently said, but unmistakable in interpretation. She was far from home. Alone and helpless in an alien culture. He could do with her as he liked.

'The British consul will find me.'

'I will make sure of that,' he said.

50

STEPHEN SMELT THE heat and dust and knew he was
nearly home. The terror he'd felt on the long journey
by van then plane had been eased by the man with him.
The man called Sam he'd seen in church. Sam had told
him everything would be all right.

'Your mother asked me to help you.'

'My mum's dead.'

Sam had held his hand then and let him cry.

'Your mum's in heaven, watching over you.'

Sam was his friend. He had taken him from that
terrible dark place, washed and dressed him in clean
clothes and told him he was going to take him home.
That it was what his mum would have wanted.

Stephen told Sam about Boniface. About his red
velvet spiders that came with the rain. They sang
Stephen's favourite song as Sam drove.

> Give me courage when the world is rough,
> Keep me loving though the world is tough;
> Leap and sing in all I do,
> Keep me travelling along with you.

When they reached the airport Sam explained that
Stephen was to be his *yaronsa*, his boy. He was to be

called Stephen Haruna. That way he would be allowed to go home.

The plane was small with a big red S on the side. It was a private jet. A friend of his mother had sent it from Kano, Sam told him. They would fly over the desert. Maybe see a camel train trekking towards Kano. Had he ever been to the camel market in Kano?

They never talked about HIM or the man Stephen had seen bent over his dead mother. He was safe now, Sam said, and Stephen believed him.

51

PRINCE KABIRU SULEIMAN greeted the arrival of police officers at his home in the West End with bemused indifference. The pleasant surroundings of the town house were in stark contrast to the city mortuary, where Bill had seen him last.

'You left the mortuary in a hurry.'

Suleiman – or Devlin, as he had been called then – nodded graciously, as though Bill had said something amusing.

'I would like you to accompany me to the police station.'

'I'm afraid that won't be possible. As you are no doubt aware, I have protected status in this country.'

'As far as *I* am aware, your name is Devlin and you are the husband of the murder victim Carole Devlin. As such I am taking you into custody on suspicion of murdering your wife.'

'My name is Prince Kabiru Suleiman.'

'My officer here,' Bill indicated Janice, 'will confirm that you came to the Pitt Street Police Station and declared yourself to be Mr Devlin. You produced a passport with the name Devlin and your photograph in it.'

The smooth demeanour faltered.

'I wish to phone my lawyer.'

'Of course. From the police station.'

Bill didn't know how long he could hold Suleiman under the name of Devlin. Long enough to parade him in front of Danny Fergus. Long enough to get a fingerprint and a DNA sample, to 'eliminate' him from their enquiries. Long enough to find out why he had passed himself off as Devlin and why he had taken photographs of Carole Devlin's mutilated body.

Suleiman was studying Bill intently, his expression malevolent. He muttered something under his breath in Hausa. It sounded like a curse.

'Threatening a police officer is an offence in this country.'

Suleiman smiled. The smile made Bill's skin crawl. He felt a strong sense of menace, yet Suleiman was simply standing before him, hands by his sides, his expression calm. Bill's thoughts jumped to Margaret. He had a sudden and irrational sense that she was in danger too.

'Sir?' Janice was looking at him strangely.

Bill pulled himself together. He stood aside to let Suleiman pass. He had no wish to have this man at his back.

'Book him in as John Devlin,' Bill told the desk sergeant. 'He'll be in interview room two.'

'But, sir?'

Bill threw the sergeant a look that shut him up. He knew Room 2 was already occupied. The quickest way to see if Danny knew Suleiman was to confront him with him 'accidentally'. In his terrified state Danny would react to anyone he knew who was connected to the case.

Bill ordered the confused constable to unlock the door.

'In here.' Bill shoved a reluctant Suleiman inside. The room had a sharp acrid scent of sweat and dribbled urine. Danny was sitting at the table, his head in his hands. He looked up as Suleiman entered and Bill got a clear view of his reaction over Suleiman's shoulder.

Danny's face went white. Suleiman tensed, like a leopard ready to spring. Bill heard him hiss like a snake.

'Fuck's sake!' Danny was on his feet. 'That's him.'

'Who?'

'The bloke with Malchie.' Danny was terrified, his face drawn back from his teeth like a death mask. He backed against the wall, as though Suleiman was coming for him. 'Get him away from me!' He put his hands over his eyes.

Suleiman had turned and was trying to push past Bill, but the constable had barred the door.

'Forgot this room was occupied,' Bill told the constable. 'Better put Mr Devlin next door.'

Bill turned to Danny, who was still flat against the wall. 'See, Danny, I told you we would get him.'

Bill nodded at Janice to turn on the recording equipment. He gave the time and place and the names of those present. He used the name Devlin for Suleiman.

The lawyer interrupted. 'My client's name is Prince Kabiru Suleiman.'

Bill spoke for the benefit of the recording. 'Kabiru Suleiman, alias John Devlin.'

Kabiru's face was impassive.

'Why did you tell us you were John Devlin?'

Kabiru was silent.

'Why did you have John Devlin's passport with your photograph in it?'

The lawyer spoke. 'My client has diplomatic immunity. You are obliged to inform the Home Office of any alleged offence.'

'I intend to charge Mr Devlin with the murder of his wife and mother-in-law and the abduction of his son, Stephen Devlin.'

'She was not my wife. He is not my son.' Suleiman curled his lip in disgust.

'Yet you asked to see her dead body. We have you on tape taking photographs of her mutilation . . .'

The lawyer looked uncomfortable. 'I must stress that the Home Office must be informed.'

'And I remind you that under Scottish Law the Procurator Fiscal's Office decides whether there is a case to answer.' He addressed Suleiman. 'Mr Devlin, you just said "he *is* not my son".'

The significance of the present tense had not been lost on the lawyer either.

'How do you know Stephen is alive?'

Something resembling fear flashed in Suleiman's eyes, then he was back in control.

'We have reason to believe Stephen was smuggled

out of this country and is currently in Kano, Northern Nigeria, with your family.'

The lawyer threw a worried glance at Suleiman.

'You have a brother called Naseem?'

Suleiman ignored the question.

'He had an affair with Carole Devlin against your father's wishes.'

Anger rippled across Suleiman's face.

'When she fled Nigeria, Naseem had you track her down and kill her.'

'Why would my client claim to be Carole's husband then photograph her body if, as you allege, he killed her?'

'If Mr Devlin, or Mr Suleiman, would agree to give a DNA sample, we can eliminate him as a suspect.'

The lawyer thought for a moment then said, 'I suggest you comply with their request.'

Bill didn't like the smug look on Suleiman's face as he gave his consent. That could only mean one thing. Suleiman didn't murder Carole or her mother. But he knew who did, and it seemed likely he had arranged to have them killed. Now the reason for his visit to the mortuary was clear. He wanted evidence that the honour killing had been carried out. That's why he'd taken the photographs.

Day 9

Tuesday

52

THEY APPROACHED THE reservoir at early dawn. The massive expanse of African sky loomed over them, bruised blue and red. The air was heavy with the acrid scent of morning cooking fires, smoke rising to hang above the shadows of roadside shacks and the more distant compounds.

McNab's certainties had evaporated in this dry dusty heat. Death was not a stranger in Glasgow, but he knew its violent forms induced by alcohol and drugs. Here, death wore a different face. One he was unfamiliar with. Talking about witchcraft in Glasgow, he could afford to be cynical. But not here. Not now.

Henry had the look of a man on a mission. His image belied someone who had lived here most of his life, yet McNab knew that Henry understood this country and its people as much as any *Baturi* could.

'John has gone on ahead. I spoke to him before we left. The two guards did not return to police headquarters. They have gone bush. The jeep was found abandoned in the *Sabon Gari*.'

Fear of punishment or fear of reprisal? McNab could only hope whoever John Adamu brought with him this time could be trusted.

As they passed through Rano, the town was slowly rousing itself in the early light. McNab thought of Carole and her house with its big verandah and flame trees. He imagined Stephen happy there, playing in the garden. Capturing red velvet spiders with Boniface. 'They will kill him now,' Boniface had said, despair and resignation on his face. Life was precarious here, and all the more precious for it. Boniface had loved Stephen. McNab corrected his tense. Boniface loved Stephen.

McNab looked out over the vast expanse of water and his heart sank. At an estimate it must be over twenty kilometres long. How could they search that length of shoreline?

'I have a motor boat moored at my weekend place,' said Henry. 'We'll use that. John's already commandeered the expat sailing club's security vessel. He'll check the Suleimans' island and any houses along the far shore. This area is well populated with fishermen and farmers. If something's going on, the local community will know.'

But would the locals be willing to talk? McNab remembered the reaction to the police when Rhona went missing. The guards tried to blame him for frightening the stall owner, but McNab thought fear of the police a more likely explanation.

After checking all the expats' weekend cottages, Henry and McNab headed out on the motor boat, leaving Abdul and the driver to drive up the lakeside as far as they could with the vehicle, visiting the local settlements this side of the reservoir.

They could hear the distant beat of another motor boat echoing across the glassy water, but the mist that clung to the surface prevented them from seeing it.

Henry headed out confidently into the lake, weaving expertly between the grey tree trunks that periodically rose from its surface. 'We'll check the island first.'

McNab wondered if he didn't trust Adamu as much as he said, or if he expected bad news there.

It took them at least ten minutes to reach the outcrop that rose like a volcano's tip from the silt waters of the reservoir. The island was nothing but rock, the bungalow filling its surface area with only a narrow strip of surrounding shore. With no trees or shade apart from a heavy overhang of thatch, the bungalow was already baking in the morning sun.

Adamu's launch bobbed a few metres from shore. McNab spotted the dark police shirts, and a figure he recognised as Adamu.

Henry pulled alongside the small jetty. 'Try not to get your feet wet.'

McNab decided not to ask why.

Adamu caught sight of him through the open window and held up a pair of sandals. 'We found these on the shore. And someone's eaten in this room recently.'

A posse of ants were busy clearing up the remains of a meal.

McNab examined the blue sandals. They looked like the ones Rhona had been wearing and were about the right size.

'These are foreign sandals. Not available locally.'

Adamu showed McNab the writing inside. Good old *Marks and Spencer*. Rhona had been here all right.

Where was she now?

'They brought her here, probably overnight.'

And took her away again. But where?

'Someone will have seen the motor boat come out here. The lake is fished night and day.' The mist had dispersed as the sun rose, exposing at least a dozen dugouts spread over the reservoir. 'The fishermen know every white man who comes here for weekends. They even have nicknames for them.'

McNab was tempted to ask what Henry's was, but didn't.

'Dr MacLeod is a stranger, a *Baturi* stranger. Someone will have seen her.'

By midday, Adamu had a reported sighting. A white woman had been picked up in the water during the night by a fisherman called Joshua.

'Rhona's alive?' said McNab. 'Thank God! What the hell was she doing in the water?'

He had the horrible thought that they had tried to drown her.

Adamu seemed to disagree. 'I think she was trying to escape the island.'

'In the dark? The woman must be a maniac!'

'Maybe,' Adamu said, 'but she did make the shore.'

'Where is she now?'

Adamu's face grew grave. 'She was taken from Joshua's compound by a man with scars on his face.'

'Stephen was terrified of a man with a scarred face.'

'The Suleiman men have followed the tradition of tribal markings.'

'It was Naseem, then.'

'Possibly,' Adamu was more cautious. 'Markings are common here.'

'Where have they taken her?'

Adamu shook his head, at a loss.

They were sitting on the small verandah that fronted Henry's shoreside cottage. It was early evening and the heat had dwindled to a manageable level. Abdul had returned with no news, so all they had to show for the day's search was that one sighting.

'God, she could be anywhere,' McNab concluded.

Henry came in. 'Tell me about the ritualism in this case. What happened in Glasgow?'

McNab told him about the deaths, the strange building on the waste ground, the skulls with nails driven through them.

'Wait a minute.' He realised that in the trauma of losing Rhona he'd never mentioned their find at Carole's house to either Henry or Abdul. 'There was a small green snake under the covers of Stephen's bed. Rhona found it. It had a nail driven through it.'

Again, Abdul seemed to be struggling to conceal his fear. 'The snake draws the worshippers to the place of sacrifice.'

'Carole's house? But what about water?'

Then McNab remembered that the house backed onto the river.

*   *   *

Their determined entry into the line of traffic on the main Rano road caused an explosion of honking horns and a few hands held up, palm directed towards the driver.

'The worst insult they can afford him,' Henry told McNab. 'It suggests he's the illegitimate child of a woman with loose morals.'

Their driver let go of the wheel with his right hand and returned the compliment to shouts of Hausa abuse.

'What about the police?'

'I'll try to get John on the mobile. We're still close enough to Kano for a signal.'

The line was bad and broke up as Henry explained their plan. McNab gathered from the exchange that John had two vehicles with him. He announced his decision to stay near the Suleiman house, just in case. Two men would follow them to Rano in the other jeep.

Night was swiftly falling as they drove up the avenue of flame trees. McNab's guts were churning, his body on high alert. He couldn't shake the feeling that it was too late. Was he approaching a crime scene where the murder had already taken place?

53

STEPHEN STOOD ON the verandah. Above him the trees sang with crickets. The line hung between the acacia trees, empty of washing. He walked through the open glass door. The louvred windows of the sitting room were open, curtains trembling in the breeze. He thought he smelt rain on the wind.

He walked slowly through to the kitchen, all the time saying, *Please be there, Mummy. Please be there.* The kitchen was empty. His mum's favourite mug had been washed and sat on the draining board. There was a smell of heat and emptiness. Tears ran down his cheeks. He'd thought if he came back, everything would be all right. That what happened at Granny's house would go away.

Sam had said, 'Trust me, Stephen. Whatever happens. Promise?'

He had promised, not understanding.

He shouted for Sam, but there was no answer, just the singing crickets and the buzz of heat and flies.

Stephen went back and stood at the open door. The creeping grass of the straggly lawn was still green. Boniface had watered the garden, thinking they were coming back.

Stephen glanced to the right. Sam's vehicle was there, but another had pulled in beside it. A man got out of the big black jeep. Stephen saw Sam appear from behind the house and approach the man.

The two stood a metre apart. Stephen could see neither of their faces.

He heard the word *uwa*, mother, and thought they were talking about his mum. Sam was very angry. Then Sam shouted, 'You said if I brought the boy . . .'

Stephen wanted to call out, but fear trapped his voice in his throat. It was the return of his nightmare. The stranger turned and Stephen saw the scars.

54

SHE SAT BETWEEN the two minders in the back seat. The smell of male sweat swamped the silty aroma that still clung to her clothing. Both men stared straight ahead, their bulky bodies allowing little room for her. Prince Naseem Suleiman, as he had politely introduced himself, sat in front with the driver.

He had declined to tell her where they were going, but Rhona suspected they were heading back to Kano.

Her repeated requests to be taken to the British consul had ended when the man to her right produced a knife and held the point to her neck.

Darkness swept past the windows, punctuated by an occasional figure caught in the vehicle headlights, or the glow of a communal fire. The car was unnaturally cool, the air conditioner turned high. Rhona's clothes had dried, but her flesh still felt damp and chilly.

Exhaustion and fear had rendered her brain incapable of logical thought, but then nothing about this case seemed logical. The man who sat in the front seat was a killer. He may not have killed with his own hands but he had ordered Carole's death. An honour killing?

How can there be honour in mutilating and murdering two women? And what about Stephen?

She had asked about Stephen as she was forced into the car. Suleiman gave her a look that suggested she would find out soon enough.

When they turned into the avenue of flame trees, Rhona knew that it would end here, where it had begun.

Glasgow was an awkward cul-de-sac Naseem had been forced to deal with. When she ran into Malchie on the waste ground, she had created a problem. The Suleiman family did not like problems. Especially those caused by a woman.

Rhona wondered how long it had taken for Carole to realise what she had got herself into. Perhaps it was Stephen and his fear of Naseem that showed Carole what the man really was. Or maybe she found out more about him than he wanted her to know. Whatever it was had terrified Carole enough to make her flee her home. But Glasgow hadn't been safe either. The world had become smaller and Naseem's family had a long reach.

There was a vehicle to the left of the house. When they drew alongside, a man appeared from the rear of the building. Rhona watched the long stride and felt a jolt of recognition.

Sam did not see her, wedged as she was between the two men in the back, the knife to her throat. Then Rhona caught sight of Stephen, standing on the verandah where she'd imagined him only the day before. He was watching Sam, disbelief flooding his face. Then Naseem turned and Stephen saw the scars.

In that moment, Rhona suddenly understood everything.

Sam was the killer and he had come to deliver his prey.

55

THE BUILDING WAS little more than a shack, used by fishermen to dry the ugly mud fish they pulled from the river. It sat on a sandbank, exposed by the nine-month-long dry season. Come the full rains it would be gone, swept away in the thunderstorms that dug fissures in the clay landscape and swelled the river to the full height of it banks.

A dugout took them across as the blood-red orb of the sun dipped below the horizon. The boatman paddled a steady rhythm, holding the canoe against the current that pulled them relentlessly south.

Rhona sat in the centre, her hands gripping the sides of the roughly hewn wood. Stephen was huddled in the bow, held tight by Sam, who faced Rhona. At her back, Naseem's henchmen watched their every move.

Sam's expression had changed swiftly from amazement to blankness when he saw her pulled from the vehicle. Whatever happened, Sam didn't want to know her, or at least be seen to know her. What surprised Rhona most was the way in which Stephen clung to him. Stephen didn't look on Sam as an enemy, but as a friend.

She couldn't believe it was just over a week since

she'd sat with Sam and Chrissy in the jazz club and discussed juju. She'd even shown Sam a drawing of the bones. The desperate realisation that she may have played into his hands scared her more than anything. He had tricked her and, even worse, he'd betrayed Chrissy.

The canoe ground over sand and the boatman jumped out and pulled them ashore. Rhona saw something pass hand to hand between him and Naseem's man. Probably more Niara than the fisherman had ever seen in his life.

Day dropped into night as they walked towards the shack. She was bundled in first, stumbling into the smell of blood and excrement. Suddenly she was back in that terrible building on the waste ground, the same decay filling her nostrils, the same overwhelming scent of death. There she'd had a powerful torch to illuminate the horror before her, here she had to imagine what lay in the shadows created by the smoking paraffin lamp. Then too she'd had an ally, McNab. What Rhona would have given, to see him run towards her, as he'd done on the waste ground.

The altar was made of red mud and topped with a skull pierced with nails. The skull wasn't human. Rhona forced herself to categorise it to stop the bile that rose in her throat. A goat's skull, most likely.

Behind her, Stephen cried out and she heard Sam whisper something to quieten him. Then she admitted to herself what she'd known all along: they had brought the child here to kill him. They had brought her here for the same reason. And she could do nothing to stop them. Everything she knew was useless here. All her knowledge couldn't prevent death.

They tied her hands together and pushed her down against the wall. When they tried to tie Stephen's hands, Sam prevented them, saying something in Hausa. He took the child to the outside wall of the shack and sat with him there, near her. It was the first time Sam looked Rhona full in the face.

He held her glance, willing her to understand something without words. But what?

The suspicion that he was trying to trick her evaporated under that stare. Chrissy was no fool. She was an astute judge of character.

Sam slipped his hand along the floor of the hut, and Rhona saw the glint of steel. She felt a soft sawing motion as the sharp blade cut through the twine that bound her.

'Be ready,' he whispered.

The hut began to fill with shadowy figures, women and men. A drum took up a steady beat. Rhona could not see their faces, but their chanting pulsed through her veins like a hypnotic drug.

A goat was brought in, bleating with fear.

Behind was a woman. Rhona felt Sam stiffen beside her. He muttered something under his breath. It sounded like *uwa*. The woman was drugged, swaying between the arms of her captors. The chanting rose, deep and resonant. Rhona's view of the proceedings was blocked by the mass of bodies, but she heard the squeal of the dying goat, the splash of the blood hitting the metal bowl and the explosion of joy from the onlookers.

A male voice called for order.

The chanting and shouting stopped.

The man spoke in Hausa. His voice had the rhythm and resonance of the chant but Rhona knew it was more. It was an incantation.

Sam sat up on his haunches and watched, the muscles on his neck straining.

As the words ended, a great sigh rose from the company. The metal bowl was passed around, and the watchers drank from it one by one. When it came to Sam, he held it to his lips. Rhona heard him whisper, 'May the blood of Jesus save her.'

The woman was the last to drink, her drugged mouth forced open to accept the blood. Then it was over. She was taken from the hut.

Rhona felt Sam relax beside her.

'Now,' he said. 'We will go.'

56

WHEN BONIFACE SPOTTED the Land Rover coming up the drive, he came running towards them, his shouts a mix of Hausa and English.

A rapid exchange with Abdul established they must go to the river quickly.

'They have Rhona and Stephen on a sandbank,' Henry translated. 'Pastor Oyekunde told him to wait here for us.'

McNab's stomach lurched and he felt a sudden surge of hope. What if he had been wrong? What if Rhona and Stephen were still alive? 'Pastor Oyekunde?'

'Sam Haruna turned up here with Stephen. He told Boniface to get word to the pastor. Boniface hitched a lift to Kano and came back with Oyekunde and some church members. The pastor found out by bush telegraph that we were headed here.'

Henry was already out of the Land Rover, the back doors open. He handed McNab a large torch. McNab would have been happier with a gun.

'Let's go.'

Abdul led the way, directing his torch onto the narrow pathway that zigzagged down the side of the escarpment between dried grass and thorn bushes.

'Watch where you're putting your feet,' Henry warned. 'This area is bad for snakes.'

Now Henry's thick socks and heavy shoes didn't seem such a bad idea.

The night was ink black, the moon hidden behind cloud. A hot damp breeze brought out beads of perspiration on McNab's face.

'Rain's coming,' Henry muttered, looking up at the sky.

As they reached the base of the escarpment, the moon swam free. Now McNab could see the river moving like thick brown sludge between high banks. In the distance a faint light exposed a sandbank.

'Listen.'

The drumming and chanting drifted eerily across the water.

'It has begun.' Abdul's face filled with horror.

The sound paralysed McNab. All the things he had heard in his life, all the violence he had witnessed, had not prepared him for this moment.

He heard Henry's heavy breathing beside him.

'We've got to stop it.'

Then another sound filled the darkness. A single male voice, deeply resonant, followed almost immediately by others. The words were in English, the rhythm African.

> *Jesus! The name high o'er all,*
> *In hell, or earth, or sky,*
> *Angels and men before it fall,*
> *And devils fear and fly.*

Pastor Oyekunde and three of his followers stood on the river bank, each holding a wavering candle, their voices trying to drown the incessant drumbeat.

> *Jesus! The name to sinners dear,*
> *The name to sinners given;*
> *It scatters all their guilty fear,*
> *It turns their hell to heav'n.*

McNab had never been a believer. He was a cynic who liked to think he was a rationalist. But in that moment he hoped, wished and prayed the singers' words were true.

'Come on!' Henry was pulling off his socks and shoes. 'God helps those who help themselves!' he announced, striding into the water.

57

NASEEM WAS STRIPPED naked, his tall muscled body gleaming like black oil, his penis erect. The chanting grew steadily louder. Rhona was shocked to feel her own body respond with a mix of fear and excitement. A man stood before Naseem, his face painted a shocking white. He tipped the metal bowl. Naseem gasped as warm fresh blood dribbled down the shaft of his penis.

The witch doctor shouted something. The words were harsh and sharp, like a command. Sam stood up, Stephen's hand in his, and walked towards him.

'Stay close,' he told Rhona.

She rose unsteadily to her feet, clutching the rope as though it still bound her wrists.

The party turned to watch the boy and the white woman led into the circle of light.

A ripple of expectation moved through the group.

Naseem was moaning, his penis still rigid.

The witch doctor gestured wildly, commanding Sam to let go of the child. Sam did so.

The world hung, balanced in a moment of time, as the witch doctor raised the machete above the child's head. Rhona roused herself from her stupor and staggered forward, then saw the flash of Sam's knife and knew what he would do.

The blade moved too fast for her to see, but she heard Naseem scream and saw him slump, blood spurting from the artery close to the severed penis.

But Sam wasn't finished.

He raised the knife again. This time it plunged up and under the lowest rib and into the kidney. Quick and efficient. The thrust of a killer.

In the stunned silence that followed, she heard the words of a hymn floating through the darkness.

> *Jesus! The pris'ner's fetters breaks,*
> *And bruises Satan's head;*
> *Pow'r into strengthless souls it speaks,*
> *And life into the dead,*
> *And life into the dead.*

Naseem's minders were trying to push their way through the confused, screaming crowd jostling to get to the entrance. Rhona grabbed Stephen's hand. Behind the witch doctor was an opening at the foot of the wall. She pushed past the wailing man and pulled Stephen to the ground, rolling him under and following.

A beam of light hit her face, blinding her.

'Rhona!' McNab's shout sent her reeling in that direction.

Stephen's eyes were better than hers in the dark. He pulled her towards the river, sinking into wet sand. The torchlight was coming from the far bank. Rhona stumbled hand in hand with Stephen into the water.

'Can you swim?'

She didn't wait for an answer but dived forward, dragging him with her. She didn't care what happened once she was in the water. She just wanted them away from the sandbank. She held the boy with one arm and kicked out into the current, remembering how the boatman had struggled to keep the canoe steady. Three powerful torch beams fought to hold her in view as the current surged south, taking her with it.

Behind her, flames rose from the shack. Craning her head back, she desperately tried to pick out Sam in the mêlée spilling from the burning building, but she could not see him. Naseem's men would never allow Sam to live after what he'd done. By taking Naseem's life, Sam had lost his own.

Stephen clung desperately to her, his rigid body pulling her down.

'It's okay, Stephen,' she said. 'You're safe now. Swim with me.'

She felt him relax as the water bore the two of them relentlessly onward and soon the beam of torches, the crackle of fire and the desperate shouts were lost in the distance.

58

THE RAIN BROUGHT her back to consciousness.

Stephen was kneeling by her side, looking anxiously down at her. His face was just as it had been in his photograph. Rhona wanted to cry. Stephen. The little face that looked down from above her desk, so she wouldn't forget what the case was really about. A lost child. But not a dead one, thank God.

'I've been looking for you,' she told him. 'We all have.'

The searchlights gradually came along the bank towards them. Then, as the beams finally skimmed across them, Rhona saw one light break free from the rest as McNab caught sight of her and ran headlong across the wet sand to where she lay.

Stephen looked around, frightened, but Rhona sat up and took his hand.

'This is Detective Sergeant McNab,' she said, 'And he came all the way from Scotland to look for you.'

'Hello, Stephen.' McNab helped Rhona to her feet. 'Thank God you're okay.'

She stumbled, the weight of her body too much for her legs.

'Let me help you,' he begged.

And just this once, she did.

They sat on Carole's verandah, sheltering from the downpour that had already turned the drive into a pond and attracted a choir of frogs. Boniface made them tea, hot and sweet and topped up with goat's milk. Stephen stayed close, following him back and forth from the kitchen. The child was in shock, but Rhona knew it was best that he stay close to someone he knew and loved.

Sam hadn't followed them into the river and, according to Henry, only Naseem's dead body was found in the remains of the shack. Searching for Sam along the bank would have to wait until morning.

'I think you should head back to the consulate. We ought to contact Glasgow. Tell them you're both safe.' Henry still looked every inch the Brit, his socks and shoes back on. Even the muddy wet shorts didn't detract from that air of confidence. 'Stephen should go with you.'

'Boniface too?' she suggested.

'Of course.'

'What will happen to him?' Rhona voiced the concern that they all shared. Stephen had no family as far as she knew. Everyone he loved was dead, except Boniface.

'He's a British citizen,' Henry said.

This meant he could return to Glasgow and be put in the care of the Social Services.

Stephen and Boniface were chasing frogs through the pond, raising their faces to the dwindling rain.

Stephen belongs here, thought Rhona.

They set off shortly before dawn, leaving John Adamu and his men searching the surrounding area for Sam. The Land Rover drove through sleepy villages, rousing with the first rays of the sun. The smell of dust had gone for the moment, washed away by the heavy downpour. From a bridge they saw the Kano River already swollen by the storm. On its beach an empty mammy wagon was being washed by its keen owner. As they entered the outskirts of the city, the sun rose in all its splendour above the russet-coloured mud houses. From the minaret of a mosque, the faithful were being called to prayer.

59

IT TOOK ONLY a few days to collect the samples from the Rarlo area for comparison with Abel's torso. While they waited for their flight back, the fruitless search for Sam continued.

Each day that passed with no dead body gave Rhona a little more hope. Stephen asked for Sam constantly, and Rhona's time with the boy in the consul's garden revealed the true story of Sam's involvement.

Sam had removed the boy from that terrible building on the waste ground. How he knew Stephen was there and how he managed to bring him home, they learned from Sam's mother.

The Haruna house was in a quiet back street of little bungalows in the *Sabon Gari*. Its garden was carefully tended. Creeping grass surrounded two guava bushes, one pink, one white, both heavy with fruit. Planted around the verandah was lemon grass, its scent pleasant in the late afternoon air. Mrs Haruna sat on a wicker chair on the narrow verandah. Her face was bruised, her eyes swollen. She rose as they approached and the movement clearly caused her great pain. She seemed very frightened.

'My son?'

Henry shook his head. He spoke to her in a language Rhona presumed was Fula, the language of the Fulani.

'It is my fault,' she repeated in English. She sat down heavily in the chair, her legs no longer able to support her.

Through the open window, Rhona saw an upright piano that practically filled the small sitting room. It was open, ready to be played by Sam, the returning son.

Gradually Mrs Haruna explained what had happened. The Suleiman family had had the local witch doctor declare her a witch. People no longer came to her shop. She was accused of harming people, especially children.

'They threatened to burn my house down. Then Naseem's men came and took me away. They beat me and threatened to kill me unless Sam did what they said. They asked Sam to bring the child home. They did not say why.'

'And he did.'

'Naseem's family arranged everything. A company plane brought them from the UK. They passed him off as Sam's son.' She looked at Rhona. 'The British do not care about Africans who leave their country, only those who want to stay.'

Sam had made them promise to lift the curse from her and set her free.

'Then he could kill Naseem,' said Rhona.

Back at the jazz club, they'd laughed at witchcraft. But Sam had been circumspect. *Lots of well-educated people in West Africa still believe in witch doctors.* Sam had come back to save his mother, but he had every intention of saving Stephen in the process.

'What about Naseem's family? Are you safe here?'

Mrs Haruna shrugged. Without her son she didn't seem to care.

'John Adamu has made it plain to the Suleiman family that if anything happens to Mrs Haruna, they will be held responsible.'

Rhona wondered if that would be enough.

She had no doubt that Naseem's family would be doing everything they could to find Sam and kill him.

If he was found by the authorities, he might not fare any better. He would be charged with the murder of Naseem Suleiman during a juju ritual. Even should Henry make a plea for Sam, it was unlikely he would avoid the death penalty under Sharia law. He couldn't go back to Scotland either, because he had aided and abetted the abduction of a minor.

How could such a good man end up like this?

In those terrible moments in the shack, when the machete was wielded against Stephen, Rhona could have killed Naseem herself. He deserved to die, for ordering the deaths of Carole and her mother, for the attempted murder of Stephen. An eye for an eye, and a tooth for a tooth. Old Testament philosophy.

She could only hope and pray that Sam was alive and safe, that he might escape the authorities and make a new life somewhere else. But that place couldn't be Scotland. His future as a doctor there was over.

Rhona thought of Chrissy and wanted to weep.

They left Mrs Haruna waiting on her verandah for the son who couldn't come home. Rhona understood now, why she didn't care about her own safety. Her life was already over.

The most difficult task Rhona had was to tell Chrissy about Sam. She'd asked Bill, when he called the consulate, if she could give Chrissy the news before it reached her through the police grapevine.

'Of course. I won't say anything until after you speak to her. You know we brought in Naseem's brother, Kabiru? Danny identified him as the man who recruited them.'

'You think Kabiru killed the women?'

'His DNA didn't match anything we had from Carole or her mother. That's why the bastard let us test him. He thought he was okay.'

So they were no closer to finding Carole's murderer.

'But the good news is he matched the fingerprint you got from the toilet seat in Olatunde's flat,' Bill said triumphantly. 'Kabiru killed Malcolm Menzies. I'm sure of it. But we still have to prove it. The plane that took Sam and Stephen over there was owned by Suleiman Incorporated. The Met have been investigating the Suleiman family for some time. They suspect them of human trafficking. Women and children from West Africa coming via their oil tankers.'

'So you've got it sewn up without me?'

'We still have a murderer on the loose.'

Finally, they talked about McNab.

'He did great,' Rhona said sincerely. 'I couldn't have managed without him.'

'Any news on Abel?'

'I've got the samples. John Adamu, our police liaison officer here, has been running a check on missing children. Advertising around the local villages. Looks like Abel isn't the only child missing.'

They lapsed into silence. Outside the Boswells' bungalow, the crickets were singing in the heat. Bill was thousands of miles away, but Rhona could sense his distress.

'Bill, tell me about Margaret.'

He cleared his throat.

'She has breast cancer. The biopsy results just came back.'

Rhona's heart jumped into her mouth. 'Oh Bill.'

'They said they caught it early.'

'And Margaret's a fighter.'

'She is that.'

There was nothing else to say.

In the end, Stephen didn't travel home with them. Henry wasn't anxious to part him from Boniface. He thought it better they gave it time. He would discuss the repatriation with the Foreign Office.

Rhona was grateful. Stephen was better off here, living in his old home and tending his red velvet spiders.

It rained on their last evening in Kano. A spectacular thunderstorm that turned the dusty dirt roads to mud. Rhona remembered what Chrissy had told her about

Sam. How much he loved living in Scotland, a country where it rained all the time. *Because the rain makes things grow.*

They were two very different people on the return journey to Glasgow. McNab said little, and she didn't mind. They were comfortable with each other at last. Rhona would never call him McNab again.

She suspected he blamed himself for her abduction, but they didn't discuss it. What she did know was that his faith in the certainties of life had been shaken.

'Africa changes people.' That's what Henry said when he escorted them to the airport. 'For ever.'

He didn't say for good or bad. Rhona believed it was for the good.

60

BILL HADN'T MENTIONED Sam in his story about how they found Stephen, but Chrissy knew he was somehow involved. Rhona would have asked Bill to say nothing until she got home. She would think it her responsibility to tell Chrissy. Which probably meant Sam was dead.

Chrissy said the words out loud. 'Sam is dead.'

It didn't make her believe them.

She set the coffee mug down without drinking any. Her stomach was churning, her mind in turmoil. Better to concentrate on work.

She had said nothing to Bill yet about her most recent findings. She wanted to be sure, absolutely sure.

She sat at the lab table, the DNA profile printouts in front of her. The match was perfect. She knew who had raped Carole before she died.

Rhona's painstaking lifting of the partial print near the door confirmed that the same person was in that room.

And the third and final piece of evidence connecting the murderer to the crime . . .

Chrissy lifted the murder weapon from the table with her gloved hand. The knife blade was very sharp.

If she ran the smooth edge down her thumb it would easily slice through the latex glove, and part her skin beneath like ripe fruit. Although the edge looked uniform to the human eye, under the microscope its pattern of indentations was obvious, and that pattern matched the wound in Carole's back and the mutilation around her vagina.

Three pieces of evidence that nailed the bastard!

Chrissy's pleasure at this was short-lived. Despair flowed through her again. She had done what she set out to do. Her job. She had succeeded. In the circumstances, it meant less than nothing.

It took a while for Chrissy's words to sink in.

'You're sure?' Rhona asked again.

'Sure about Malchie or sure I'm pregnant?'

'Chrissy?'

'I'm sure. All tests are positive,' she said with a half laugh. 'I'm definitely pregnant. And Malchie definitely killed Carole and her mother.'

She busied herself fetching the lab reports and handing them to Rhona.

'I ran Malchie's profile against everything we had, including the ones from the . . . Nigerian Church of God.' She stumbled over the words.

'Chrissy, please . . .'

'I'm fine.' She shook her head. 'I couldn't believe it when his DNA matched the semen in Carole. Then I checked his footwear. You would have been proud of me,' she told Rhona. 'The partial footprint by the kitchen door was an exact match for Malchie's trainer.

They found his knife on him. It matches the blade markings of the murder weapon.'

'He was only fifteen.' Rhona couldn't think of anything else to say.

'He was an evil psychotic bastard who liked fucking with women.'

Rhona watched Chrissy disintegrate in front of her eyes.

'I'm glad he's dead. I want them all dead.'

Rhona reached out to her.

'I want Sam alive. Alive and here with me.'

Rhona gathered Chrissy in her arms.

'I want him here with me.' Chrissy gave a wail of despair, her body heaving with sobs. 'What am I going to do without him?'

Rhona held her tight and let her cry. Rhona cried with her; for Sam, for Stephen, for Bill, for Margaret and for Chrissy herself.

Going to the lab had been a displacement activity. Rhona had told herself that she needed to see Chrissy in the flesh, explain the whole story, check she was okay, before she went home.

She expected Chrissy to be upset when she told her about Sam, but nothing had prepared her for the news of Chrissy's pregnancy.

Sam would have made a great father, *would* make a great father, she corrected herself, if he ever got to see his child. Chrissy might decide to terminate the pregnancy. It would seem like the easier option. Somehow, Rhona didn't think Chrissy would choose that path.

Bringing up a child as a single mother would be difficult. A mixed-race child in Scotland would have plenty to deal with.

Rhona hated herself for thinking that way. Sam had saved Stephen's life. He'd saved her life. Any child of his would be precious.

But it had to be Chrissy's decision. And she hadn't given up hope that Sam was still alive.

She spent a couple of hours in the lab, looking at Chrissy's reports, checking the results. There was no doubt. All the data they'd collected at the first murder scene matched Malcolm Menzies.

He killed the two women and mutilated Carole. If the white van was involved, as they suspected, then someone helped him remove Stephen, and take him to the building on the waste ground. If it wasn't Kabiru, then it was another of his followers.

Rhona remembered her own fear of Malchie. Perhaps her instinct for evil ran deeper than she realised. Malchie got his kicks from tormenting and torturing women. She'd seen the evidence of that in his mother. She'd experienced it herself. And any psychotic leanings he had were exacerbated by his association with Kabiru Suleiman and the strong dope he'd been using.

Kabiru had given Malchie the opportunity to act out his fantasies. But when Kabiru thought the boy had betrayed him, he faced the same fate as his victims.

'A stupid wee bugger. Wanted to be a hard man,' Karen had said of her brother. A hard man who became a murderer.

* * *

Chrissy went home early. Rhona offered to go with her, but she refused.

'I'm going to tell Mum about the baby.'

'It's early yet. Maybe you should wait.'

'There's no point. I'll never live at home again. Mum'll be okay. Wait till she hears the father's a committed Christian . . . or a black bastard, as my dad would say.'

'I'm sorry.'

'Don't be. I'll see Sam again. Maybe not in the flesh but . . .' She didn't finish.

Rhona wondered if Chrissy was intent on telling her mother so there would be no question whether she should have the baby. Her mother would never countenance an abortion, even if the father was an African.

'I think I'll ask Pastor Achebe to christen it. That'll really piss off Dad. There's only one thing worse than a gay bastard, and that's a black one.'

The old Chrissy, wonderfully irreverent, was fighting back.

Sean was walking along the path through the park. He walks like a musician, Rhona thought, then wondered what she meant by that. Rhythm. There was rhythm in everything he did, like Sam.

He was coming to look for her at the lab because she hadn't come home. He must have asked Bill for the details of her return flight.

A stab of pain went through her at the thought of Bill. She hadn't spoken to him since she landed. There was a strategy meeting tomorrow morning. But they wouldn't be talking about Margaret at that. Maybe there was nothing left to say. All she could do now was be his friend.

Sean had paused at the bridge over the Kelvin and was staring down at the water. Rhona thought of the first time they had stood together on that bridge. They had only just met. She was avoiding him, not because she didn't like him, but because she did. When she agreed to see him again, he looked so pleased that she felt like a tune he had just played.

Rhona put on her outdoor coat and went to meet him. Africa changes people, Henry had said.

It had certainly changed her.

Easy Kill

By Lin Anderson

The fifth thrilling novel in the Rhona MacLeod series.
Turn over for an extract now . . .

I

THE CAR WAS flash, and looked brand new. As it pulled up, the nearside window whirred down.

'Hey you!'

The vehicle had drawn up in the darkest part of the street, avoiding the improved visibility of the safe zone. Better lighting and multiple cameras made the punters nervous.

A hand appeared, waving money at her. Still Terri hesitated.

'Are you fucking working or not?'

Terri took her time approaching, trying to get a look at the man before she committed. She preferred regulars. She knew what they wanted. She knew they would pay.

She was near the car now. Terri stumbled, her ankle going over on one high heel.

'Careful,' he called, suddenly solicitous.

Terri bent to look in. The guy's face was in shadow but he looked harmless enough. Three twenty-pound notes sat on the passenger seat. When she opened the door he scooped up the money, freeing the seat for her.

'There's an alley further along,' said Terri, indicating an opening a few yards ahead.

The man pulled away from the kerb, swiftly and purposefully, throwing a quick glance at a nearby camera.

'Not around here. I like my privacy.'

He dropped the money in her lap.

'What does that buy?'

Terri told him, keeping to the normal rates, not telling any lies in case he was testing her. If he was a regular punter, he would know anyway.

He nodded, seemingly satisfied.

The city lights flowed past in a blood-streaked blur. They were heading out of the centre. Despite her misgivings at leaving the zone Terri felt her body relax, soothed by the combination of Valium she'd taken before coming out and the stuffy heat inside the car.

'You'll have to take me back afterwards,' she said.

He didn't react, his profile impassive.

'I have to get back,' Terri insisted, imagining being thrown out miles away.

'One fuck a night not enough for you?' He smiled, but not at her. 'You need how many? Six? Ten fucks a night?

Terri tensed. Talking dirty was sometimes the fore-play. For those who could not perform it was often the whole play.

'How many?' he insisted.

'I have six regulars on a Wednesday night.'

'Six fucks,' he nodded to himself. 'Not a problem.'

They were approaching traffic lights. Terri decided if they changed to red, she would get out of the car.

He zoomed through on amber.

'Look,' she said. 'We don't have to go any further. There's plenty of places around here.'

The punch, when it came, knocked the air out of her. He put his hand back on the wheel as though nothing had happened.

Terri tried to draw breath into her lungs, gasping and wheezing. 'Please.' She whimpered, retreating as far as she could.

He glanced in his rear-view mirror. 'Say, "I need six fucks a night".'

Now his left hand was gripping her exposed thigh. She yelped.

'Say, "I need six fucks a night".'

She said it quietly.

'Louder.'

Terri repeated it, louder this time.

They were on the Kingston Bridge crossing the River Clyde, going west. A sudden thought struck her, she was heading towards home. She'd told her mum she would visit this weekend, and she wanted to keep her word.

He had fallen silent, intent on the road. Terri slid her hand into her bag and felt for her phone. A spasm of fury crossed his face as a sudden drilling noise indicated an incoming text. Reaching across her, he tore the bag from her hand, lowered the window and threw it out.

He took the next exit without indicating, doubling back towards the city centre. Terri kept thinking that as long as he was driving he couldn't hurt her. She tried to compose herself and plan how to get away. She had been in difficult situations before and survived.

2

THE HOTTEST AND wettest July so far on record had turned Glasgow into a warm bath. Had the skies been blue and the sun shining down on the sandstone city, its citizens would have relished this evidence of global warming. After all, it would save a trip to Spain to top up their tans. For the last week, the skies had been perpetually dark and grey, rain a semi-permanent feature, in all its west coast forms; smirr, Scotch mist (an understated steady drizzle) and full-blown tropical downpour, known locally as stair rods.

This morning it was Scotch mist that clothed the eastern side of the city, its magnificent cathedral and neighbouring graveyard – the Necropolis, affectionately known in Glasgow as the City of the Dead.

Two mounted arc lights brought occasional glimpses of a forensic team moving among the mausoleums and ornate graves of Glasgow's rich departed. In their white suits they could have been spectres, or some alien species looking for evidence of human habitation among the tombstones.

The corpse that had brought them there was once a young woman. Sniffed at by a fox on its night-time forage, nosed by one of the roe deer that grazed the luscious grass, it had finally been found by a shocked jogger, who made a point of running to the top of the Necropolis every morning before breakfast. That was something he wouldn't be doing again in a hurry. The flies had got there before him, lifting in a black cloud on his approach. Flesh flies and bluebottles had arrived minutes after death, to deposit their maggots or eggs in all the natural orifices. A little later, standard houseflies had joined the party.

Dr Rhona MacLeod, chief forensic for the Strathclyde Force, crouched next to the body, her white-suited figure indistinguishable from the other members of the forensic team. Above her, a pinnacle-shaped gravestone declared this to be the last resting place of one *Edwin Aitken, a merchant of the city, respected father and citizen,* whose family sorely missed him.

The young woman usurping Edwin's grave had no name as yet, and apparently no means of identification. Her clothes suggested prostitution, but there were plenty of girls out clubbing in Glasgow wearing even less.

A skirt of flimsy plastic masquerading as leather was drawn up around her waist, a striped top pulled up to expose her breasts. A black nylon bra, knotted around her neck as a ligature, was the probable cause of death, but there were also six bloody puncture wounds clustered in the shaved genital area. The violence hadn't ended there. The stiletto heel of the red sandal, missing from her right foot, had been inserted in her vagina.

The body had lain in this spot since the early hours of the morning. It had been discovered at eight-thirty and by then patches of lividity, caused as the blood sank to the lower parts, had fused together into larger purplish areas that still blanched under pressure. There was no exact science that could establish the time of death, as there were too many parameters affecting the state of the body. Lividity offered some indication, as did infestation. True flies were holometabolous, metamorphosing through four distinct stages: egg, larva, pupa and adult. Left in the open like this for a couple of weeks, infestation would have reduced the corpse to skin, bone and cartilage.

The area was already cordoned off, the incident tent in the process of being raised, which would stop the inevitable rain from washing away the evidence and hopefully keep any more flies at bay.

DS Michael McNab was Scene of Crime Manager, his dark auburn head visible now alongside that of DI Bill Wilson, Rhona's friend and mentor. Bill's face looked as grey as the neighbouring granite headstones. Michael, in contrast, looked like a man who had just been for an invigorating run.

Rhona glanced up as the nearby bushes parted to reveal another forensic suit, filled out a little more than her own. Chrissy McInsh, Rhona's assistant, looked down at the violated corpse. Compassion clouded her eyes.

'Poor cow.'

'Did you find her pants?'

Chrissy shook her head. 'Probably not wearing any.'

'Or he took them as a trophy.'

There had been eight murders of Glasgow prostitutes in the last ten years, with only one conviction. None had occurred since the safe area had been established. Until now. Three of the previous victims had been found without underwear. One had been dumped naked. Extensive police enquiries had led nowhere, except to establish that the unsolved murders were not likely to have been committed by the same man. Which meant there were eight uncaught murderers walking the streets of Glasgow.

'They are shite, killed by shite; who gives a shite?'

'Chrissy!' said Rhona, shocked by her assistant's bluntness.

'Not my opinion. A quote from one of our police colleagues a few years back.'

'Who?'

'Press didn't say, but I have my suspicions.'

If the victim turned out to be a prostitute, which looked likely, they would have a hard job finding her killer. When a prostitute was murdered, it was nearly always by someone she didn't know. No relationship between the murderer and victim meant the circle of potential suspects was limitless. Men using the services of prostitutes didn't volunteer information, since many had girlfriends, wives and families who didn't know about their little hobby. The public weren't interested, unless the death involved an 'innocent' young woman out jogging or walking her dog.

'Is she a user?'

'Probably,' Rhona replied. 'There are marks on her inner thigh.'

'The press will go for "junkie prostitute found dead in graveyard" and the punters will go to ground.'

There were an estimated 1,200 street prostitutes in Glasgow, compared with 100 in nearby Edinburgh. The high number reflected the poverty, deprivation and drug problems of the west-coast city. Most decent Glasgow citizens wished the problem would disappear. It gave the city a bad name.

'We can't be sure she was a prostitute,' protested Rhona.

'Odds against it don't look good.'

'Morning ladies.' As he approached, DS McNab gave them a big smile, aimed predominantly in Rhona's direction. Chrissy raised one eyebrow at her boss, but Rhona ignored her.

'If you can step aside for a moment, we'll get the tent up.'

'You're a bit late. We've been here twenty minutes,' Chrissy said.

The DS looked Chrissy up and down appreciatively. 'Have you put on some weight? It suits you.'

It was a remark Chrissy would normally have furnished with a cutting reply. Not this time. Rhona saw a flush creep over Chrissy's cheek, and stepped in to defend her.

'Can I have a word?'

McNab was happy enough to speak to Rhona alone, although that wasn't her intention. She merely walked him to where DI Wilson stood with the Procurator Fiscal, whose job under Scots Law was to determine whether a crime had taken place.

Chrissy looked relieved to be let off the hook. So far only Rhona and Chrissy's mother knew about Chrissy's pregnancy. According to Chrissy her mother had taken it pretty well, but hadn't built up the courage to tell the family priest yet, let alone Chrissy's father and brothers. All hell would be let loose when the news broke, especially when the men found out who the child's father was.

At close quarters, Bill Wilson's colour was an even more pronounced grey, a tone more in keeping with a strung-out heroin abuser than a healthy man in his fifties with a loving wife and family. Rhona gave him a worried look, which he chose not to acknowledge. She knew what was eating at Bill, but she wasn't sure who else did. Bill didn't allow worries over his personal life to be discussed on the job.

The Fiscal acknowledged Rhona with a nod, then said his swift goodbyes. Not many Fiscals appeared at murder scenes, particularly when there was little doubt that a serious crime had indeed taken place. Rhona imagined Cameron heading back to his nice air-conditioned office and wished she could return to the peace and tranquillity of her forensic lab. But that wouldn't happen for some time yet.

'A bad business,' said Bill. 'I thought creating a safe zone had made a difference.'

'It had,' replied Rhona.

'Not for this one.'

'What do we want the press to know?' McNab asked.

Bill thought for a moment. 'I've a mind to say nothing about prostitution until we're sure. Let's give them *Young woman found brutally murdered after night out.'*

That way they might get forty-eight hours of public interest in the case, before the truth was revealed. Bill was taking a gamble. He could just as easily get on the wrong side of the press. Alienating them meant no high profile for the case and less likelihood of finding the killer. Female street prostitutes, especially junkies, were the most threatened and abused members of society. No one cared when or how they died.

Rhona looked over anxiously at the crime site and was relieved to see that the tent was up. DS McNab had given up waiting for his private conversation with Rhona and was back on scene. The Necropolis was a hive of activity. Inner and outer cordons prevented the public from getting too close to the *locus* of crime, but the steep rise of the ground offered the more inquisitive a bird's eye view, if they were prepared to climb to the top of the hill, or, even better, scale one of the higher monuments.

Rhona made her way back to the tent. Forensic samples taken from the body *in situ* were vital. History was littered with cases where not enough forensic material had been gathered, leaving the prosecuting lawyer with the job of trying to prove a case largely on circumstantial evidence. If the murderer had left any trace of himself on the body, or the immediate area, she wanted to find it.

Chrissy was already inside, working her way over the surrounding area. She glanced up gratefully as Rhona entered, then went back to what she was doing.

Rhona knelt next to the body. The filtered light of the tent softened the victim's features. The woman's face was still thin, her cheekbones prominent, but the expression appeared more peaceful.

She left the ligature in place. It was better removed in the mortuary, keeping the knots intact. You could tell a lot from the way perpetrators tied knots. Rhona took samples from below the fingernails and bagged the hands. Then she concentrated on the mouth. As she swabbed for traces of semen, she found a small metal crown. Any contact with the crown, perhaps during unprotected oral sex, would have left scrapings of DNA. Rhona sampled it, then moved to the wounds in the genital area. The irregular edges and evidence of tearing and bruising suggested they had been made by a blunt force instrument, like a chisel or screwdriver.

Rhona carefully extracted the shoe and studied the six-inch heel. The end looked similar in dimension to the wounds. She bagged and labelled the shoe and set it with the other exhibits. Vaginal and anal swabs would be taken at post-mortem. Sperm deposits could be retrieved up to twenty days after intercourse had taken place.

Closer examination of the inner thighs suggested the victim was a drug user. Rhona checked the bare arms and found the same. Needle sites weren't the only wounds on the body. There were clusters of sores on the front of the thighs and lower arms.

Rhona called Chrissy over. 'Take a look at this.' Chrissy accepted the magnifier and directed it on the wounds.

'She could be a tweaker,' she said after a few moments' study. Tweaking or skin picking was a common side effect of using crystal meth or methamphetamine hydrochloride, where the addict imagined there were bugs crawling under their skin. Chrissy shook her head. 'If she did this to herself, she was living in hell.'

Her sampling of the body complete, Rhona examined the surrounding area. The earth was well trampled with no obvious individual footprints and no discarded condoms. Chrissy confirmed the same on her patch.

'If he used a condom, he took it with him,' she said.

When the mortuary crew had bagged the body and loaded it into the van, Rhona was free to examine the exposed grave. Until now the prominent smells had been a mixture of fresh blood and the acrid odour of urine and faeces expelled through fear, shock, or death itself. Now that the body had been removed, Rhona realised she was picking up another scent.

She sat back on her haunches and took a deep breath. Most of the Necropolis graves were grass covered, but not this one. Built into the hillside and fronted by a low stone wall, it lay constantly in shadow. Here there was no grass, only dark earth and a sprinkling of weeds.

Rhona bent closer to the ground. The smell was definitely stronger there. A terrible thought crossed her mind. One she hardly dared contemplate.

'Are there any police dogs on site?'

'I think so.' Chrissy looked at her quizzically. 'What's up?'

'Not sure yet.'

Outside the tent the drizzle had developed into stair rods. There was no sign of Bill, and Rhona assumed he had returned to the station to set up an incident room. McNab was standing near the inner cordon, apparently oblivious to the downpour.

Rhona called out to him.

'What's up?'

'I need a police dog. The soil under the body is disturbed and there's a strong scent of decomposition.'

'This *is* a graveyard.'

'The man buried here is too long dead to smell this bad.'

The cynical smile disappeared from McNab's face.

'You think there's something else buried there?'

'Let's see how the dog reacts.'

He nodded, serious now. 'I'll radio one in.'

3

THE DOG WAS already working its nose as it entered the tent. On release it made straight for the grave.

They watched as it grew ever more excited, sniffing and pawing at the surface.

'What do you think?' Rhona asked the handler.

'She smells something all right.'

Rhona checked with McNab. 'Do we need permission to excavate?'

'We'll worry about that later.'

Rhona began to remove the earth cautiously with a small trowel, aware of what might lie beneath. It took a little over four inches to establish that something was buried there and by then the putrid smell was strong enough to gag on. McNab, reading the expression on the handler's face, sent the relieved man outside.

Eventually an object distinguishable as a finger began to emerge from the damp soil, swiftly followed by another. From nowhere, the first fly appeared and made an attempt to land. Rhona swatted it away.

Gradually the full hand lay exposed. It was badly decomposed but recognisable as female, a small gold ring biting into the rotting flesh of the middle finger.

Chrissy muttered 'Jesus, Mary and Joseph' under her breath.

Rhona stood up. 'Okay. Looks like our perpetrator has killed before.'

McNab stared down in disbelief. 'He knew the body was there?'

'He knew all right,' Rhona said with conviction. 'Why else bring his victim to this particular grave?'

'I'd better call the boss.' McNab pulled out his phone.

'Bill's going to love this,' said Chrissy.

By the time Bill returned, Rhona had exposed the face and upper body, both in an advanced state of decomposition, but there was no mistaking the ligature around the neck, fashioned from a bra.

'Our man's got a trademark.'

'If the knots are tied the same way.'

'How long has the body been buried?'

'A shallow grave. Hot weather and plenty of rain. At a guess, maybe a month.'

Bill let a sigh escape. 'There could be more.'

Young women engaged in street prostitution appeared and disappeared regularly. Many were homeless and went unregistered. Most were outcasts of society.

'We should use the dogs. Check the rest of the graveyard for disturbed earth,' Rhona suggested.

She didn't need to look at Bill's expression to know how many man-hours that would need. There were 3,500 tombs in the City of the Dead.

'What about this one?'

'I've contacted Judy Brown at GUARD. I'll help her expose the body and get it to the mortuary.'

'Do we call Sissons back?' Bill said.

'I don't think we need a pathologist to determine death has occurred in this case.'

It was a feeble attempt to be light-hearted. Bill acknowledged it with the ghost of a smile. The truth was you couldn't succumb to constant angst in this work. You accepted the horror and got on with the job, even if it meant developing a ghoulish sense of humour.

GUARD, the Glasgow University Archaeological Research Department, supplied the experts needed for dealing with concealed bodies. Judy Brown certainly had the experience, having worked on mass graves in the Balkans, Angola, and more recently Iraq. Thankfully, after a further period of careful excavation, Judy's trowel hit metal. The iron grave-covering lay a couple of feet below the surface.

'He couldn't have buried another one here even if he wanted to.' Judy's long dark hair was drawn back and fastened with a comb under the regulation hood. Smears of dirt marked her face and mask where she'd brushed aside some stray strands. 'The official graves here are twelve feet deep and brick lined. There'll be more than one member of the Aitken family sharing their patriarch's resting place.'

'I bet he never imagined two scarlet women lying on top of him,' Rhona said.

'I expect he preferred them alive,' Judy replied cynically.

The exposed remains followed the same pattern as the one above ground. A short skirt drawn up, the chest exposed, the ligature and stiletto.

'No pants again. Could they have rotted away?'

Judy shook her head. 'Unlikely in the time this has been in the ground.'

'So he collects them?'

'Or they don't wear them. Certainly makes things quicker.'

Rhona stood up, her knees protesting at the length of time she'd crouched. Judy joined her with a groan of relief.

'What about transport?'

'There's a mortuary van waiting,' Rhona told her.

'Let's get some fresh air, then.'

The evening breeze skimming the hill was a welcome relief from the stench inside. Rhona dropped her mask and took a deep breath. She had been inside the tent most of the day. The penetrating smell would have impregnated her clothes and hair, despite the suit. The only solution was a long hot shower.

McNab was still on duty, although Chrissy had long since gone back to the lab. He supervised the removal of the corpse, then joined Rhona and Judy.

'So, not a mass grave then?'

'Only if you count the Victorian layers,' Judy said.

McNab gave Judy an appraising look and Rhona hid a smile. You could always depend on Michael McNab to eye up the ladies. She was just grateful his eye was no longer on her.

'The dogs pick up on anything?' she asked.

'Not so far. We'll have another go tomorrow.'

'I'd better be getting back.' Judy stepped out of her white suit.

'I wondered if anyone fancied a drink,' ventured McNab.

Rhona shook her head. She did fancy a drink, but not with Michael McNab, and besides, she fancied a shower more.

McNab looked directly at Judy.

'Maybe, but I need to go back to the base first.' Turning, so McNab could not see her face, Judy looked quizzically at Rhona – should she?

McNab was fun and had been pretty good in bed. Rhona hoped her expression conveyed at least that much. She left them to their decision-making and headed for her car, which was parked what seemed like miles away.

Dusk had rendered the Necropolis eerie and silent as the throb of the police generator faded into the distance. Out of the harsh glare of the arc lights, the shadowy gravestones stood sentry on Rhona's walk back to the Bridge of Sighs. Below the bridge, a yellow stream of headlights flowed down the road built over what had once been the Molendinar Burn.

The victim had crossed here to her death, just as other victims had made the more famous crossing in Venice. Rhona's mood was growing as dark as the day. She remembered what Bill had told her once, earlier in her career. The only death to fear, he'd said, was your own. It was a strange thought for him to voice, considering how much he worried about the well-being of his two teenage children, and now his wife Margaret.

A line of police vehicles was parked in Cathedral Square. Once inside her car, Rhona called Chrissy.

'Go home,' Chrissy told her. 'I've logged and stored everything. I'll see you tomorrow.'

Rhona found herself readily agreeing.

She drove westward through the city towards a sky bruised red and blue. It looked both beautiful and ominous.

Rhona found herself craving the small ordinary things of life, as far away from violent death as was imaginable. The sounds of the flat when she would open the door, sometimes a hushed silence, sometimes music. The soft mew of the kitten. Its purr of pleasure as it greeted her arrival. Rhona's skin prickled in anticipation as she slid her key quietly into the lock.

Tonight there was music, but no sign of Tom the cat. She stood for a moment in the hall, breathing in its familiar scents, then went in search of the occupants.

They were both in the kitchen. Sean stood facing the window, listening intently, the kitten cradled in his arms. Something in his stance stopped Rhona from interrupting.

The music was jazz piano, a tune Rhona was unfamiliar with. A padded envelope lay on the table. Nearby was an empty CD case. Musicians often sent Sean samples of their work, hoping for a gig at the jazz club. Rhona assumed this was one of those occasions.

As the track drew to a close, Sean turned, sensing her presence. He placed the kitten on the window seat, where it curled itself into a tiny ball.

'That was Sam playing.'

'Sam?' Rhona's heart leapt.

Sean indicated the envelope. 'The CD arrived this morning.'

Sam Haruna, the father of Chrissy's unborn child, had been forced to flee during Rhona's last big case, uncovering a child-trafficking ring in Nigeria. The men chasing him were both influential and ruthless, and if Sam was still alive he was in great danger.

Rhona picked up the envelope, postmarked London, three days before. 'He must have made it back to London. I have to call Chrissy and tell her. She'll be over the moon.' Rhona pulled out her mobile, but Sean stopped her hand before she could dial.

'I think we should wait.'

'Why?'

'This recording could have been made at any time. It doesn't prove Sam's alive now.'

'Who else would send the CD, if it wasn't Sam?'

Sean didn't have to answer. The Suleiman family were as powerful in the UK as they were in Nigeria. If they suspected Sam was back in Britain, then all his ties were here in Glasgow. His job, his church, his girl-friend. They would do anything to flush him out. The muggy heat of the kitchen suddenly seemed suffocating, as though West Africa had followed Rhona home.

'We can't tell Chrissy until we're sure.'

Sean was right. It would be too cruel, especially now.

'There's something I haven't told you,' said Rhona.

The kitten, sensing her mood, rose and stretched with a plaintive miaow, jumped lightly down and came to rub itself against her legs.

Sean waited.

'Chrissy's pregnant.'

A series of emotions played across Sean's face, and Rhona convinced herself that envy was one of them.

He shook his head in amazement. 'Sam would have loved that.' He corrected himself. 'Sam *will* love that.'

Rhona couldn't meet Sean's gaze. She'd purposefully kept this news from Sean, telling herself it was early days yet. Chrissy didn't want everyone to know. All lies, of course. Chrissy had no problem with Sean knowing about Sam's child. It was Rhona that had the problem. Ever since Sean had expressed his desire to have a child, one drunken night after his father died, Rhona had been torturing herself about it. When she'd challenged him sober, Sean had told her to forget it. That all Irishmen were maudlin in drink. But Rhona couldn't forget it, because the words had been said, and drunk or not, Sean had meant them.

'Rhona . . .'

'I'm going for a shower,' she said abruptly.

Rhona felt Sean's eyes on her back as she left the room. It was at times like this she wished she wasn't in a relationship.

4

LEANNE WOKE AT nine o'clock on Thursday morning, knowing something was wrong. Two sleeping tablets had rendered her practically unconscious, leaving her with a dry mouth and swollen tongue. She always took two when it was Terri's turn to go out. That way she didn't lie awake worrying about her.

The lurch in Leanne's stomach when she saw the empty place in the bed beside her sent her to the toilet. She retched in the sink, then turned the tap full on, rinsed out her mouth and splashed her face. In the poor light of a low-wattage bulb, her frightened face looked back at her, white and distorted. Leanne stared down at the healed sores on the blue-veined tributaries of her inner arms, testament to Terri's determination that they should both get clean.

Leanne gripped the sink, as her legs lost what little strength they had. By rights the two of them should have woken curled together, Terri at her back, arm circling Leanne, hand cupping her breast. Leanne shut her eyes, the pain of wishing like a knife in her guts.

After a moment she straightened up, went for the mobile and rang Terri's number, desperation growing with each unanswered ring.

They'd agreed from the beginning. Stay safe, call if in trouble. The phone slipped from Leanne's hand as the trembling became an uncontrollable shake. A cold sweat swept over her, rattling her teeth. She hugged herself to control the tremors and tried to think through her fear.

Wednesdays were regulars. The stall guy from the Barras market who gave Terri pirated CDs. The old man who smelt of piss and called her Marie. Wednesdays were quiet, never more than six, then home. But Terri hadn't come home.

Leanne tried the mobile at five-minute intervals while she dressed. Each time it rang out, she prayed for Terri's voice to break the endless ringing, only to hang up in despair.

She made herself a heavily milked tea with two spoonfuls of sugar, Terri's cure for just about everything, hoping it would quell the mixture of hunger and nausea that gnawed at her stomach. While she sipped it, she put on the radio and listened to the Scottish news. Dread was replaced with hope when there was nothing that might be linked with Terri.

Outside the flat, warm damp air prickled Leanne's skin, as she headed for Terri's favourite spot. On her right, the distant trees on Glasgow Green stood thick-leafed under a thunderous sky.

The network of dismal streets that made up the east end of Glasgow's red-light district, looked even shabbier in daytime. When Leanne reached the entrance to Terri's alley she hesitated, afraid of what she would find. When she finally plucked up the courage to enter, she picked her way across cobbles slimy with wind-blown rubbish and a scattering of used condoms. As her eyes became accustomed to the dimmer light, she was relieved to see the alley was empty.

Someone had vomited in Terri's doorway, splattering orange gunge on the scored wood of the door. On a nearby wall someone had spray-painted, 'Fuck you!' in red.

Leanne walked the length of the lane, looking for any sign of Terri, but found nothing. On the far wall was the mounted camera that was supposed to keep Terri safe.

Leanne passed the police station on her way to the free food van. Even now, she didn't think of going inside and reporting her fears for Terri's safety. A missing prostitute with a drug problem wouldn't be high on their list of priorities. And she was still hoping that Terri would turn up some time soon.

The van was serving breakfast. The smell of frying bacon hung in the air as Leanne approached. There were half a dozen folk in the queue, two of them women, neither of them Terri. Leanne scanned the faces, registering the ones she knew. Three of the men were strangers, the fourth a regular visitor at the van. She was relieved to see the elder of the women was Cathy, still on the game at forty-five going on sixty, everyone's pal and confidante. Her companion looked barely eighteen and hung on her arm like a wet dish-cloth.

'Have you seen Terri?'

Cathy registered Leanne's worried expression immediately.

'No. Why?'

'She never came home.'

The girl beside Cathy was stoned, her eyes glazed. There was a bruise on her cheek the size of a walnut. A cold sore on her lip had lost its scab and was seeping. Leanne realised Cathy was the only thing keeping the girl on her feet.

'She needs some food inside her,' Cathy said. She took a firmer hold on her friend, preventing the girl from swaying. 'You checked Terri's spot?'

'There's no sign of her.'

'Her phone?'

'Not answering.'

Leanne knew what was going through Cathy's head. Terri had bought a fix and was flaked out somewhere until the trip was over.

'She's not using.' Leanne said.

Disbelief flickered across Cathy's face.

'She's not,' Leanne repeated, more to convince herself than Cathy. 'Did you see her last night?'

Cathy thought for a moment. 'In the queue for the food van. Then she headed off like the rest of us.'

They had reached the front.

There were two people serving – an earnest young man with red hair, and an older woman called Liz, who all the girls knew and liked. Cathy ordered two bacon rolls and two mugs of tea.

'How about you?' Liz asked Leanne.

Leanne shook her head. 'I'm looking for Terri. She never came home last night.'

Liz turned to her colleague, who was wrapping Cathy's order.

'You manage on your own for five minutes?'

As soon as Liz emerged from the van, she hugged Leanne. The motherly embrace brought tears to Leanne's eyes. She had to bite her lip hard to stop herself bawling like a baby. Cathy had propped her companion on the steps of the van and come to listen.

'Terri was here last night. Ate a good meal. I saw to that. She left around nine thirty.'

Cathy chimed in, looking as concerned as Liz. 'I'll check the drop-in centre. See if she's been there.'

'And I'll ask everyone who comes to the van. Have you got a photo?'

Leanne took out her purse and extracted the one picture of Terri she had. She hesitated before handing it over.

'I'll stick it in the window. It'll be safe there,' Liz said. 'Has Terri ever gone off before?'

Of course she had. Just like Leanne herself had done. But things had changed since they got clean. Since they got together.

Leanne shook her head. 'Something's happened to her.'

'What about the police?'

Fear gripped Leanne. She'd spent too many nights sweating in the cells and paid too many fines.

'How about if I go?' Liz said.

Leanne looked at the woman's kindly expression and wanted to kiss her. 'Would you?'

'Give me your phone number. I'll go as soon as we finish here.'

When Leanne left the van, Terri's photo was already stuck to the glass with Sellotape. If anyone had seen Terri after the food run, Liz would be the one to find out.

Despite this, Leanne didn't feel any better. A sense of dread was churning at her empty stomach. Instead of going back to the flat, she cut through Bain Street to the Gallowgate, and from there up Barrack Street. Some punters didn't like the brightly lit district and took you somewhere less obvious. The area, close to the brewery, was popular for that reason.

A police car passed her, heading up John Knox Street towards the Necropolis, quickly followed by a mortuary van. Leanne watched their progress with mounting alarm, registering the line of parked police vehicles, and the white shape of an incident tent half-way up the slope of the Necropolis.

Worry brought Leanne to a standstill. What if the hive of police activity had something to do with Terri?

Final Cut

By Lin Anderson

*Final Cut is the sixth book
in Lin Anderson's Rhona MacLeod series.*

When Claire regains consciousness after a stranger causes
her car to crash in a snowstorm, she is frantic to discover
that her nine-year-old daughter Emma is missing from the
back seat. Then Emma is found in the woods nearby,
unharmed but cradling a child's skull. She claims it 'called'
to her – and she can hear another voice nearby . . .

Meanwhile, forensic scientist Rhona MacLeod is trying
to discover the identity of a corpse found badly burnt in a
skip. The body is wearing a soldier's ID tag, but DNA tests
show it's not him. When DS Michael McNab asks for her
help identifying the remains Emma found, they discover
the two cases are linked in ways they could never have
imagined . . .

'Inventive, compelling, genuinely scary and beautifully
written, as always'   Denzil Meyrick